Nikki Dudley

ellipsis

Sparkling Books

A CIP catalogue record for this title is available from the British Library.

Cover image © Shutterstock/maksimum/Eugene Grabkin

2.1

BIC code: FH

ISBN: 978-1-907230-18-9

Edited by Anna Alessi.

First published in hardback in April 2010 and reprinted in June 2010. This edition August 2010.

Printed in the United Kingdom by Blissetts.

For more information visit our website *www.sparklingbooks.com*

Acclaim for *Ellipsis*

From the opening sentence, *Ellipsis* is strangely engaging: what is it about a red scarf that could make someone choose someone else? And what if that choice turns out to have been thrust on the other as some premeditated plan?

Lyrical prose intertwines with an elegiac and introspective narrative. Rather than being pretentious, there is an earthy, inviting undertone to Dudley's text, despite the curious storyline that plays with initial impressions and twists them around and around again.

This is a work of literacy rather than prosaic shelf fodder. Think artsy, melancholic and slightly bewildering and you'll be near enough to understanding *Ellipsis.*

Excerpt from review by *The Truth About Books*.

*

Well, how could I resist a novel that shares its name with the punctuation mark I overuse the most?

Ellipsis is an interesting debut from Nikki Dudley that (happily) never quite settles into the shape you might expect.

What's particularly striking about the central mystery is less the actual events of the plot than the way Dudley plays with the reader's perception; one is led to conceptualise the story in a particular way, then finds that it's not the right way – but it's hard to shake off the original interpretation, so strongly has it been established. And the ending produces a further twist that leaves us on shifting sands once again.

As its title suggests, *Ellipsis* revolves around gaps in knowledge – in the reader's knowledge of what happens, and in the characters' knowledge of events, people, and even of themselves. And those gaps add up to an intriguing, satisfying read.

Excerpt from review by David Hebblethwaite.

The Author

Ellipsis is Nikki's first novel, she is currently working on her second. Nikki also writes poetry which has been published in several magazines including *streetcake,* the online magazine, of which she is joint editor. She lives in London where she works in publishing. Her interests are reading and travelling around the world.

Dedications

For my Mum and Dad. Thanks for being my best PR and for the inspiration.

And to Joe, for helping me believe in myself and for thinking up the most exciting plots for everyday life.

Acknowledgements

A big thanks to the following: my whole family, who have made me stronger and helped me to achieve; Pip and Martin, for their backing and for some amazing adventures; Sam and Megan for their friendship and critiques; my good friends for keeping me smiling; Parliament Hill School, for providing me with a good grounding as a reader and a writer; all the students and lecturers on the Creative Writing BA and MA courses at Roehampton University, who helped me develop as a writer (in particular Louise Tondeur and Leone Ross for 'growing' my fiction); the members of authonomy.com, who provided valuable feedback; Andy Sweetman (DNA Graphic Design) for helping me realise my front cover; and lastly the team at Sparkling Books for supporting me and my novel.

"The boy stood on the burning deck..."

Felicia Dorothea Hemans

ellipsis (Gk 'leaving out')

Cuddon J. A., (1999), *Dictionary of Literary Terms & Literary Theory,* Penguin Books, London

Chapter 1

Red Snake

I chose him because of the red scarf.

My palms sweat. Dirt from the walls is smudged across them and slithers in the folds. There is a faint smell of kebab in the air and an excited murmur moving down the platform like Chinese whispers. I wonder how distorted the message will be by the time it reaches my end.

Can you hear it too, Mum? Do you think they're whispering about me?

There are other scarves too, red and white combined and I guess that a football game must have taken place. Yet, his scarf is different. It is pure red, the red people affix to the badge of fiery passion, the badge of cold-blooded murder, without the interludes of white to dull its beauty.

He is unique. I've watched him for weeks now and the time has finally arrived. The clock says 15:32 as casually as ever but it secretly signals to me: this is the correct time. It is not destiny; it is careful planning and the instinctual knowledge inside.

Mum, this is the moment.

Now, my breath barely disturbs the stillness of the cavern the swarm of strangers are gathered in, all awaiting the rush of wind that will open up the arteries, revive us. Everybody appears lost, shuffling on their feet, staring at the same grotesquely large posters until they become less overpowering, fiddling with buttons, holding their phones and longing for reception. Anything to avoid eye contact.

My favourite moment is the shared objective, the upraised eyes facing the same direction, the temporary and forced community as the wind invites the dusty air to dance, flings the litter in celebration. All I can do to keep calm is count the seconds down in my head. Even when I think of you, you are bouncing in my mind.

The only details I know about him have been gathered through observation from afar. This is actually the closest I have been to him in three weeks. From here, I can smell his sweat weaving with his aftershave. I can also see how he has missed a belt loop and a tiny bald patch in the back of his hair, perhaps where he has a birthmark.

Are you excited too, Mum? I know you've been thinking about him when we've been trying to sleep. Now, we're so close...

He is reading one of those trashy papers that have stormed the city. The wires of his iPod headphones are coming out of his ears and snaking down his chest to his jacket pocket. If he knew what is about to happen, would he change the song he is listening to, faintly nodding his head, and not struggling to remember the throwaway words? Would he fling down that paper and rush off to buy his favourite book?

It is the scarf that ensnared me. I had been wandering the streets three weeks before, in another dimension of thought or nowhere at all. Then, it flashed at me, like a camera suspending a moment in time. It is a snake that has coiled around my attention and shot its venom into my blood. I latched onto the scarf and followed it all the way home. The rain tried to bully my eyes closed but I stood firm, keeping them set on the scarf weaving through the grey world. When he reached his house, I stood outside for another half an hour, smiling, pouring with gratitude.

Since then, he has been my daily plot. Today, he has thrown his scarf on haphazardly, perhaps being late or not wearing it for warmth but simply out of habit. I can only guess who bought it for him. His girlfriend? His mother? An old friend or relative who put no thought into a present for him? Or perhaps he chose it himself and red is also his favourite colour.

Despite following him, I recall very little about his appearance and when I try to remember three days later, I won't have a clue. I can guess that he has black hair but then I can also guess it is blond. I can say he's short or maybe tall. I can say he is black, white or Asian. Yet the fact is; I haven't paid attention. When the photo appears in the paper, I will look on it as fresh-eyed as everybody else.

What I remember most is a sense of him, a presence. He is like a positive image in a photograph where the rest has been inverted. Even more peculiar is the sense that he is aware. Sometimes I have caught him pausing in the street, as though to let me catch up. Another time, when he was trying on clothes, he seemed to single me out in the mirror and mentally ask my opinion.

The countdown begins to flash: **STAND BACK TRAIN APPROACHING**. My chest implodes and the rest of my body springs alive. All I hear is a harmony of sounds: beating inside and the roar of the train.

Step forward.

Peer into dark.

Wind hisses at hot skin.

Folding newspapers.

Roar gallops in heart.

Eyes of light emerge.

Monster creeps closer.

A unison of feet.

Red scarf flutters.

Spring forward.

Head slightly turns.

Outstretched arms connect.

Eyes of train wide.

Mouths silent words.

Falling.

Newspaper flailing.

Reach out.

Touch the scarf.

Train screeches.

Screaming.

Monster engulfs.

Faces press up to windows.

Scarf a ball in fist.

I breathe. Stop. Think: *Right on time*. As he fell, his lips moved in the shape of these words: *Right on time. Right on time. Right. On. Time.*

Mum, did you see?

Chapter 2

The Phone Call

At 15:32 a day later, Thom Mansen stops. He drops his pen as though it has stung him. He pushes away from the desk and stretches his legs. He doesn't pick up the phone even though it cries out. He stops and cannot find a place to start again.

He wonders what his boss would say if he went to his office and said, "I've stopped and I can't begin again". Would he himself be able to explain this? He doubts it. He doesn't feel hungry yet, he doesn't need to piss, and life is unusually 'fine'. In fact, his boss even suggested a promotion might be in the works and he hasn't argued with his girlfriend in months.

So he is lost.

Perhaps he has some rotting disease that works its way to the surface inside out and that's why he feels strange. Perhaps his heart has stopped and he has unknowingly passed into death at his desk whilst helping Mrs Rayder understand that her policy does not cover the death of her beloved tomcat, Bubbles.

He laughs into the air. "Shit", he mumbles, knowing it's entirely possible for this to be the case. Yet, hearing his own voice reassures him that he is still in a physical realm of existence, not in a twisted form of limbo where everything is similar to the life he has been leading up to this point.

The pen lies on the pile of paperwork. He stares, narrows his eyes, screams at his hand to move forward a few inches and clutch it. But his hand ignores him. His eyes begin to ache and tire in their sockets. He closes them for a few moments and reopens them.

Yet, he still doesn't move. He begins to panic and thinks he's having a stroke or an unworldly force is possessing him. But he knows he has to meet Emma later at the restaurant. Will he make it? Will his body simply imprison him here throughout the night? He would much rather be with Emma, having sex, talking about nothing.

He sees the light of the phone glaring at him. There are incoming calls on four lines. He is sure one of them is the old man who phones every day, pretending to ask questions about his housing policy, but in reality just wanting to connect with another human being. Apart from that, it could be any one of the thousands of customers, waiting to chew an ear off.

"Come on Thom, get yourself together!" He shakes out his shoulders. He smiles at his progress and prepares to get back to his day. However, he now finds he has no desire to pick up the pen, to continue signing the rejections on policies, to hear another customer saying "of course I read the fine print" when they haven't, to continue in any way at all.

He goes through every part of his job specification in his mind and cannot put a tick by any of the duties. He watches the other people walking by his office through the glass, like a helpless goldfish not functioning at the same level or speed. They are all busy – moving papers, picking up phones, and chatting about who's shagging who this week. What is stopping him from doing the same?

He imagines if any of them cared enough to notice him, what they would see. A man, who is clean-shaven, has straight and recently cut brown hair (which curls at the sides if he doesn't monitor it), a straight tie, a dribble of ink trailing from his lip that he doesn't know about. Thom complies with every rule about uniform in the employee's handbook; he is the physical representation of company policy. Would they know he hasn't moved for five minutes? Would they assume he has been working up until the moment they happened to glance in?

Although his body is functioning again, Thom's mind is suddenly heavy. His head drops into his chest like his neck has dissolved. A depression pulses through him, makes his chest rise and fall in a pitiful sigh, makes his body sprawl out on the desk like a person who has just suffered a heart attack. He watches his breath make a mist on the wooden face of the desk.

Abruptly, the phone stops wailing. Then ten seconds later, it rings again.

He grabs hold of the receiver. He balances it on his face which is still flat against the desk and awkwardly muffles, "Hello. Thomas Mansen".

"Thom. It's Richard".

Thom shoots up as though someone has electrocuted him. "Rich, what's going on?" It's the voice... He can tell from the first syllable, the downward direction of the tone.

8

Richard delays, his breathing heavy for a moment. "Thom... it's about Daniel". Thom is sure Richard is crying, or perhaps he has a cold. "He's dead". Crying, then.

"What?" Thom stutters, then again, "*what?*"

"He fell under a train. Yesterday". Richard's words are so direct, poisoned darts that keep hitting him. Thom's chest starts to tighten; his bones are shrinking like clothes washed at the wrong temperature. "I'm sorry I didn't call earlier. Aunty didn't take it well, *obviously*... I had to call the doctor", Richard adds, making Thom feel like he has been squeezed out of his body and now lingers somewhere above the desk, not knowing the way back in. *He needs to get to Aunty Val.*

"Oh", is all Thom says.

And then he listens to Richard, talking about the funeral, an inquest, the reading of the will and asking can he come and can he bring Emma, and Aunty Val would've called herself but she is still crying, and she needs him there. Tonight.

Chapter 3

The Note

Highbury and Islington station. 15:30 Sunday.

It is Daniel's handwriting. Thom recognises the way Daniel crosses his Ts with slanted lines, the way the top of his zeros never quite meet. *Not meet,* met. Daniel won't be in the present tense anymore.

At this, the note in Thom's hand starts to shake and he buckles onto the bed.

Thom supposes he should know better than to snoop in Daniel's things. Looking in Daniel's possessions is similar to how it had been trying to relate to him in life. Thom feels like he is swimming against the current and he has found a small piece of flotsam, but it instantly falls apart. This note could be written in Chinese, for all the sense it made.

There are so many drawers in Daniel's room, small ones for tiny secrets, large ones with small compartments inside; large ones ordered in such a way that no one would dare touch a thing. Thom can smell Daniel's authority. Invisible foot soldiers are standing guard around the room, willing to die in order to protect his classified information.

Yet here Thom is, having been compelled by the only drawer half open, like a partly opened wound. He shouldn't be in here anyway, as Aunty Val and Richard haven't even managed to open the door a crack. He is trespassing because he knows Daniel won't be able to stop him. He wants to see the magician's secrets that have bemused him for so long. He has poked around in this drawer and his hand has seemingly come out dripping with blood and sticky with pus, and all he wants to do is stuff everything back inside and close it up.

He refocuses on the note.

This is the time and place he died.

Thom shivers and tosses the note away at the thought. Yet moments later, he slowly leans closer to it and re-reads it at least ten times. He is a mouse tiptoeing around a mousetrap.

What do these words mean? Was Daniel meeting someone? And were they involved with his death? Was it suicide even? Or is this merely a coincidence that he wrote down *this* time and place, when they just so happened to denote almost to the minute, his death?

Thom feels his stomach groaning in part shock and part confusion. He rushes to the toilet and vomits. This has happened before, only a few times in his life – well, the worst times if he is honest. However, although he has clearly vomited up most of his breakfast, the questions remain inside Thom like ulcers, nagging and ugly. He washes out his mouth with cold water and makes his way back to Daniel's room.

The note is still there. Thom doesn't know why the note shouldn't be there still, but perhaps he would prefer it to disappear;

leave him alone to be sad about Daniel. The last thing he needs is more questions. Whenever somebody dies, there are enough questions anyway. All he can think about is the last time he'd been in the hold of this endless interrogation, when he'd just turned twelve, and both his parents hadn't come home. He'd vomited then too. A few times in fact.

Oddly enough, this room is where Thom was transported that night. He vaguely recalls Aunty Val kissing him goodnight whilst Daniel watched from the doorway, having been evicted for the night to the sofa. Thom felt unsettled then by the clatter of the railway that ran behind the house, but over the course of his adolescence it became as natural as birdsong.

In this moment however, the sound of the railway makes him feel nauseous. Although thankfully, he has nothing left to eject. He looks down at his suit and, seeing a vomit stain on his left cuff, rubs at it anxiously. If he turns up at Daniel's funeral covered in vomit, surely he may as well smear it over the coffin. After all, they were more than just cousins, yet not quite brothers.

Now that Thom thinks properly, he wishes he had known Daniel as well as he did Richard. Although, he and Daniel were the same age and even shared the same birthday, it seems these things merely gave them more reason *not* to bond. Instead, as soon as Thom arrived after his parents' deaths, he and Richard, who was two years older, fell into a closer friendship.

Thom tried with Daniel, yet Daniel didn't seem interested. Whenever Thom pictures their shared birthday parties, Daniel is set back in some way, a step further from the table where everyone was singing 'happy birthday' or at Christmas, Daniel waited until everyone else had torn at their presents frantically and only then, he carefully chose one to begin with.

And what is the last thing he had said to Daniel? He searches through his memory and can only come up with a brief conversation at Richard's last birthday party. Daniel was standing by the front door. They exchanged pleasantries about general health and jobs. And what is it that Thom said to him? His last proper words to his cousin; face to face?

"Daniel, do you know where Aunty Val is?"

"In the kitchen". He nods towards the house. His smile acknowledges what they both feel; a need to find an exit as fast as possible, a sad knowledge that they will never linger with each other.

"Thanks. Speak later".

Yet Thom didn't speak to him later. And he never would again.

Thom wishes now he had tried harder. If not to be closer to him in life but for this moment, in order to understand this note, to understand why Daniel had written it so precisely and had left it in the only half open drawer in the room, as if he knew...

Chapter 4

Lips Stick

He isn't wearing the scarf in the photo.

When I first see the photo in the paper, I only glance at it and feel my body collapse inwards. Tears gather at the corners of my eyes at the absence of it. I instantly pull the scarf towards me and hold it up to my face, kiss it; smell his aftershave and his sweat, to pretend I am still following him. I have thought of him at 15:32 each day and probably always will.

After hours of comforting myself with the scarf, I allow myself to examine the photo. Before this, I have enjoyed merely remembering his presence and I think seeing his photograph, probably some false one from his graduation or a family holiday, will spoil the essence of him that I can feel if I close my eyes. Concentrate.

When I finally set the page in front of me, I scrutinize it. Apparently, he was twenty-four years old. Apparently, he had short brown hair that threatened to curl at the sides. Apparently, he had a scar on his left cheek about three inches long. Apparently, they are appealing for witnesses.

I am wrong though; in guessing it would be a cheesy family photo. Part of his face is covered in shadow as though he is a nocturnal animal peeking out at the daylight and there is no smile, only a faint fizzing up of a smile hiding behind his pursed lips. His eyes are dark brown and, for a moment, my heart accelerates, so convinced he is actually looking at me. In the same moment, I see his eyes as he hung in the air. Yet this is all invention because of the photo. The photo has brought him back to life.

Now, I see the only detail that is clear to me: those lips, speaking to me, pronouncing each word. He had been so precise, inserting them into my memory like he'd penetrated me and caused an embryo to grow inside and begin to kick.

Right on time.

I thought perhaps I misunderstood or imagined them but underneath the doubt, I feel certain. He wanted me to know. Perhaps the only thing I misinterpreted is why he seemed aware, not because he stood out, but because he knew who I was, my intentions, and my actions. Even before I knew? Perhaps my crazy notions that he slowed down and waited for me and looked at me in that mirror weren't so 'crazy'.

I close the paper and look at the walls. Yet all I see are his lips, curling and sneering. His menacing face is projected onto every surface, daring me. The only place I can't see him is in the television, which instead reflects my image. So I sit cross-legged on the plastic wooden floor and look into the tiny screen.

There isn't much choice about where to go here. It is a bedsit with only a small bedroom, and a kitchen along one wall sectioned off by a stained curtain. The toilet and shower are a few doors down, shared with three others. It's so small in there, every time I get out of the shower, I nearly stand in the toilet.

They tell me this place will be good for me, to get me back on my own feet, to get away from the place where it happened. Nobody asked my opinion and my estranged brother has gone ahead and sold the house, refusing to give me my share of the money until I feel 'more balanced' as he puts it.

How can he decide that for us, Mum? How can he take away our home?

So, here I am, in this place that is not only the definition of scum, but also a place where things come to die. I have several potted plants, all of them refusing to live, no matter how much I water them and ask them what else I can do. There is a dead rat in the corner and dead insects that were feasting on the rat's carcass, before they, too, died. I don't move any of it. I look at the rat and the insects sometimes, feel the dead leaves between my fingers and remember I am alive and feel superior.

Oh, what would they say if they knew their ploy to put me on 'the road to normality' has landed me here, in the house where everything is dying or already dead?

However, the worst thing isn't the death rate. The worst thing is the landlord. He smells like road kill and every so often tries to have a 'chat'. He knocks clumsily on the door and says, "Hi sweet cheeks", exhaling a bottle of whiskey over me. He always manages to talk his way in, pretending he has some issues about rent or the building to discuss, and as there is nowhere else to sit, we always end up on the bed. He then says things like "I love your soft hair" and runs his hand through it, making my curls moist with sweat and "that's a very… very… .nice top" when he's really looking at my cleavage. When he tries to grope me, I always throw him out.

16

I'm a tough girl so I don't mind.

I have to cope with these things because you can't protect me now, Mum.

Although, if he does it again, I may have to kill him.

Chapter 5

The Dead, Silence

Thom is surprised during the funeral. No one seems to have known Daniel. Thom himself spends the whole funeral in a daze, thinking about adjectives for Daniel, only realising it's over when Emma squeezes his hand. She looks great in her black dress. If it weren't so inappropriate, he would take her to the car and distract himself with a good dose of indecent exposure.

By the time they watch the curtain devour his coffin, Thom has thought of only useless adjectives for Daniel. He was mysterious, elusive, and witty. He always seemed like he knew more than everybody and he probably had. That's what drove a wedge between Daniel and everybody else. That's why during the funeral there are few tears. The entire room is suffocated with only one feeling: guilt.

The wake is at Aunty Val's house. Thom feels the pieces of furniture he grew up with are stabilisers. He can't help but think he has missed seeing it more than he has missed seeing Daniel over the last few months. The tired grey sofa in the living room is so old and so used that you can see the mould of people's arses. His is the one in the middle. Aunty Val doesn't care much for decoration as she always tells him people are more important than houses.

Therefore, she doesn't care (especially today) that the wallpaper in the living room has started to peel at the seams and that a stain has grown on the ceiling the colour of tea from when Richard always spills his bathwater. The mourners walk mud into the living room and nobody complains.

During the wake, Thom drifts between everybody, trying to catch snippets of conversation about Daniel. Yet, everybody seems to be discussing the food: "These sausage rolls are tasty", or the weather: "It's warmer than I expected it to be", or where they bought the clothes for the funeral: "It was a bargain, especially as I'm only going to wear it once..." Worst of all are the people who are saying nothing at all. The only bit of shocking information is that Mrs Launder's dress, which looks like shit, apparently cost her one hundred pounds. She has clearly been robbed.

Thom slumps onto the nearest thing for the second time that day and rests his head in his hands. Emma appears a few minutes later, kissing him on the ear. She sits across from him, pushing a cup of tea in his direction. He gives a faint smile and takes a sip, then pushes it aside.

"How are you?" she asks, reaching across the table to touch his hand. He is conscious of the dried sick on his sleeve but hopes she won't notice it.

"Fine", he says automatically.

"No. How are you *really?*"

"I'm *really* fine", Thom pauses and adds, "I've just been thinking about how little I knew him".

"Don't people always think that when someone isn't around anymore?" Emma counters, thinking this isn't serious. He hasn't told her about the note, which has crackled in his pocket throughout the day, so loud at points that Thom wonders why someone hasn't heard it.

"This is different".

"How?" She is leaning forward.

"I'm not sure". He shrugs, chickening out. Sometimes, he is worried that he finds it hard without a script for every eventuality, a line to satisfy people when they want clarification. Emma lets him get away with it for now. She doesn't say anything else. She just pulls him closer and kisses him on the lips, deliberately, hard. She holds his face an inch from hers for a moment, saying she is here for him; she will wait, until he understands himself.

Chapter 6

Red Pen

Nobody notices when I slip upstairs during the wake and go into his room. I tag onto the group again when they arrive back from the funeral and mill amongst the people who knew him. I wonder about the connections in this group. Who loved him? Who has come out of guilt? Who is tagging along like me? What would these people say if they knew his murderer is here?

I check all the rooms on the second floor and decide which one is his. The first one obviously belongs to a woman, judging by the lacy bras. The second has a letter in it addressed to Richard Mansen. The third is a guest room or a storage room, where old furniture that will probably never be used again is waiting, hopefully. The other room is a bathroom so it only leaves the last door, which doesn't look any different from the others, but the wood is pulsing when I press my hand against it. There is a secret message written along the wood that only I can read.

His room is plain. The walls are white, the carpet a dull brown. There are several sets of drawers, all light MDF wood. One of the drawers is slightly open but not enough to see inside. A large antique looking wardrobe sits behind the door. His bedspread is white with only one black line near the top, showing where the head should be. The spread is creased and one corner is folded back like an eyelid permanently open.

I sit on the bed, clutching the scarf in my fist and try to imagine him sitting beside me. I imagine the speed and heaviness of his breath in the silence, the size and presence of his body, the depth the bed would sink under his weight. Would he say something to me? Would he whisper or speak in a loud deep voice? Would he pronounce the Ts in his words?

The only thing I am certain about him is that he made me kill him.

I had believed it started with me but the chain began somewhere before that, and I have to find out where and when. This is why I am here in this room, listening to the clattering of the train and the murmuring mass of people below. I am a trespasser, the murderer transforming into an investigator. I'm going back to the start of the flow chart to discover the direction and force behind each move.

The open drawer seems the nearest place to begin. It is one of six drawers, all about 5cm by 5cm, in a set beside his bed. I edge towards it, feeling like it's a landmine waiting for me to add stress and unknowingly kill myself. Yet I still stick my hand in, with my eyes closed.

Nothing. I feel nothing. I think my hand must have gone numb. I peer inside. The drawer is empty. I tug open all the other drawers in the set and find the same. They are all empty. I jump to my feet and begin flinging open all the drawers in the room, the wardrobe, checking under the bed, opening the cupboards above the wardrobe, even pulling back the bedspread in the hope of finding something.

Yet I find everything is empty. There is nothing in this room. He was never here. The only discovery I make in the room is a small red pen mark on his bed sheets and the only object in the room is the angry bedside radio, which is screaming red numbers at me and they happen to be, 15:32...

I wilt onto the floor. The carpet smells new. And I notice, belatedly, the faint smell of paint. He has completely erased himself from this house. He has pressed backspace on the keyboard and removed his life. And this all seems to add to his words as he fell.

He planned it. He chose me. He moulded me.

Mum, how did this happen?

15:32 hadn't been instinctual. It had been as set as the train tracks onto which I pushed him.

Chapter 7

Aunty Val

After the wake is over, Thom agrees to stay the night. Emma leaves because she has to go back to work the next day. He says goodbye to her at the door and, as her car pulls away, he has to grasp onto the door handle to stop himself from waving to her.

Inside the house, the lock sounds like a bullet. This is followed by soft crying from upstairs and the clatter of plates that can be heard from the kitchen. He decides Aunty Val is the priority of the two.

He tiptoes upstairs, wincing at the creaks he should have remembered were there. It is instilled in him that death is quiet; something the living shouldn't flaunt themselves in the face of.

Aunty Val's door is open. He stands outside for a moment and peers in, instantly smelling the sorrow, hanging in the air like smoke clouds. The walls seem to be quivering in disgust, the paint flaking like dead skin.

"Hello", he whispers through the crack in the door and slowly moves his head through.

Aunty Val gasps. A fresh tear is rolling down her face, an afterthought, because now she has turned white as paper. She is breathing hollowly, holding herself up with her arms. Then after a few minutes of looking at him, proof-reading his features, she gulps in air and starts to cry again.

It's only now that he springs into action and rushes to her side, taking her in his arms. She is crying words into his body, something like "your voice" and "Daniel". Thom doesn't want to think about what she is saying though, feeling his heart begin to shiver behind his rib cage, so he presses her into him until her words are too muffled to hear. It isn't the first time someone has mistaken his voice for Daniel's but this is the only time when it scares him.

Yet, almost thankfully, she is too concerned with crying to continue moving her mouth, and her lips forget. She sobs onto his neck and he remembers sobbing onto hers for a week after he'd first moved here. He knows from those times to let her finish, let her run out of water, and let her moans grow muted, disappear.

When these things happen, she looks up at him shyly. Thom tries a smile but even his mouth knows it's stupid. She leans her head on his shoulder. He thinks her eyes are washed out, as if somebody has diluted them. They used to be a much stronger green. He knows it's to be expected but when he thinks back to a month ago, when he last came to visit, he'd noticed it then too. She has let her hair go grey, when usually she keeps it coloured a medium blond.

Aunty Val always keeps herself well dressed and maintained. He always thinks of her saying, "You've got to keep up the hard work if you want to look good". She is fifty-two and looks good for it, although she is always embarrassed when a man shows interest in her.

25

So did this neglect start a month ago? Or even longer? He hasn't visited as much as he should have. And if this neglect had been occurring before Daniel's death, then why? Had she been worried about Daniel? Perhaps this supported the theory that he committed suicide. But would he have? Thom guesses they are questions he can ask later (and some which he cannot) but now he has no right to bother her.

"He's really dead", is how she breaks the silence. It seems obvious but Thom feels like it stabs him in the ribs then. She is right, he can't argue. He can only nod, trying to breathe.

"Did you like the song we chose?" she asks.

"It was good. Did Daniel like it?" he blushes.

"It was one of his favourites", she confirms, and he feels himself smile, glad that at least one person feels certain regarding Daniel. She is the kind of person who always takes notes and stores them in a mental filing cabinet, in order to refer to them later. Thom on the other hand keeps forgetting people's birthdays and buying Emma gold jewellery when she only likes silver.

"I'm sorry". He throws in a worthless phrase to secretly apologise for not knowing Daniel and now it's too late.

"I'm too young to be losing kids", she says, adding, "like *you* were too young".

"Let's not talk about that", he dismisses, and kisses her forehead.

"But I want to", she croaks, wiping her nose on her sleeve. He can't help but find this uncomfortable, especially as she has always been so strong for him, more so than with her own children. She faces him and holds onto his arms at the elbows, pressing down, needing to make her point. "I know it's different but I thought you would be the best..." Her lips rebel against her, muffle her words. "I thought you would understand *this*..."

"Okay", he interrupts.

"No Thom, please", she begs, "I *know* you hate talking about it".

"It's not the same", he tells her, wriggling in her hold.

"But it was wrong too". She is staring at him, searching. "Your parents shouldn't have died then and Daniel..." she falters again, "shouldn't have..."

"What do you want me to say?" He cuts over her, unable to go back, even for her. He has never been able to discuss it properly. The week he cried himself to sleep is the closest she ever got to it. The closest anybody has got in fact. Even he struggles to get near to his feelings about it all. Perhaps back then, he asked somebody why or what happened or some question that didn't matter like what happened to the car but he hadn't opened a showroom to let everyone examine his feelings. Perhaps, this is his problem. Perhaps that is why he has a job where he always knows what to say because there is a handbook.

"I don't know what I want you to say", Aunty Val eventually admits. He moves and puts his arm around her, pressing her shoulder against his.

He thinks about work, about the people who phone about a loved one's life insurance, how they've lost that person and to really rub it in, they have to argue with him about the clauses in the contract. And so he says what he says to them (because he isn't a bastard), "I'm sorry. I'm *so* sorry. I'll do all I can".

Chapter 8

The Reading

Thom is only beginning to recover from the funeral when the reading of the will pops up like an uninvited relative. He doesn't even remember he has to attend until Aunty Val shakes him awake in his old bed, three days after the funeral, where he has been having nightmares for most of the night. She says they're leaving in an hour.

He turns on his side and stares at the wall. He sees the faint remains of the treasure map he and Richard drew on the wall the first summer he'd been here. Daniel insisted it was too simplistic and went to draw his own, more complicated and realistic map. Two hours after they finished their hunt, Daniel appeared with a five-page map, complete with cryptic clues. He and Richard could make no sense of it and resorted to mocking him instead.

This is how Thom feels now. Like he is standing in a map, an infinite number of pages long, trying to find somewhere familiar, somewhere he can start from. He can't help thinking he has lost the solution page to the puzzle that had been Daniel. But as soon as he returns from the solicitors, he is determined to find at least an impression in the wet sand, however small, that will lead him somewhere.

The solicitor is a well-spoken man and all Thom can remember about him is his twitching moustache that nods along to his every word. A desire to laugh jabs at the back of his mouth throughout the reading. Yet Thom is sure that laughing will be inappropriate and it is so quiet in the office that the clock could be arrested for excessive noise. Its only competition is the shuffling of papers on the solicitor's monster of a desk for five minutes, and the formalities of death, voiced softly by moustache man.

The solicitor, Thom, Richard, Aunty Val and a shrunken prune of a woman, who has yet to identify herself, occupy the room. Aunty Val's husband left when Richard was two and Daniel not even born, and no one cared to find him. In this room were the people that Daniel wanted to share himself with, or share his possessions with, which were probably just as estranged from him as most of them felt.

After reading the obligatory paragraph, the moustache moves on to awarding prizes, for knowing Daniel, for loving Daniel, for caring he is dead. Yet Thom misses most of the information. He drifts away until he realises the moustache is addressing him.

"And to Mr Thomas Mansen, I leave *this* key". The moustache slides a key across the desk, as though he is passing him a bribe. "I hope he finds his gift as thoughtful as I hoped it would be".

Thom takes the key, weightless in his hand, contradicting his heavy frown lines. Why did the comment about his *gift* seem loaded? After all, what twenty-four-year-old has a will anyway?

Aunty Val and Richard have passed by, without event. Then focus turns to the prune woman. Her face is a fruit gone bad, folding and collapsing into itself. Her skin is a landscape of rough ground filled with ditches. She stares at the moustache throughout, squinting, holding a handkerchief. Thom doesn't remember seeing her at the funeral.

"I leave Mrs Mary Tray, the sum of two hundred pounds, to spend as she pleases". The moustache has concluded, abruptly. The woman, Mrs Tray, doesn't flinch or express any emotion. She continues to sit for a further ten seconds, Thom counts, then excuses herself with a graceful wave and hobbles out of the room. The rest of them watch, on the edge of words, silenced by the resolve of the door.

"Thank you for attending the reading", the moustache says, dismissing them. The three of them, a small fabricated family, help each other up.

The reading of the will means more questions. Thom has a desire to put his hand up, like a schoolchild, and wait for somebody to ask him what he wants. Perhaps that way, someone will have to answer him and he won't need to think anymore.

Chapter 9

Postbox

I have been watching them for twelve days. After the emptiness I encountered in Daniel's room, I have latched onto them, not knowing where to go or what to do anymore. They fill up the emptiness with their sorrow, their quiet desperation, and their connection with the dead.

I stand outside their door everyday from about 8am to 9pm, following each of them separately or together when they leave the house, learning about their habits and lives. I hate when I have to go home and try to sleep, when all I can think about is where they might go and what I might miss. Sometimes I do follow them until the early hours of the morning and survive on only a few hours sleep before running through the streets, excited and breathless, to see them again.

The woman constantly has a stringy tissue creeping out of her hand and down her wrist, like a bandage she hasn't been able to remove since it happened. She looks like she has been on a drinking binge. Her hair is a tangled mass of wires; her lips are the colour of pale ham, her body a faltering argument that she used to be winning. She often goes shopping and usually returns with two or three bags from Sainsbury's. She has twice visited another woman, about the same age, in a house around the corner. She and this woman appear to drink tea together and watch Bargain Hunt. She has several times broken down in the street and had to be collected by one of the men living in the house. She is Daniel's mother.

The first man is called Richard. He doesn't look like Daniel. He has darker hair and a slightly chubby face. His eyes seem to be smiling constantly, despite anything else. He usually wears jeans and t-shirts and often has a screwdriver or some other tool on his person. I presume he is an engineer or a mechanic. He often stays in at night and only a few times walks past me, holding hands with a blonde-haired girl who wears short skirts. He sometimes smokes on a bench on the corner of the street and stares up at the sky.

Richard is the one who spoke at the funeral. I watched him from the shadows at the back of the church, watching the sorrow unfold, watching the tissues gathering like flags of surrender. He hadn't said as much as I expected him to, he hadn't filled out Daniel's personality, he hadn't seemed anything but extremely sad that he couldn't perform better.

It was nothing like your funeral, Mum.

There were more than three people at this one for starters. At yours, there were no pictures, no eulogies, and no communion in the face of death. Perhaps it had been this way because of the circumstances; perhaps because people didn't know how to face me when there were two people from the hospital waiting outside to take me back when it finished.

I miss you.

The second man is the one I am interested in. He didn't speak at the funeral. And from what I have observed, he doesn't speak much generally. He has walked beside the mother almost every time she has left the house; if only to drop her off and leave, then return to pick her up. He has sat in the living room of the house staring at the wall and I have watched him, wondering if all he sees in the paint is Daniel's face also. He has stood in the front garden three times, separating his m & m's into colours and eating them in order: brown, blue, red, green and yellow. I don't know what this means yet.

He looks uncannily like Daniel. The same dark menace haunts his eyes, although he doesn't seem to be relishing in it like Daniel, as the photo in the paper seems to portray. They have the same coloured hair and over the last few weeks, the curls threatening Daniel in the photo, have crept up on this look-alike, along with fuzzy lazy stubble. Yet, this man doesn't have the same presence as Daniel and I think he would hate it if he did. When he walks down the street, he bows his head and avoids eye contact with everybody. He keeps his right hand in his back pocket when he isn't using it. He makes me want to shake him awake, punch him in the nose until he realises he's bleeding; tell him Daniel is dead and not him. I feel like I have committed two murders.

It takes almost two weeks of watching for him to finally take action. The key he has been randomly slipping out of his pocket and examining, so intently that I'm sure he could identify it in a line-up, finally springs him into action, a delayed mechanism.

He rushes past me so fast that I have to completely turn my back and pretend I am reading the notes about delivery times on the postbox. This has been my way of hiding whenever one of them passes by. Sometimes I am so transfixed by the postbox that I cannot leave. I stroke the smooth chipped paint, press my fingerprints into these chips, and think about you. I often think about hugging it but somebody always interrupts and pushes their unimportant letter into its mouth and I wish I could get inside there so easily, hide in the darkness and feel the red body encompass me, a new womb for the one that I have lost.

Chapter 10

Storage Lock Up Number 11

Shit.

The lock up is filled from floor to ceiling with huge bookshelves. The bookshelves are arranged like a labyrinth so when Thom turns around the first corner, he fears he will never find the way out. He begins to wonder if he should have told Aunty Val where he was going. The fluorescent lights in the ceiling are partly blocked by the shelves and the light is scattered awkwardly, as though the light is coming through unevenly spaced floorboards and he is trapped beneath.

The thought of floorboards reminds Thom of the numbers on the door. 11. They are like two exclamation marks with a dash on the top left. When he arrived at the door, he pressed his two fingers against them but felt nothing. Why did he feel drawn to these numbers, these simple shapes?

The woman on the desk told him the lock up had only been acquired three months before. Yet, there is a smell of rotting food, especially the strong stench of banana. Thom wonders if he will stumble upon a disgruntled monkey who has been unable to find the way out, who will promptly kill him. Although would it be the worst thing?

Along with the banana, there is a dusty air that can be seen swirling around him whenever he passes a slot of light. The light also reveals some of the contents of the bookshelves that, apart from the expected books, are clearly full of numerous unrelated items. To name a few of them, there are empty cardboard boxes, cracked ornaments, ripped pieces of paper and notebooks, old car parts, rotting food, pots of ink, perfume bottles and these are just the things Thom can make out initially.

Thom thinks about the moustached man's words: "I hope he finds his gift as thoughtful as I hoped it would be". If Daniel's thoughtfulness created this dark labyrinth which smells foul and looks like a rubbish tip – *why?* What did he want Thom to get from this? Or is it possible that somebody else had come in here and sabotaged the contents?

Thom reasons that it's not impossible that somebody broke in here and sabotaged it, but it is unlikely. Although if the note is a clue that Daniel had been in some kind of trouble, it is a justified suspicion. Overall however, Thom thinks perhaps he is reading too much into the note, the key, *everything*. The only thing he needs to do is find something in this lock up that makes sense, between everything that doesn't.

He decides to start at the end, that way he is working his way towards the exit and not working his way inside, deeper into the labyrinth. He has no concept of how big the lock up is because he cannot see the walls. Every space is occupied with a shelf, a path is marked out with other shelves jutting out in various places. He is suspicious that the shelves are leading him somewhere he shouldn't be going.

Each bookshelf has ten large shelves. They are made from quality wood and each detail like this makes Thom feel increasingly uneasy. Why did Daniel pay so much to have all these shelves put in? Was it just for his benefit? Thom lets the question float around in his brain but drowns it with his present task. He kneels on the floor, his jeans instantly browned with dirt, and rifles around on the first shelf.

His hands come back blackened, full of scratches from un-expected items hiding underneath others and smelling of filth. He came in a well-dressed and clean man and he will leave smelling and looking as dirty as a man who has been homeless for several months. He imagines the look on his boss' face if he'd gone to work in this state, and it brings a smile to his face. Although, his smile quickly sours into a frown. Can he ever really go back there?

There is nothing of interest on the first shelf, or not that he can tell. He moves onto the second and the next and the next, plucking out the objects that he thinks mean something, whilst in his head the mantra repeats: *you could be wrong you could be wrong you could be wrong you could be wrong you could be*

Chapter 11

Red Slippers

I am stupid. Whenever I think about how I lost you, guilt punches me in the stomach and I have to tell myself to breathe again, just breathe. It happens every day; sometimes once, sometimes repetitively like a song on constant repeat, niggling at my nerves. At times, I can convince myself it is our neighbour's fault, for interfering, for believing I am crazy.

Our neighbour is a middle-aged man, who 'worked' from home, which actually means he watched his precious street like a child he couldn't allow to grow up. He knocks on our door to find out why the rubbish bin hasn't been taken in for five weeks. When I open the door a crack, my eyes are squinting because they aren't used to the sunlight. I haven't been out since it happened. I have cooked meals for two and one is always left uneaten. We are steadily running out of food but I'm not concerned. Every day is an ordeal, a bloodying battle from morning to night; a dam rebuilt and knocked down.

I don't see his nose twitching. I don't realise that the smell, from both of us, might be suspicious. Myself, smelling unwashed and neglected. You, smelling cold, removed. I am unaware. My senses have become trapped in little boxes inside and they have been jumbled up. I smell objects. I touch the aromas and emotions around me. Right then, I can touch my neighbour's confusion. It is blue, a spotted cluster that bangs against the door, trying to see what is hidden.

I tell him I've been ill and slam the door.

I hear him shout, "Are you crazy?" It is a question I will hear many times and a question I will ask myself when I am alone in that minimal room without personality, afraid to give me anything, for fear I will somehow use it to injure or kill.

Inside the house, the air is filled with brown flakes that constantly cry from the ceiling and swirl around me. As soon as I wake up, they begin, and gather on the floor until each step is like trudging through mud. The sadness is an algae corrupting our house, the place where you are ingrained on each floorboard, each blemish on the paintwork, each smudge on the window. I go around and touch everything, feeling your presence throbbing, seeing the beat physically making the surfaces and objects rise and fall.

You are in the bedroom. I visit you every hour. You are always cold, never reply to my questions, and don't even look toward the chair in which I sit. Yet I won't leave you, I know you'll be back to your old self soon. I know your skin will redden, wrinkle, contract and slacken with expressions, in time.

If only you would eat again. Each night I call up that dinner is on the table, but you never appear. Sometimes I leave the food on your bedside table but when I return, you haven't touched it. I get angry and tell you I won't bother making you food if you're just going to waste it. Although I know tomorrow, I'll make it again. And I know soon, you *will* eat it.

It's been just the two of us for six years now. Michael left for university when he was eighteen and never returned. I went to the local university and stayed at home. You and I always got on so well and I didn't want you to be lonely. And this is my home. I'm not ready to leave. Screw Michael anyway, he hardly visits and he hasn't been able to look me in the face for months.

You've been brilliant recently. I've been depressed. I've been afraid to go out, afraid to look in the mirror. Every time I stop for a moment, all I see are those angry muscles pressing me down, Harry's eyes asking for forgiveness yet determined, violent words thrusting into me, my defences pricked and flooded.

I don't know how to live without you. You've been nursing me for the last three months and now I am nursing you. We don't need anybody else around. I didn't even think of taking you to the hospital.

It was five weeks before, when I opened the door and found you lying with one side of your face squashed against the floor, a line of blood neatly dried on your chin. When I moved closer I noticed your neck was bruised, the skin flaccid like a sock that had fallen down, your skin chalky. You were sprawled out like a star, legs pointing towards the door. Your fluffy hair dashed over your eyes. I thought you must have been unconscious and hoped you weren't concussed. One of your red slippers had somehow travelled several feet away and the other was beneath you. I collected them and put them back on.

I carried you upstairs and put you to bed, pulling the covers right up. I kissed you on the head and told you you'd feel better in the morning. You didn't say anything.

In the night, I woke up and thought I saw your slippers underneath my door. You often check on me in the night and I always catch you just as the door closes, your red slippers flashing in the crack under the door, before I turn over and go back to sleep. That night, I strained to hear the soft bump of your bedroom door against the doorframe but there was nothing. I crept across the landing and listened outside your door and there was nothing. Only silence. I told myself I must be going crazy and went back to my room.

Two days after the neighbour knocked, I lost you.

Chapter 12

Objects

Thom sits in the dark with his eyes fastened. He knows he can open them if he tells his brain to send a message to the muscles and nerves surrounding his eyes, yet he doesn't. He lets his facial muscles lie comatose, like caterpillars inert but full of potential.

He feels an object with his shaky fingers. He has spent two days looking over the objects collectively and hours scrutinising each object's every feature. With this brush it's the plastic body with rubber welts that has embedded the pattern into his palm, the stubbly beard that has pressed into his pores until they sting and remind him of his own unkempt face, the curled lip of its head like a sneer. He has devoted hours to using all his senses to analyse this object and now he has spent half an hour holding it in his hands, expecting the lights to suddenly blind him.

It is several minutes later, when he begins to wonder, why the hell is he holding this washing up brush? Why out of all the contents of that lock up, did he deem this specific object important? Was it instinct that drew him to this object or untold desperation?

Questions again. And where have all the answers gone? Thom wonders if he should place a missing 'answers' report. They seem to have camouflaged themselves in the scenery, the people, the words all around him, and he can no longer distinguish them. The answers he once recognised so easily in life have grown and their adult forms are so matured, he cannot pick them out in a line up.

He drops the brush onto the floor and it thuds against the collection of other items gathered there. The train grumbles outside the window as though it's hankering for food. Thom jumps to his feet and yanks the window wide open. He screams.

It's a loud high-pitched scream. An animal gnawed apart by a metal trap, or a hedgehog disorientated and screeching for rescue.

The train doesn't respond. The train continues to clunk onwards, on its set path, unaffected by this one man's pain from a window beside the tracks. The passengers inside the train probably don't notice his cry and if they do, they probably imagine it's a rowdy schoolchild playing with another nearby. Or if they're listening to music, they probably think it's part of the music that they've failed to notice before. If they see him even, they presume he is merely shouting to somebody he knows or he is insane and they turn away, back into the safety of isolation.

Thom wonders if he should talk to somebody. He has barely communicated with anybody since the day he heard the news. The news of Daniel's death seems like the last thing he heard clearly. The normal sounds of everyday life seem duller like he is sub-merged in water. The world is an art gallery where he walks amongst the pieces yet he is not a part of them.

There is a random series of knocks on the door and Richard pops his head in. Thom is relieved that he is no longer alone with the pile of objects, as though they have been bullying him and he is glad he now has someone to fight with him. Although as Richard settles himself on the bed, Thom kicks the pile beneath the bed as he pretends to rearrange himself.

Richard is a mixture of two extremes and he displays them within the first thirty seconds of sitting down beside him. He fidgets with his hands and his lip twitches, a lizard bouncing on legs like mattress springs. Then, he throws his head back and gives a long extended yawn, gulping in air like an addict.

"How you going, Thom?" Richard asks and pulls at his ear lobes. He pulls at them every few minutes. Thom has never figured out why. Perhaps it is nervousness. Perhaps it is merely an unfounded habit. Perhaps he just likes how the skin of his ear lobe is so soft. Thom has no idea of the reason or the cause, yet he knows Richard will do it, as he knows the sun will rise tomorrow.

"I'm okay. You?" Thom isn't looking at Richard. In fact, to an outsider, he looks disinterested. Similarly, Richard is tracing the lines of the pattern on the duvet.

"Yeah", he says slowly, not sure how to answer even a simple question. Perhaps he is merely lying like Thom is. Neither of them probes any further though. They leave it at the words they use to fend off queries, to keep people from digging underneath the pretence worn like clothes every day.

"Rich..." Thom begins, scratching his stubble, "do you think he jumped?" The words claw out of his throat, each letter stabbing him, breeding in size as he tries to arrange them in order and make sense.

"What?" Richard frowns. His head suddenly filled with ditches reminds Thom of Mrs Tray and he remembers he must find out more about her.

"What do you think?" Thom persists. Richard looks down at his lap. Thom loves Richard. He can't imagine how he would've survived his teens without him. Yet, Richard has one major fault, which is his need to believe that life is as it seems.

"I don't know". Richard shrugs. Thom feels like he has snatched a treasured toy from a child. Richard tugs his ear lobe a few times in a row.

"So you haven't thought about it?"

"I guess I haven't..." Richard mutters, glancing at the door, which is still slightly ajar. "I haven't thought much about... you know..." He slaps his hands against his knees and a moment later, adds; "*trains*". It is a whisper that could be misinterpreted as 'chains' or 'lanes' or anything else that rhymes with it. Only Thom knows because he has the context. This is the first time he has felt superior with the knowledge he has. *Small victories.*

"Was Daniel okay? Before it happened?" Thom ventures, a feeble attempt, as he knows he should've asked much earlier. Richard closes his eyes, thinking.

"It's hard to tell. I mean, we both know how strange he could be". Richard rubs his head as though he is massaging a bruise.

Thom hates to see Richard massaging that invisible bruise so he shakes his head. "Don't worry mate. Let's leave it, *for now*". He can't drag Richard into turmoil too; it wouldn't be fair. Not now, anyway. He needs to find out more.

Richard looks at him like he has been given a reprieve and stands up. For a moment, Thom thinks he is going to leave the room but he walks over to the window and heaves it open without flexing a muscle. He reaches into his pocket and pinches his packet of cigarettes out, flipping it open and sucking one out between his lips. He turns round and raises an eyebrow.

"Want one?"

Thom doesn't smoke. Yet, a moment later he finds himself cautiously watching a flame move towards his face, making his eyes cross. He sucks on it tenderly and instantly exhales, as Richard taught him when he was fourteen and they first tried smoking at the back of the garden.

"I know it's a stupid thing to say but I *do* miss him", Richard says, glancing at Thom. "But the worst thing is I can't remember the little things he did". Richard grimaces at the window panes.

"Don't feel bad", Thom tries to comfort him. Yet there is no reason behind the words, no weight for Richard to grab onto.

"I haven't cried you know… since it happened".

"I vomited", Thom volunteers, sheepishly. They both chuckle but the chuckle is dry and brief. Thom moves towards the window and tries to flick ash through the gap but he misses, and it falls onto his jeans.

"You're a shitty smoker". Richard grins. Thom starts to protest but eventually shrugs, trying to brush the ash away. "Sometimes when I'm smoking", Richard starts, watching Thom closely, "I imagine I'm being watched". Richard rolls the cigarette between his fingers and flicks his eyes towards Thom, squinting as if Thom's judgement will scald him.

"What?"

"I just mean, like in films, when the guy's sitting on some bench somewhere and it's just him and his cigarette..." Richard gives his a long kiss, moving his eyes along a train snaking past outside. "It's like one of those moments, when they're thinking about everything that's happened over the course of the film and the audience are either really happy for them or thinking *God, they're fucked*".

Thom thinks about this for a moment and wonders what the audience would think of him, a pathetic smoker, with jeans he's been wearing for five days that are now smudged with ash.

"So, *which* are we?" Thom asks, hopefully. Richard pulls at his ear and leaves a temporary red blotch there, like the spark of his cigarette, slowly fading.

"I can't decide yet", Richard answers, disappointing them both.

Chapter 13

Blood

She can't ruin everything.

I won't let her come swooping down on my new life, my new friends and take me back to that room where the walls won't even talk to me. The only person who talks is her: about *her* thoughts and feelings, *her* family life, *her* next delightful holiday from work with all the trimmings. When she should have been asking me about something, *anything* and not smearing her perfect life all over my room, like shit to taunt me by having to smell it every day that the lock turned in the door.

I guess at least her self-fascination got me out of there. And seeing her again now, smoothing her hair in the murky mirror in the hallway leading to my bedsit, I know nothing has changed. She sucks the end of her pen desperately, like a baby controlling a dummy, then pauses to check if she has any ink on her lips and being satisfied, stuffs it in again. Doctor bitch Rosey.

After our first meeting, I decided she must've changed her name to *Rosey* because it is so fitting. It can't be a coincidence. Or perhaps her name coerced her into being such a deluded, ignorant donkey. She is the literal translation of rose-tinted glasses.

I watch her from the bottom of the stairs, her nagging pen harassing the clipboard and paper she carries with her. I'm sure she is making some official note about me not answering her calls and failing to be present for a follow-up appointment. If I could, I would push her in front of a train. And perhaps I will… I can't let her disturb me, now I have a new family to look out for, now that they need me to help them cope with Daniel's death, now that I need to find out how he managed it.

I am just beginning to tiptoe away like a mime artist when the landlord's door opens.

"Thanks so much", a voice says. I halt. His face immediately floats into my head. I think: *run!* Yet, my knees seize up like cogs unable to turn. For a moment, I imagine he won't see me, like when we used to hide under the kitchen table and giggle, pretending we were invisible until you grabbed our legs and pulled us out. I am six again and he can't see me either.

Yet he does. I have my face turned towards him, my legs and body still facing the door. He backs out of the landlord's flat, clearly knocked back by the stench of sweat, his breath and the collection of half-dead fish swimming in shit. I recognise his nose that is exactly like mine, slightly bent on the bridge and pointed up a millimetre or two at the end. I notice the stubble he has left to fester and stray, his hair creeping over the top of his ears like ivy.

I see my brother.

"Michael", I say. It's not a question. It's not the start of a sentence. It is nothing at all. It is as though he is a familiar object I am trying to articulate in a new language.

His eyes are wide, blood shot. He grabs onto the banister, a lost child doing the sensible thing and waiting for somebody to find him, and he plants his feet firmly on the ground. The landlord burps and closes his door.

It is only us now, two animals afraid to start a fight, too afraid to find out who is the fittest, who can survive. I think I love him still. I think I still love.

Mum, your kids are together again.

He is looking at the door behind me. It is a black hole that will swallow me up and he will not be able to find me in that darkness. I wonder if he can ever detach himself from what he thinks is right and cry with me for the loss. He never talked to me about you; all he did was dress up like a fraud and act his way through the funeral and every conversation we've shared since.

"Hi", he croaks and coughs, trying to regain his power. The noise causes the dust in the air to pirouette around us. I am entranced for a moment but shake myself awake when I see him staring at me. I wish he would hide with me again. I glance over at the small table by the door and realise it's far too small for the both of us. I just want to share stories with him and pretend we're on a submarine looking at all the fish on the seabed, pretending every time your legs pass, you are an enemy submarine that we have to fight with.

But Michael doesn't play anymore. He takes people away from their home they've always lived in, he tells his children their Aunty is mad, he works at a bank and owns a red BMW, he stands in hallways and doesn't know what he should say to keep me there.

"You're going bald", I say and watch his lip tremble, like a fishing line bobbing as a fish takes the bait. He lifts his head upwards, his pointy nose keeping face.

"How are you?"

"Wonderful. And you?" I smile like the Joker from Batman, manic and sad. Perhaps I am bipolar, insane?

"You can tell me how you are…" Michael pauses, for effect, "truthfully?" He always does this. He loves to separate his sentences to really emphasise his point, to pretend he is a diplomat. I wish I could scream in his face just to make him turn white and scare that smug undertone out of his words. At the same time, I wish I could fall into his arms and ask him to tell me why I pushed that man.

"Why are you here?" He doesn't think fast and the silence wraps around us like anaesthetic numbing bodily function. We are speaking quietly, secretly and, so far, the evil Doctor hasn't heard our reunion. In fact, I think she is in my bedsit, poking around in my things, trying to understand me for the second time.

"I'm here. That's what matters", Michael says, taking a step towards me. He strokes the banister tenderly as though he is comforting me. Yet my skin only feels cold.

"That's a poor way of not answering the question". I stare through him. Although trying to keep such a flat expression only makes me want to laugh.

"The doctor asked me to come", Michael finally explains. Yet his words are no surprise and I wonder why he even bothered to verbalise them.

"Do you miss her, Michael?"

"Who?" He bows his head.

What a traitor, Mum!

I want to kick him in the teeth and watch each tooth swim in blood and slide away from his gums. I want to watch his lips inflame with hardened skin and struggle to form words that he uses to create scrawny excuses and reasons. I can't think of a way to express these thoughts without actually carrying them out so I don't speak. Instead I turn towards the small table that has innocently witnessed our meeting and I grab it by its top. With my arms straightened to their fullest, I watch him watching me and I think *the tables have turned*. Then I smash the table into the wall.

One of the table legs breaks and I let it fall to the floor. I only wish it could be his face, his identical nose smashing irreversibly. I'm not sure who looks sadder – him or the table. Then in the next moment I hear the Doctor shouting from the top of the stairs and Michael lifts his face like a soldier following orders.

I run. The door opens up and swallows me. Michael chases me into the darkness, calling my name, weaving through people, calling my name and getting stuck between the cars. Michael shouts my name and I cry because he is calling me and I want to go back and ask him what he wants.

Michael, Michael, do *you* need me?

Chapter 14

The Notebook

Thom opens the notebook. The first page is blank and he is on the edge of relief, feeling like he is peeping into his girlfriend's diary. It has taken him two days to even get this far but it's time, after his complete failure with the other objects he chose from the lock up. Thom reasons he shouldn't feel bad about looking at this notebook though. After all, Daniel left him the lock up and its contents. So, this notebook is his property and he has the right to read every scribble and word it contains.

The second page is full of writing. The handwriting is an angry scrawl, not like Daniel's usual composed hand. In this notebook another side of him seems to have taken over or he was too excited to put on a charade, even for himself. He notices the rest of the notebook is full from quickly flicking through the pages. He begins to read:

I am wandering around without belonging, without stable identity or a true family who love me. From the outside, I'm sure I appear just like anyone else. I'm sure I look like a clean pane of glass but the glass is hiding what's really there: a stormy sea that is swallowing me up. Sometimes, I can't even breathe and have to really concentrate on normal everyday actions.

I'm afraid of myself. I don't trust my body or my mind anymore. I have begun to hate people. It's because I'm different, that's all. I keep losing people and I wonder whether it's all my fault.

Perhaps I was born to live alone. Although I have no one I can really ask this question, no one listens to me anymore. My family say they love me but I know they secretly wonder about me, whether there's something wrong with me.

I have no idea what to do anymore. I spend hours sitting alone and planning ways to escape. Then I change my mind and go back to living like I have been. I wish someone would help me.

The bottom of the page has blotches of ink on it and Thom guesses Daniel's pen broke. Thom feels weighed down by the words, weighed down by guilt for not helping Daniel more when he had the chance. But would Daniel have accepted his help?

Thom doesn't understand how Daniel could've felt this way. Why did he feel so alienated from his family? Why did he feel like he was losing his mind? If anything, this notebook supports the idea that Daniel had actually thrown himself in front of that train. Perhaps the note Thom found is an indirect admission from Daniel that he committed suicide.

Thom wonders how he will even begin to tell Richard and Aunty Val.

Thom flips through the notebook, catching glimpses of the same angry scrawl continuing throughout and sometimes, just pages filled with scribbles or others completely heavy with biro covering every inch. Then Thom sees something that makes him freeze. He has reached the last page and written in much clearer ink are the words: *property of Thomas Downing.*

First, Thom throws the notebook at the house and it slams against the ground.

Second, he sobs into his ink stained hands.

Third, he looks at his hands and wonders when his hands and his brain disconnected and wrote these hopeless words...

Chapter 15

The Woman

Ten minutes later and Thom is no closer to understanding the notebook and how his name, his *real* name appears in there. Is it possible that Daniel merely took a notebook belonging to Thom and wrote in it himself? Or had Daniel written it and for some reason, put Thom's name in there on purpose? Otherwise the only other possibility is what he feared: that he wrote it himself.

He thinks about the words in the notebook like *belonging* and *losing people* and *alone* and they swarm around his head. The words were a shock to read and Thom realises it isn't so much because Daniel may have written them but because they sum up many of his feelings about his own life.

Thom *does* feel alone, even when he is surrounded by others. Since Daniel's death, he has taken his solitude to extremes and it has been easy to do so, because most people in his life barely notice him or can be bothered to hear how he really feels. And there have been times when he has wondered about Aunty Val, Richard and Daniel, and whether he is an unwanted extra. Other times, he has been sure they all love him.

It dawns on Thom then, that he can think of a perfect time when he could have written these words. Immediately after his parents died, he suffered from complete shock and distress, not sleeping properly and often finding himself doing things without realising it. He lost grip on life for a while and slowly, Aunty Val and Richard mainly, recovered him. But what if during the time when he'd been so confused, effectively 'losing his mind', he wrote this? But it all sounded so adult, so informed – could his young self really have written this?

It is possible, Thom decides. This would explain his name being written as *Thomas Downing*, his name given to him by his parents. He took Mansen after their death, when Aunty Val adopted him and as far as he knew, had tried to use it as soon as it was confirmed. The period between him losing his parents and the adoption wasn't that long, as the authorities had deemed it necessary. It had been perhaps six months to a year at most. So that is the only period where Thom could have written those things, although his confusion and anger remained with him like an ulcer, obvious and sore, for much longer.

Thom realises the more he turns it round in his mind, it is possible he still thinks these things even now, he has diluted feelings to the same effect at times. He shouldn't feel sorry for Daniel at all, he should feel sorry for himself.

Thinking again of Daniel, Thom wonders if Daniel read this. Did he leave it in the lock up so that Thom would find out how he felt and perhaps to let him know he'd been depressed too? Is this another link to the suicide theory? Or did Daniel just want to upset Thom for some unknown reason?

Thom wants to believe Daniel's intentions were good. He can't quite fathom the other possibility, it makes his head become groggy and makes vomit rise in his throat, like the day he found the note. He wonders whether he should've saved the vomiting, as he can't think of a suitable way to respond to the notebook now. His only option seems to be to amputate a limb in disgust.

In that moment, as Thom is grimacing about the prospect, he sees the arm peeping out from the side of the house. He wonders if Aunty Val or Richard are hiding there and are too ashamed to come out, having witnessed him crying. He gets to his feet quietly and tiptoes towards the side of the house. Yet as he gets a few yards away, the hand whips out of sight and Thom guesses the owner of it has begun to run.

Thom chases past the house and into the front garden. He sees his target, a woman with dark curly hair and a skirt dragging behind her, fiddling with the gate. Thom dives towards her and grabs her around the stomach, pulling her to the floor. They make a collective groan as they tumble onto the grass that hasn't been mowed since the funeral and has grown wild, tickling their bare skin. A piece of grass prods up Thom's nostril and he sneezes.

The woman is limp underneath him and he wonders for a panicked moment if he has knocked her unconscious. Yet when Thom looks down, he sees her blue eyes watching him with unwavering interest and not the fear or guilt he expects. He moves away, scratching his stubble as he separates himself from the woman, suddenly conscious of it. She eases herself up casually, as though she is sunbathing on the beach, not having just tried to escape him.

He is about to speak when she yanks at her elbow and frowns at a small cut that is slowly oozing blood. She makes a noise of disapproval and looks up at him. For a moment, he feels like a boy-friend who has forgotten to buy her an anniversary present and then remembers; she is the one that owes him an explanation.

As Thom looks down he notices her skirt has ridden up around her legs and he sees her smooth thigh and above that, the edge of the red knickers she is wearing. Thom gulps on air and looks away again, pretending to check his knee for damage.

"Thom", he says after a moment, involuntarily, like a hiccup.

She is quiet for a moment and then replies, "Sarah". Thom thinks there is something strange about the way she says it, almost as if she has plucked it out of the air or it is a name she has always loved and has now chosen it for herself.

Thom manages to smile at her, despite the awkwardness and the lack of explanation. They have only managed two words but Thom feels better. After about thirty seconds of more silence, she smiles back. The gesture has clearly been thoroughly considered, some-thing she doesn't want to give away easily. Therefore, Thom appreciates it.

"Hello Sarah", Thom says, checking to see if she flinches at the name. She does nothing, just continues to stare at him as though he is an alien object that has landed in her path. When he moves his hand towards her, she jumps back. Thom points at her elbow and she understands and offers it to him. His sleeve soaks up a little of her blood and he moves it away, thinking about how much they have already shared in such a short space of time.

"Why were you crying?" Sarah asks, surprising Thom. He had no idea anyone saw him in the garden and he wonders what she must think of him. He hesitates for a moment, his gut spinning like a Catherine wheel, shooting off in all directions.

"My cousin died", he tells her, feeling his tongue struggling with the words. His saliva has turned to wallpaper paste.

"I'm sorry", she says automatically, emptily. Thom almost laughs; her voice is like a glacier splitting his body in half. Even stranger than her tone is that he likes it. He is sick of people cooing him like a baby. Sarah is bashing him over the head with a rock instead.

"Please come in. We can wash that". He gestures to her elbow.

Flicking her curls out of her eyes, she nods and Thom pulls her up.

Chapter 16

Red Mug

"How did he die?" I ask as Thom places a mug of tea in front of me. The mug is red and I am instantly intrigued by it. Thom pauses for a second in front of me, unsure what to do with his body, unable to let go of the mug handle. I reach over to lift the mug into my hold, desperate to feel the colour pulse into me but I miss and touch his hand instead. He looks up, almost blushing and then throws himself backwards onto the sofa. I grit my teeth. After all, it isn't him I intended to touch; it is the colour.

"Hit by a train", he answers. He doesn't say Daniel fell, or jumped or was pushed because he doesn't know. Only I know the truth. In the papers it says the case is still open but there have been no developments. Apparently, they can't find the footage from the station for that day. So I am still free for now. I am free and I wonder if I care either way.

"Were you close?" I stare into my mug, without giving him any attention. I fear that looking too closely into his eyes might remind me of Daniel too much. They have the same colour eyes and the way Thom's lips move when he speaks takes me back to that moment, when Daniel mouthed those words: *right on time.*

"I've lived here since I was twelve", he gestures to the room with his hands. "But, we weren't especially close", he admits, playing with his knuckle.

"Why did you live here?" I am wondering aloud and after I ask, I think perhaps 'normal' people wouldn't be so direct. Thom seems slightly stunned for a moment but quickly recovers; as though it is something he has programmed himself to do. I concentrate on separating the strands of my hair and examining them, waiting.

"My parents died".

My head jerks up, my mouth involuntarily jarred open. "Oh God..." I moan; my features running downwards like a painting soaked with water. My stomach is jumping. I can't believe what I have done to this man. He has experienced enough pain already. Yet I hadn't thought of anything that day, I just killed Daniel, whether he planned it or not.

Mum, how can I live with this?

"Do you believe in God?" he asks softly. I wonder if he is going to tell me he is at peace, he understands that God has a plan and therefore, he is dealing with all these lost people.

"No", I say, no explanation.

"Me neither", he agrees abruptly. I wonder for a moment why he brought it up. Is it just because I mentioned the word 'God'? Does he think I am a hypocrite for using the word when I have no belief in the concept?

Thom takes a gulp of his tea, completely unaware of my paranoid musings and burns his tongue. "Shit". He uselessly tries to cool his tongue with his hand and sucks in air. He doesn't notice me moving until I'm beside him. I want to cuddle him, for his parents, for his cousin, for not cuddling Michael. Most of all, right now, I wish it was you. This is the first time I have wanted to perform this action for years and I have no idea why Thom is the person I want to do it with.

I lift my arms and look at them as though they are not connected to me. Thom notices and forgets about his tongue for a moment, perhaps wondering if I am going to show him my wings or start a puppet show. His tongue still darts in and out of his mouth though, and I am suddenly drawn to it. I am looking at the lips that look so familiar and want to touch them, feel how soft they are.

I lean towards him and he doesn't move, curious perhaps. I wonder if he thinks I'm going to tell him a secret or blow on his tongue or spit in his face. His eyelashes flutter uncomfortably. I am a floodlight blinding him. Yet he doesn't move, even when I press my lips against his. At first, it is a still kiss as though I'm trying to give him CPR but it deepens and my tongue flickers against his for a moment. It feels hot against mine and I wonder if his tongue is burning mine by proxy. His stubble scratches my lips and, as I kiss him, I think I am remembering *something*… a red bedspread, the stench of lavender clashing with disinfectant… then I forget.

As I release his mouth from my hold, he uses his hand to stay upright on the sofa. Perhaps he fears he is in danger of simply falling to one side. I can see his lips trying to form words, his throat bulging with speech but he fails and only shakes his head. I start stretching out my curls, not focussing on him.

"I think God is a comfort blanket for people", Thom finally says.

64

I have no idea why he is returning to the subject. It feels like the kiss hasn't even happened.

"It wouldn't make you feel better about your cousin…?"

"Daniel", Thom reveals, not realising I already know, and adds, "no".

"Why not?"

"Why did you do that?" he asks, almost aggressively and I wonder what is so offensive about my question.

"What?"

"Before… the kiss", he croaks.

"I don't know", I answer, honestly. I draw my legs up to my chest and rest my head on them.

"I have a girlfriend". Thom finally remembers.

"Okay", I say, surprised by how unaffected I feel.

"Emma", Thom emphasises.

"Okay", I agree, cold again. I suppose he thinks I should care but I don't. I don't have any real feelings for him, I just wanted to touch someone again. It doesn't matter who he is.

"Daniel…" Thom says, out of nowhere. "Sarah… You remind me of him, *a bit*". Thom's eyes are wide as though he isn't the one who made the suggestion.

"Really?" I smile faintly.

"You surprise me", Thom admits; his forehead growing more wrinkled with each word he says. I have no idea why he is telling me this.

"In a good way?"

"I hope so", Thom whispers, his eyes focussed on something in his head. I wonder if he is thinking about what he was reading in the garden, the thing that made him cry. "I've only had nasty surprises from Daniel".

I am afraid I have ruined this man. Although when I think about it, I remember Daniel's hint that he planned for me to push him in front of that train. Has he left similar puzzles behind for his family, particularly Thom? Am I meant to confess to save him from this torment?

For a moment, I nearly say the words. I nearly tell Thom, his lip trembling like he is standing in the snow, *it was me*. *IT WAS ME!* I am the murderer who took him away from you. Then I think the word 'murderer' is too strong and that can't possibly be what I am. I just need to look after them. They need me. Someone needs me.

"You'll be okay", I finally tell him and he stares at me hopefully, like when I was a child and you told me the gerbil wasn't dead, he was just sleeping. And I wanted to believe you so much.

Chapter 17

The Red Stain

When Thom waves to Sarah as she gets to the corner, he is practically in the garden a millisecond later. Yet before the notebook, he shrinks. He takes steps towards it but appears to be moving further away. It looks like a person who has jumped from a building; pages bent and twisted at awkward angles, opened with the words bare like a person's body ripped open on impact.

He kneels beside it, a parishioner atoning his sins, a man humbled by greatness. He touches the pages, feels the ink impressions that are harsh and definite and tries to press them flat. Yet, he can't force them to retreat; they are as strong as the day they were written.

Thom sags against the back of the house and drags the notebook onto his lap. He smoothes down the pages and closes it. Even the cover isn't familiar to him. It is brown mock leather with a circular pattern moulded onto the front cover. It has a red stain on the back, which means nothing really, as it could've come from the lock up where it had been buried underneath a shelf of rubbish.

Why did he know nothing about this?

Thom can't read the words again, not now anyway. He just holds the notebook in his lap and traces the pattern with his fingers until he becomes aware, an indeterminate time later; that someone is in the kitchen. He grabs onto the window sill and hauls himself up, peering in through the net curtains.

He sees Aunty Val. She is at the kitchen table, carefully counting and stacking her penny collection into even piles. Thom can already see when she will finish, the piles of coins in straight piles across the table and an odds pile in the far corner. Then she will sweep them into her hand one by one and replace them in the jar. Counting the pennies calms her and she keeps them around as a form of comfort. Thom can remember only two times the pennies were counted *and* taken to the bank. Once, when Daniel decided to go to university and another, when Richard wanted a moped.

The only other times Thom remembers using them is when the three of them used to play bingo together. They'd separate all the coins into even piles (or as close to); each put some in the middle and then draw cards from the deck. Thom always loved to be the caller, it made him feel grown up and responsible. Daniel hardly ever called "bingo!", even if he had the cards. He never wanted to attract attention but he still played – why? – nobody knows.

Thom is almost happy for a moment but the notebook grows cold against his hand, stinging him back to reality. His fingers tense around its body. It is a small snake that has slithered through his fingers and frozen in his hold.

Thom turns the doorknob and flings the door open. As the door flies open, it smashes against the table and the coins shudder, the piles jutting out of shape like vertebrae knocked out of position.

Several of the piles spray over and mix with the piles next to them. Thom feels like an artist who has ruined the paints by mixing all the colours together.

"*Sorry*", he whispers, placing the notebook on the table and pushing it towards her with one finger. It presses against the pennies and moves them in unison like one of those machines at the arcade, where you try to get your two pence to push some money off and create a chain reaction.

Aunty Val is silent. She is still staring at her fallen pennies. They are parts of her castle, falling down around her. Her mouth is twitching at one side and her hands are flat on the table, as though she is awaiting instructions. So Thom delivers one: "Read it".

Aunty Val plants her hands on top of the notebook and plucks it from the demolition, not causing a single penny to move a fraction. Her collectedness makes Thom envy her. Although, he wonders if she can retain it after sampling the contents. Thom waits as she opens the notebook to the first page with writing on, and her eyes begin to scan the words.

Five minutes pass before she puts it down and gathers her hands together in front of her, looking up at him. "And what is this about?"

"You've never seen *that* before?" Thom snarls, shaken by her lack of concern.

Aunty Val shakes her head and says, "Why? Where did you get it?"

"That's not important. What's important is that it has my name in it". Thom flicks open to the offending page and lets Aunty Val take a quick peek before slamming it shut. "How can that be explained?" Thom demands and wishes she will miraculously have an explanation that will calm him, which will make this whole wild set of events fade into the background and leave him to move on.

"I didn't know you thought of yourself as a *Downing*, after all these years". Aunty Val frowns, showing the first real sign of distress about the notebook but Thom can't help thinking she has missed the vital point.

"I didn't write that! Or… I don't remember writing it".

"What do you mean Thom?"

"I mean that I found this and I have no recollection of ever seeing it before or writing in it. Now, does *that* make sense to *you?*"

"Maybe you wrote it when you were younger", Aunty Val says plainly. She makes him feel like he has a splinter but is making it out to be a six-inch knife wound.

"I did think of that but I just can't remember doing this… at all".

"You were very upset then. You hardly spoke for a month and saw a counsellor". Aunty Val pats Thom's hand, dismissively.

"A counsellor…" Thom thinks for a moment. "Oh yes… I did, *didn't I?*"

"At least you remember that". Aunty Val smiles gently, a parent figure trying to encourage a pathetic attempt by her child.

"But why don't I remember this?" Thom slams his fist against the table and makes some of the coins jump in fright. Aunty Val doesn't flinch though. He feels bad for acting angrily when he notices the tissue poking out of her sleeve, reminding him of how fragile she still is.

"Did you really feel those things?" Aunty Val ventures, "the drowning, the fear we didn't love you, all of that...?"

"No", Thom interjects, "well, I don't think it was that bad".

"We always loved you the same", Aunty Val half pleads.

"I didn't ask you about that", Thom dismisses her and looks down to avoid seeing a tear carving its way down her cheek. Before Daniel's death, he rarely saw her cry. Now, it is a daily event. He can't handle it; it makes him want to run until his body twists in pain.

"Do you think someone else could have written it?" Thom mutters, still facing the table. There is a moment of definite silence from Aunty Val.

"Who do you mean?"

"I don't know. Anyone. Someone else". Thom focuses on her hand that is gripping the edge of the table.

"You're scaring me Thom", Aunty Val tells him. "You've been very quiet lately and now *this*. Has Daniel's death brought up old feelings about your parents?"

"Oh great!" Thom shouts, standing up and sweeping the notebook and coins from the tabletop. There is a sound of clinking and thudding as they hit the floor. "It's me who's the crazy one?"

Thom spits. "There's all this shit lying around that I don't understand and you don't notice anything because all you do is sit around and wallow for fuck's sake!" Thom doesn't take a breath. Aunty Val's jaw has sagged, bringing out the wrinkles in her neck. Thom lowers himself onto the chair again. It has been years since he lost his temper this way.

"I know you're upset so I know why you did that. I just ask that you give me the same respect". Aunty Val holds back the tears and gets to her feet. Thom springs up to follow her but her turning to face him cuts him short.

"Please clean up those coins", she says and strokes the side of his face. Thom grabs her hand and kisses it and she nods, knowing what he means. Thom feels comforted by her but at the same time, sees how her eyes flicker under his gaze.

Thom wonders what Aunty Val would say if he told her all the parts he knew, about the note and the lock up, and whether she would still call him crazy then. Thom also wonders why he doesn't want to tell her, why he is keeping Daniel's secret for him, when he isn't even here to know about it.

Chapter 18

Red Door

I try to return to my bedsit the evening after I meet Thom for the first time but standing on the corner, I can make out Michael sitting in a car opposite the building. I am surprised he is wasting his time and partly touched by his presence. I wonder if Doctor Rosey is hovering too but decide she probably has better things to do.

There is no way I can sneak in. Michael has completely cut off my access to warmth and shelter. I have no choice but to make the streets my home for the night. I wrap the scarf tighter and walk in the opposite direction.

I think about Michael sitting in the car. Does it mean he cares about me? Or is he doing it for the good of society? After all, he considers me mentally unstable and probably dangerous. I'll bet that Doctor's been stirring up his fears too, putting detonators all over his mind.

It would be so easy to walk over to his car and ask him to help me. It would be so easy to let the doctors take me back to the hospital, keep the door closed 22 hours per day, make me swallow flavourless pills until I forget my identity and forget the sadness that hovers over it.

Yet, I am needed. Thom needs me. His family need me. They don't realise what I can do for them. Take today for example, I made Thom forget for a moment, I made him come out of his pain and confront something completely different. This is why I know I'm meant to help that family, why I know I have something special to share with them.

Without you, I have to find somewhere to be. You understand don't you, Mum? I'm not forgetting our family or you.

At the same time, I can't deny that spending time with them may give me the opportunity to find out more about Daniel. There are so many questions about him that need to be answered. I have made no progress in discovering what he meant when he said those words, before the train smashed him to pieces. In his destruction, all the answers shattered, like a plate thrown against a wall and scattering into dark undiscovered corners. You never find all the pieces when that happens. There is always a shard someplace that the eye misses.

Overall, the only thing I know for certain is that I need to be with them. And without thinking, this is where my feet take me. I find myself staring at the house, which looks like an old woman, deflated and sagging. The door is painted red; something I have failed to notice, but the paint is peeling and flaking away in defeat. The curtains are half pulled in some windows and completely open in others. No one cares whether it is day or night. This house is in mourning too.

When I go in there again, I'll open and shut those curtains for them.

The thought makes me smile as I take residence on the bench opposite them, wrapping my coat around my body. My ankles are exposed and soon become cold but I close my eyes. In the darkness, Daniel wakes up and I start to follow him.

Chapter 19

Red Scarf

Thom walks down the stairs the next morning, a flash of red stopping him by the hall window. He squints at the figure curled up on the bench opposite the house and instantly starts to run. He fumbles with the door and races across the street, nearly tripping over the rough grass in the front garden.

He reaches the bench, gasping for breath. She is wearing a large overcoat that has fallen open, revealing her bare legs and a few inches of her stomach where her top has ridden up. The blood red scarf is around her neck and trails over the side of the bench, looking as deeply asleep as she is.

Thom kneels down beside her. He considers tucking her curls behind her ears but as soon as he reaches towards her, his arm feels heavy and he lets it drop. Instead, he rests his fingers on the wooden slats, a few inches from her.

"*Sarah*", Thom whispers, too quietly at first, then louder a few more times. She begins to rock from side to side, a boat gently nudged by the current. Then as he persists, she shoots up as though he has shot her in the spine.

"Sarah, it's me", Thom says, grabbing onto her wrist. She jolts again but exhales heavily when she sees him. After a few moments, she even smiles and Thom feels comforted and cold in the same instant.

Sarah folds her legs towards herself so Thom has space to sit. Thom watches Sarah grasp the scarf in her fist and pull it towards her.

"How are you?" she mumbles. Thom almost laughs at her mundane question.

"I'm fine. And you?" Thom humours her.

"Fine", she answers, in a tone that is hard to doubt.

"What are you doing here?"

"I came to see you". She looks at him sheepishly and quickly refocuses on the scarf, pulling at the loose threads at the bottom.

"You did?" Thom leans forward.

"Yes. I just enjoyed our chat yesterday so much", she says in a voice so flat Thom gains nothing from it. She must mean it though, otherwise why would she put herself in a position where she could be humiliated? All of it is another puzzle. It seems she is just as empty as Daniel. So why does she fill him with so many emotions?

"I like your scarf". Thom gestures. Her head snaps up instantly.

"You like red?" She turns towards him and presses her fingertips against his arm. He doesn't answer straight away, enjoying even the minute pressure of her skin against his. He imagines he can feel her pulse beating with his own.

"I love red. It's very bold".

"It's a passionate colour", Sarah adds urgently.

"Yeah I guess it is. We associate it with such strong emotions, contradictory ones at that: love and hate", Thom agrees.

"And sex and blood", Sarah tags on again and Thom sits back, unnerved by her words. She falls silent and leaves Thom thinking of how she is one of those people who cuts conversations in half, but is not bothered when social interaction is stopped short, like a film paused in the middle.

"You're wearing the same clothes as yesterday", Thom mentions.

"So?" She shrugs. It's a good question, Thom reasons. Why should she have changed her clothes? But then he notices her elbow, still blotted with blood and the grass stains on her knees.

"Did you go home last night?"

"Of course", she spits out air heavily.

"Where do you live?"

"Fennel Street", Sarah answers sharply. Thom snakes his hand along the edge of the bench and touches her shoulder. She watches his hand vigilantly, as though it is not connected to Thom and may attack her.

"You look like you stayed here all night. You can tell me, if you did…" Thom squeezes her shoulder. Shaking his hand off, she brings her knees up to her chest.

"I don't even know you". Her words are muffled by her knees.

"That's true but there must be a reason you're here". Thom puts his hand between them, his hand making a star against the wood.

"I did stay here last night", she admits. One of her hands dances along the edge of the bench.

"Why?" Thom asks, trying to catch her gaze. He wants to get closer to her, understand why her honesty makes his blood rush in all directions, causing it to collide and explode like atoms splitting.

"I'm having trouble with my landlord". She shrugs and he watches her hand, still doing gymnastics on the edge.

"We can't have you sleeping on the street", Thom tells her. He reaches forward and grabs her dancing hand, clasping it tight, afraid she might try to escape. Yet she squeezes his hand in return.

"You should stay with me – I mean, *us*".

"I can't. We don't know each other". Sarah gives Thom a coy smile.

"Stop saying that". Thom pulls her to her feet, for the second time in two days.

"Just come inside and meet Aunty Val. She'll fix you some tea".

Thom feels her hand spasm momentarily but thinks it is only a reflex.

Chapter 20

The Mother

I watch her from the hallway as Thom talks in a whisper, explaining my presence. She glances towards the hall a few times and fiddles with her hair and her cardigan, obviously more annoyed she doesn't have time to fix herself up rather than the fact that Thom wants to invite a complete stranger into her house.

Yet, Thom doesn't think we are strangers. He likes me. He told me we *do* know each other. And he's right. We should be together. We should all be in this house, supporting each other, finding answers about Daniel.

I don't feel prepared as she walks towards me. I see everything I have observed from afar zoomed in: the cracked texture of her soggy tissue, the separate strands of her wiry hair scooped into a clumsy ponytail, the wideness of her pupils and the crowd of emotions leaving her eyelashes clumped together in a wet huddle.

"Hello Sarah". She offers me her hand, without hesitation. I take it and her touch is like a blowtorch slicing through my body. I stumble for a second and press against the wall, avoiding her face. If I look into her face...

"Are you okay honey?" the mother asks. She is looking at me like I am her own child or a beloved pet she is about to get put down. My vision finally stabilises and I'm forced to stare into her eyes. It is although I fear she will instantly know my secrets, but she does not. Apart from being full of water and emotion, her eyes are soft, making my feet steady again.

"This is Aunty Val". Thom smiles; unaware of the turmoil I have just recovered from. This moment is the happiest I have seen him and perhaps the happiest I will ever see him.

"It's nice..." I splutter, "to meet you". I realise I am still clutching onto her hand. She is a scaffolding for me but I am aware that I have to let go. Her hand drops to her side and I wonder why she seems fascinated by me, staring and smiling like a cheesy billboard.

"Shall we go into the living room?" Thom suggests. We all go inside and sit down together. Val brings us tea and custard creams. As Val mixes in my two spoons of sugar, I remember you. I smell the perfume you used to wear and how it lingered beside me when you had to go back to the kitchen, having always forgotten to bring the milk.

Chapter 21

Curls

Her curls are like ribbons of dark chocolate, only blacker. Thom follows them around the room and when they're not there, he imagines their circular pattern curling into the edge of his view like paper burning, dissolving as quickly as it is seen. Everything seems to look like them too – the shadow of the curtain rings against the light, the winding grain of the coffee table, even the shapes he makes in the sky when he joins the stars together...

Thom doesn't know why he can't stop thinking of those curls. Even the few seconds when he manages not to, his thoughts turn to the edge of her red underwear he glimpsed beneath her skirt the day they first met. Then, he gladly returns to the curls before he can begin to blush or think of Emma.

Thom hasn't spoken to Emma in days, maybe even over a week... It's been eight missed calls, that's all he knows. He sits in the kitchen and watches the phone dance around the table until it either stops or plummets to the floor. He would almost feel relieved if it smashed apart but it has remained strong, unlike him. That's why he doesn't answer her. He can't think of anything new to say. He could easily listen to her small talk and pretend to care or he could say "Yep. Still grieving here". And then what? Would that satisfy her? And for how long?

Emma is far away; a distant planet that he knows exists but has no interest in exploring at present. Knowing she exists is enough. Yet if it's enough for their relationship, he can't tell.

In a similar vein, Sarah has become almost a fixture over the last few days. Sometimes he doesn't notice her at all, only her curls, as though they are a completely separate entity. Perhaps his fascination with her curls is only a distraction from his fascination with her. But he can't think about that right now either. Thom has to admit though, she has been a comfort. Sometimes he has been sitting in the dark without realising it and suddenly the room is flooded with light. Sarah isn't there but he hears her soft footsteps disappearing from the scene. Thom has ignored his body's needs at times too and Sarah has carefully deposited food near his door just as his hunger seems to have reached its peak.

Sarah seems to know Thom better than even he does. Yet she keeps her distance. The door to the living room where she sleeps is usually closed with little sound inside, and when she does appear, she helps Aunty Val with the washing or sits on the sofa with her legs pulled up to her chest. She looks like a fugitive, always afraid to be discovered. And maybe she is. He doesn't even know her; he just wishes he did.

Richard has barely spoken to Sarah. He tells Thom "I'm not sure". "Sure about what?" Thom asks and Richard just shakes his head. He is acting like a dog who always barks and growls at someone, with reason or without, no one can ever ask the dog for its opinion. And Richard won't give Thom one. He can't mistrust

Sarah on such a vague impression from Richard. Although, it's not like Richard to have a vague dislike for someone, without some foundation at least.

Thom is no closer to Daniel. He often puts out all the objects he found in the lock up on the floor and rearranges them, hoping they will suddenly fit together and unlock something. Yet they don't. He has re-read the note a million times, until the paper looks a hundred years old, but still it has revealed nothing more than the words written on it. He hasn't even looked up Mrs Tray yet, the mysterious beneficiary. He will do that soon.

Every morning he wakes up and feels like the world is a rhino sitting on his chest and he loses his determination all over again. It takes him hours to breathe easily again, to function. But tomorrow, he will make some progress. He knows Daniel must make sense to someone and every puzzle must have a resolution. Thom can't believe that reason will betray him on this one.

Chapter 22

Swelling Blood

It is the fourth time I have stood in Daniel's empty room, including the time I snuck in during his wake. I have been staying at the Mansen's house for four days now, steadily becoming a fixture, whilst Daniel wilts with each passing day. Or does he?

The family and I are still transfixed on him. He is like that book, *The Catcher in the Rye,* because after you've read it cover to cover, you're not really sure what happened when someone asks you years later. And it seems neither the family nor me are really sure what happened with Daniel. Was it our stupidity, or was Daniel a genius who left behind an unsolvable puzzle? Or was he simply an ordinary man who wanted to die?

I sit on the bed. As I think about what his death has done to me, I realise it has awoken me again. For several years before his death, there are entire weeks and months I cannot recall. I have no idea of the length between my leaving the hospital and meeting him in the street. Even the days when I stalked Daniel seem a blurred series of photos, merging into one continuous film.

Yet since the moment I watched him fall, every sense has been on alert. I have smelt the sadness radiating from the house, touched the vibrancy of red, heard the guilt slinking after the family like a venomous snake, and watched depression grow from stubble to a beard on Thom's face. And I'd tasted him. I'd tasted Thom's guilt and confusion like heavy wallpaper paste gluing his tongue down, causing his words to huddle at the back of his mouth in a sticky trap.

I want to open Thom up. I want to cut his words free and examine his feelings; their colours, their textures, the way they fit together and interlock.

The door flings open then.

"What the hell are you doing in here?" Thom whispers loudly and checks behind him as he closes the door. "Aunty Val wouldn't like this at all", he adds.

I stand up and touch his arm. I notice that whenever I touch him, he stares at my offending body part with either disbelief or reluctant intrigue. "I'm sorry. I was just curious", I say gently. His lips are taut like they are two sizes too small for his face. Although, he tries to smile and appear casual by placing his hands in his jeans pockets, shuffling from one foot to the other.

"It's okay", he mutters, not convinced.

"I'll get out of here", I reassure him. He nods but as I start towards the door, his hand shoots out.

"I'm sorry… if, I frightened you". He squeezes my arm with one hand and then raises the other to grab hold of my other arm. He is holding me like I am a person who needs shaking.

"I just wouldn't want you to touch his things". Thom's voice breaks. "It's *too* soon to be touching… his things, his… life".

"Have *you* looked in any of the cupboards or drawers Thom?" I ask, without thinking, regretting it as soon as I see his face. In an instant, his wet sadness is wiped off and replaced with frown lines.

"Why would you say that?" he asks, his grip tightening. He seems more distressed than he should be. He is biting his lip and already he has punctured them, a dot of blood marking his front tooth. "Why would you say that?" he repeats; both his words and his grip harder.

"I'm sorry. I just wondered". I shrug and try to pull away but a second later; he releases me anyway.

Thom walks over to the chest of drawers by the window. He looks over at me, a child asking for permission or seeing how far they can go without being told off, a person testing another's love for them by putting themselves in a dangerous situation. And all I can do is say nothing and wait for the inevitable.

Thom opens a drawer. He lets out a small yelp and for a moment, I hope that he has found something; a severed hand, a blood stained shirt, a weapon. Yet, when I look over his shoulder, there is nothing. Only the wood that the drawer is made of.

Thom catches my eye again. He has started to shake, a tree battered and relenting in a violent wind. He keeps my gaze as he places his hand on another drawer handle and slowly eases it open, a drawn out yawn and finally, he turns towards it.

Another yelp.

I know what he is feeling now. His heart is probably racing faster, his mind filled with the colour of that wood. Worse for him, he probably knows exactly what should be in that particular drawer and all of them. Whereas, I only expected something, anything...

Like a sense of déjà vu, he begins flinging everything open. He finishes the chest of drawers in five seconds, moving onto the drawers beside Daniel's bed, and flinging open the wardrobe. All empty. Gaping holes in everyday life, empty shells that are now devoid of function, life departed from the body it once filled.

There are no words for Thom. He is screaming like a baby who cannot understand anything yet. He is pushing the chest of drawers over and pulling the curtains down. He is punching the mirror on the front of the wardrobe and kicking the door in until it cracks in half, like broken ribs.

I watch the destruction of the empty room. I watch the blood swelling out of his knuckles and forget the whiteness of the room. The red is beautiful and I'm surrounded by it, a calm sea lapping against my brain until I realise, the lapping of the sea coincides with my pulse.

I remember. Thom. He is sobbing on the floor and smearing the carpet with blood, like a child finger painting. He picks up the slithers of glass and throws them at the wall but they only chime quietly and fall to the floor.

I dive towards him and take his hands by the wrists. I press them into my chest and don't let go. His blood soaks into my chest and I feel like he has taken a knife and slit my chest open.

I am alive. Mum, I am so alive. And Daniel is still dead.

Chapter 23

Mrs Tray

The empty room tears a hole in Thom, literally with his slashed hands and, in another sense, perhaps intellectually. Either way, he has to mend this hole somehow. The only way he thinks this might be achieved is by getting some clarification, on anything he can. So he contacts the solicitors the next morning and after a bit of negotiating, he feels his hand moving in the shape of letters and when he replaces the phone receiver, he has an address.

Mrs Tray. The woman with a face like deteriorating fruit. The woman who silenced them all with the door. The woman with no reason for attending the reading, according to those who were meant to know Daniel. Yet clearly, they had been standing much further from him than they realised.

All night, Thom dreamt of falling through an endless white hole. Not the standard black hole dream, but a *white* hole. Obviously, the blank walls of Daniel's room were taunting him. The walls that have been painted recently, without anyone being aware. They are hiding Daniel's secrets. His room is a huge void, only filled now with Thom's blood and the smashed glass.

And now here Thom is, trying to get the woman with a face plagued with holes to fill his own. Perhaps she, as no one else has so far, will turn the whiteness of his mind some other colour. Even pearl would be something.

Mrs Tray lives in a cluster of flats designed for the elderly. It's a small community with a well-kept green in the middle that the flats surround. There is nothing remarkable about her front door. It is painted green but the green is like her skin, cracked and faded past its original state. He finds her name on the bell and presses it several times.

It's only now that Thom ponders about Mrs Tray. Is she a friend of Daniel's? If so, how did they meet? Perhaps she is a relative of one of Daniel's friends or girlfriends (though Thom isn't aware of many). Perhaps they met accidentally and formed a friendship. Or perhaps they had been having a sordid and frankly, creepy affair. Thom relishes this idea for a moment but he fails to laugh. Whatever the details, there has to be something helpful he can find out here.

Thom hasn't noticed the door skulking open and he jolts slightly when Mrs Tray's cratered face floats ahead of him. She is smaller than he remembers and this time, she props herself up with a wooden walking stick, the texture as knotted as her hand that appears to have shrunk around the top of it permanently.

"Mrs Tray..." he says. It's the beginning of a sentence but he has no idea how to complete it. He hopes she will rescue him or ask him who the hell he is or invite him in without a word, yet she only stares. Her eyes are the colour of faded bark and they examine him closely, as though she is waiting for him to pounce.

"I'm Thom", he tells her finally. He wants to slap himself across the face. His stupid name means nothing to her! Perhaps he shouldn't have come. Maybe the answers he seeks so hard are also the thing he wants to run away from.

"You were at the reading of the will", she says. Thom feels like she has thrown him a piece of driftwood in the sea. Her voice is much softer than he would have anticipated and, even more surprising, is the gentle Irish twang to it. Her raspy face has given him false impressions. He should know better than to trust his own judgements at the moment, he keeps getting tripped up whenever he does.

"Yes. That's why I'm here!" Thom exclaims, too excitedly for the subject matter. He composes himself and holds his hand out. "Thom Mansen. Sorry". Her hand moves upwards in slow motion and Thom finally grasps it. In situations like this, people often say 'pleased to meet you' but Thom isn't sure he is and doesn't want to lie to the woman.

"You'd better come in", she says, neither pleased nor displeased. It's all very lukewarm. Thom shrugs to himself and lets himself in. She directs him to a lit doorway down the darkened hall and ushers him ahead of her, the slow thump of her walking stick pursuing him.

"Sit anywhere", she shouts ahead and Thom sits himself in an armchair near the door. He digs his fingernails into the fabric and waits for the unknown to catch up with him. He closes his eyes, his blood thumping inside his head, the rhythm smashed by the door. Once again, her work is decisive and unquestionable.

"I wondered if anyone would come", she sings without trying and lowers herself, with some effort, into a chair facing him. He tries to look as disinterested as she does, hoping that it will have the strange effect of drawing truth from her. Thom has found this sometimes works with people (especially those who were trying to make fraudulent claims) who, so desperate for some clarification, end up spilling their secrets.

On the table he sees a pack of cards set up for solitaire. She is playing three-card draw and Thom instantly respects her a little more. What is the point of playing one-card draw? It is one of his pet hates.

"You took longer than I expected actually", Mrs Tray says and folds her arms. If anyone saw her now, they'd say she looks like any harmless elderly woman, yet Thom believes she is hiding something. Her face is full of nooks and crannies where she can conceal things.

"I've had a lot to do", Thom claims. When he really thinks about his words he wants to laugh. What has he actually achieved? He's failed to get out of bed, sat around in the darkness, invited a strange woman into his home, and sliced his hands open. It isn't exactly the traditional definition of 'progress'.

"I imagine so. Do you play by the way?" She gestures to her cards. Thom nods and leans forward.

"The seven of spades can go over there". He wonders if he should've said it but she nods gratefully and performs the action.

"Sometimes all it takes is a fresh eye". She smiles but Thom gets caught up in her words, a wind stuck in a pipe, rattling and whistling. A fresh eye? Perhaps that is all he needs.

93

"Do you live alone?"

"I'm alone", she answers. The two words are small and quiet, yet they seem to pull at Thom's lips and like a puppet, he mouths them a few times: "I'm alone".

"Did you enjoy your inheritance gift?"

"Why would you call it a 'gift'?" Thom cocks his head, like a detective in a film.

He wants her to know he mistrusts her, but even he has no idea why. Some detective...

"Well, didn't your friend, Daniel, call it a 'gift' in his will?" Thom is disappointed that the explanation is so simple and picks up on the fact that Mrs Tray referred to Daniel as his 'friend'.

"He was my cousin", Thom tells her. She nods quietly, perhaps having suspected it and folds her hands in her lap. She gives Thom none of the usual 'I'm sorry' and merely waits.

"How did you know him?" Thom asks finally.

"I didn't", she says, "not really". The words are simple but Thom feels like his eardrums are pressured for a moment and he doesn't believe he really heard them. *I didn't* – what does that mean?

"I'm sorry?" he asks; using the phrase he expected from her.

"I didn't really know Daniel", she repeats, more forcefully. Thom watches her lips move and churns the sentence around in his chaotic brain, filled with all the things Daniel left behind.

"But why were you there? At the reading?" Thom splutters.

"He looked after my husband. In the hospital", she explains.

The hospital! Finally, something Thom knows about! For several years, Daniel worked full-time at a hospital for those with mental health problems. He'd only taken a job as an administrator at first but later worked as a mentor for several patients. He hadn't spoken too much about it to Thom but Aunty Val often passed on stories. Thom often wonders how Daniel found contentment in the job, as he seemed to have limited empathy for others and preferred to be alone. Yet, Daniel spent around three years there and Thom heard of no complaints throughout that time. Why he left, Thom isn't sure. Yet it wasn't long before he died, perhaps six or eight months at the most.

"Your husband was a patient then?"

"Yes. He spent several years at the hospital but before Daniel arrived, he was making very little progress". Mrs Tray stops for a moment and smiles to herself. The gesture and its relation to Daniel seem foreign to Thom.

"Daniel helped my husband greatly. I think he finally felt like someone was listening and even that helped a little. But like I said, I didn't really know Daniel. I heard a lot from my husband, when he felt able, and met Daniel only a few times myself", she pauses. "He seemed like a lovely lad though. He was quiet, shy, but he helped my husband so much. I think my gratitude embarrassed him".

"He helped your husband?" Thom is asking himself to believe it, rather than asking her to clarify. How could someone who hardly said a word to his own family help a mentally ill man?

95

"Yes. So when he sent the letter, I had no reservations agreeing to his request".

"His request?" Thom repeats. Thom can't construct his own words; merely regurgitates those of others instead.

"He sent me a letter, several months ago. He asked me to attend a meeting".

"The reading of his will?" Thom surges forward with his words.

"As it turns out – yes", Mrs Tray verifies. Thom sags backwards, his body jolting and struggling to function normally. Just breathe, just beat, just swallow.

"Did Daniel commit suicide?" she asks. Thom stares at her for a moment, wondering if she is really asking *him* a question. He thought she might have the answers but here he is, on the spot, as it were.

"I don't know", Thom says, "I've wondered..." His throat is getting smaller. He starts to cough like a cat trying to retrieve a hairball. Mrs Tray pours him a glass of water from a jug he hasn't noticed and he gratefully gulps it down. His hand shakes so much that he spills it down his shirt. "Sorry", he gargles as he slams the glass down on the table. "Do you still have the letter?"

Mrs Tray leaves the room and returns a few minutes later with a perfectly crisp envelope. It has been torn open with an old-fashioned letter opener, judging by the perfectly straight tear across the top of it. Thom looks up and Mrs Tray nods her approval. He plucks the letter from inside and places the envelope neatly on the table beside him. He unfolds it and Daniel's handwriting instantly drowns him.

Dear Mrs Tray,

I realised it's been a few months since I contacted you. I hope you are coping with the loss of your husband, a great man whom I have missed greatly since I left the hospital. Thank you for inviting me to the funeral, I was happy I was able to see him off properly.

I would have come to see you but it's just not possible right now. So I'm afraid I have to ask you a favour by letter. I know it's not polite to ask something of you, especially as my friendship was solely with your husband. Yet I have no choice and as you're related to someone I trusted, I feel like I could ask you and perhaps you would find it in yourself to help me.

It's a simple request. I need you to attend a meeting that will probably occur within the next month. The address is enclosed on a business card. You will probably be called nearer the time. I just wanted to ask you personally. Please be there.

Yours, Daniel

"He invited you to his will reading in advance?" Thom asks, holding the letter away from him as though it's diseased. All Daniel's paper trail seems to be offending him.

"I know. I don't understand it either", she says. Silent for a moment, she finally adds, "I guess he must've known one way or another he was going to die". The statement is the next obvious step but it knocks all sound from the room. It winds the situation and, for a few seconds, nothing and no one moves or breathes or comprehends.

"I found a note too", Thom reveals finally. He hasn't told Emma, Aunty Val or anyone else since he found it. It has burnt its every curve and line into his brain but he hasn't said it out loud. Until now...

"What did it say?" She is just as intrigued as he is about hers.

"It had the time and place of his death". Thom winces. He doesn't know what effect the revelation will have. He's been dreading it since he found it.

"Oh goodness". She shakes her head.

"So he knew", Thom vocalises their thoughts. "He either jump-ed in front of a train or he was pushed by someone he knew".

Thom feels an inappropriate waterfall of relief beating down on his shoulders and back. He wants to close his eyes and let it beat him unconscious. "I thought I was going crazy". Thom wants to scream and smash everything in the room apart. He wants to punch his way through the wall and draw blood again. He thought he felt confused but all he feels surging through him like a current is anger. Anger pumps into his heart and gets stuck, inflating it until it buzzes like a threatened beehive.

"It sounds like you have a lot to find out", Mrs Tray tells him. He has to clasp onto the chair in order to stop himself from hitting her or throwing something at her. *Obviously* he has a lot to find out, stupid bitch. That fucking bitch comes along with her sob story and one letter and starts telling him what to do. What does she know?

"I'm sorry about Daniel. I was so sad to hear about his death and now, it all seems so… sinister", she adds and puts her hand on his knee. Thom stares at it, wishing it would burst into flames.

"Can I have this?" Thom asks abruptly, snatching at the letter. Mrs Tray withdraws her hand quickly and nods.

"Please do". She heaves herself out of the chair and walks towards the door. "It was nice to meet you Thom". Thom realises he has overstayed his welcome and probably frightened the woman. He would usually apologise but all he wants to do is lash out so he keeps his mouth closed, for fear of bees flying out of him and stinging her to death.

On his way out, he merely nods at her and crumples up Daniel's second letter until the creases mark the inside of his hand like a tattoo.

Chapter 24

The Stranger

Thom dives into a parking spot just outside the house and turns the engine off. He lets his body flop. After all the adrenaline that has been surging through him the last hour, his muscles haven't relaxed once. He wouldn't mind now if a huge spaceship fell out of space and crushed him. It would save on a lot of emotional turmoil and he wouldn't have to tell Aunty Val that her son was either murdered or planned his own death. All the questions she would ask him – why? What happened? What made him do it? How could he leave us all to deal with this? Thom has no idea, not one, to share with Aunty Val.

Mrs Tray had seemed an unimportant character. Yet she has really opened the can of worms, as such. She confirmed that Daniel had premature knowledge of his death. Either suicide, planned murder or even some psychic sense – Daniel knew. And now Thom knows. Thom knows and his heart feels like a steam engine in his chest, wheezing and coughing itself onwards. If he closes his eyes, he isn't certain he will open them again for hours or perhaps days. Yet when he does close them, it is alarmingly white so he is forced to open them again.

There are still things that make no sense. The notebook for one. Had he written that or had Daniel? And the lock up. What did the effort of doing that and the objects inside reveal? And the emptied room. Why would Daniel empty it and how did he do it without his family's knowledge? Aunty Val clearly hasn't noticed yet, as she hasn't mentioned it.

Thom jumps at a knock on the window. At first he thinks he imagined it but when he notices the shadow over his lap and the steering wheel, he lifts his head and sees a man standing there. This isn't a yellow line and he isn't blocking a driveway so the man's intentions are unknown to him. Thom unwinds his window.

"Yes?"

"Do you live in that house..." the man interrupts himself with a glance over his shoulder, "*that* house over there?" Thom pulls himself up and looks at where the man is pointing. Yes, that is his house. He can't see anything wrong with it – no fire, no broken windows, nothing visible from the outside. Is there something wrong? In the same vein, this man doesn't look like a fireman or a policeman, unless he is plain clothed.

"Yeah", Thom answers casually. He doesn't want this stranger to know he is alarmed and confused. The man keeps looking around. It seems he expects to be caught out by someone or he is about to reveal a secret to Thom.

"I've seen you going in and out of there", the man says. He is bending over to speak to Thom. Thom can see a defined bend in the bridge of his nose. His hair is a black lump of frizz and something about it seems familiar to Thom. *Familiar hair*? What is Thom thinking?

"I need to ask you about someone", the man finally continues. He is trying to get something out of his pocket but his hand seems to be shaking. Thom backs away slightly, yet doesn't roll up the window.

"I've seen you together", the man mumbles whilst he continues to struggle. Finally he pulls out a folded piece of paper. He opens it up. It is a photo. He hands it to Thom. "Do you", he pauses deliberately, "know her?"

The man looks excited, almost manic. Thom looks at the photo carefully. Of course he knows her. She is much younger in this picture. Her hair is shorter but her intricate curls still wind around his attention. She looks happier. Now, he always senses sadness in her. But he could hardly judge her for that; he hasn't been a barrel of laughs lately...

"Why are you asking this?" Thom pushes the photo back at him, reluctant to give in so easily. The man helplessly takes it back, but glances at it before placing it back in his pocket.

"I need to find her", he answers briefly. No explanations, no hints that he knows her well or is concerned about her. What does this man want with Sarah?

"Look, I don't know her that well. We only met once", Thom tells the man and makes a move to exit the car. The man pushes the door shut again and Thom wonders then what this man might do.

102

"She's been in your house…" he fumbles. "I know she has?" The man persists with a question, although Thom isn't sure it's not just the tone of his voice. His voice is bordering on a whine.

Thom opens his door again and this time, the man doesn't block him. Thom locks the door and turns back to the man. "If you know, then why are you asking me anything?"

"She'll just run if she sees me", he confesses, sagging against the car.

"What have you done to her?" Thom asks, feeling the adrenaline begin to pulse through his blood again.

"I'm trying to help her", the man insists. He grabs onto Thom's arm but Thom immediately shakes him off.

"I think you should leave; whoever you are". Thom begins to walk towards the house. Yet, the man chases after him, grabbing at his shirt. Thom spins around and bats at the man with his hand. "Just fuck off. I don't know what you want and I can't help you, okay?"

"You think she's fine but she's ill. I know her. I promise I just want to help". Thom can't decide if the man is genuine or whether he just believes his own lies.

"What's her name then? You haven't even said anything personal. How do I know you know her?"

Thom and the man are standing in the middle of the road. The sun is starting to set and the impending darkness doesn't seem attractive to Thom in his current situation. He has to get away from this strange desperate man.

"Her name is Alice", he says softly and Thom instantly starts to turn. The man stamps after Thom. "But I bet she told you her name is something else, didn't she?" His words chase Thom across the street and will never fully be lost inside his mind. "Let me ask you, does she seem strange to you? Does she talk about her family? Do you know that much about her?"

The man won't shut up so as Thom reaches the gate, he flings round and aims a punch at the man's face. Luckily, the man ducks and Thom misses. Thom doesn't really want to hurt him; he just wants to scare him away. Like a moth head butting a light bulb continuously, this man is becoming irritating.

"What are you doing?" the man shrieks.

"I told you to leave. You haven't convinced me of anything and you're wasting my time", Thom says the words but still inside, the moth keeps crashing into the back of his eyes and he knows he won't sleep much tonight.

"I don't want her to hurt herself or anyone else". The man seems weary now.

"You don't even know her name". Thom puts the front gate between them.

"That's not important. What about the other questions I asked you? What about them?" The man looks like someone dying pleading for a cure. Thom could easily give him a glimmer of hope and give into the doubts he has dismissed in order to have an easier life. He *has* wondered about her: why she acts so coldly, where she appeared from. Yet Thom is too tired to trust this man, too battered to let something else in his life fall apart.

"She has a lovely family. She's shown me pictures". Thom watches his words pull down the edges of the man's mouth like weights. Thom stares at him for a few more moments and turns away.

"I won't give up", the man vows to Thom's back.

"Do what you like". Thom shrugs. Thom opens the front door and slams it behind him, almost in Mrs Tray style. As he laughs at the comparison in his head, he looks up the stairs and sees Sarah watching him. Thom doesn't say anything, just returns the stare. He wonders if he should have protected her or if she will shed her skin and prove to be the monster the stranger warned him about.

Chapter 25

Red Scars Beneath

He is bound to have them: questions, doubts. He hardly knows a thing about me; only the obvious physical attributes and a few snippets of information that can barely fill half a page. And when he sits down beside me on the steps, so close that our knees and thighs are squashed together, and says, "There was a man asking about you outside", I know he finally has to ask. At the same time, I know it's finally time for me to lie.

"What did he ask you?" I question, managing a convincing mask of concern.

Thom is instantly the gentleman, saying: "I didn't tell him anything".

I should've known he would be on my side. He is a sweet man and I can't help but reach up and touch his soft stubble. Like always when I touch him, he opens his mouth slightly and freezes, waiting for the moment to pass.

"So what did he want to know?" I ask again and Thom turns his head, making my hand fall away.

"He said he knew you. He said you were ill and you need help". Thom says the words cautiously and still doesn't want to make the air throb with awkwardness or cause the stairs to creak underfoot. He glances at me from the corner of his eye, trying to gauge my reaction.

"That's strange", I say casually. Inside, the drum of my heart thuds quicker.

"I couldn't tell if he was lying or not", Thom pauses but quickly continues, "are you in some kind of trouble, Sarah?" He is more concerned than playing the detective.

"I told you, I'm a little behind on my rent but that's all". I give him a sheepish look. He nods understandingly.

"He said your name is Alice", he adds and lets the name hang in the air for a moment. He seems to be watching it to see if it attaches itself to me or to see if I make a move to claim it.

"Alice? That wouldn't suit me at all". I laugh. Thom chuckles a little but it doesn't fit his mouth properly.

"Sarah does suit you", he agrees.

That's exactly what I always thought. I even wanted to change my name by d-poll but I had never done it. I'm glad I can be who I want now.

Do you mind that I left my name behind, Mum?

"Did you ever call Daniel 'Dan'?" I ask.

"No, it didn't seem to fit". Thom shrugs. "I guess nicknames are familiar and playful. Daniel didn't really go for that type of thing". Thom picks at the skin around his nails as he picks at his memories.

"That's sad", I say quietly.

We fall silent and listen to the house, humming and creaking.

"Aren't you going to ask what the man outside looked like?" Thom asks abruptly. I almost believed we had left the subject behind but Thom is scrutinising my every pore, line and muscle for weakness.

"Oh… I meant to ask". I fumble slightly. Thom seems a bit suspicious for a moment but he gives me a brief description nonetheless: short black frizzy hair, the beginnings of a beard, a brown overcoat, and a bend in the bridge of his nose. I shake my head in response and say, "I don't know who that is, sorry". Thom seems disappointed but nods again.

"He had a picture of you", Thom adds. He has been quiet for a few minutes and I have been listening to his puckered breathing. He seems distressed about something, unable to even let the air slip easily through his windpipe. What is wrong with my Thom?

"He did?" I ask, unable to think of anything else just then.

"Yeah. It looked like you were a bit younger in the photo", Thom pauses. "How do you suppose he got that?"

I have to think fast. At that moment, I hate Michael more than ever.

"I didn't want to tell you about this but I suppose I have no choice", I hear a voice saying. Thom is looking at me with keen interest and I realise it's my throat that is vibrating with sound. "About two years ago, I was raped". The words hang in the air like poison gas and neither of us knows whether to breathe in or out. We stare straight ahead for a few minutes.

"You were raped", Thom repeats. I know he instantly believes I am weaker. Everyone does when they hear that. So many people didn't know how to speak to me afterwards, that's what made it more isolating.

You kept me alive, Mum. I wouldn't have survived without you. But you aren't around to pull me out of the quicksand anymore; I just keep sinking until even the numbness doesn't feel anything.

"What does this have to do with that man?" Thom asks quietly but his fists are already wriggling with his assumptions.

"He was my boyfriend but we broke up". The lie feels like fur on my tongue. I want to stick my fingers down my throat and make it come gushing out. I want him to see the blackness inside but at the same time, I want him to love my black curls instead. "He didn't take it too well", I add. Thom is biting his lip so hard I can tell there is blood gathering beneath his teeth. It is slowly throbbing out of him like the blood that oozed from his hands in Daniel's room. I resent him for a moment, for being able to see some of his pain in the burnt scars beneath his bandages whereas my scars are inside, hidden beneath the bandages of my skin.

"That man hurt you", he says but his teeth and his clenched expression muffle his words. I nod and this is enough to answer. Being so close, every movement is like an earthquake between us.

It all happens so fast. Before I can blink, Thom is on his feet and has managed to jump most of the staircase. He is advancing on the front door, his body arched like a hedgehog preparing to defend. I

109

stumble after him and manage to reach him just as he grabs at the door handle. I push him against the wall.

"That won't help anyone", I tell him but he squirms underneath me. His head is so furrowed I want to shake him. I want to make him look sad again. Anything would be better. "Please Thom", I say and press my face into his shoulder. He smells of sweat and cold.

In the next moment, I feel him push me away gently. He has stopped shaking. His anger has been replaced by concern for my gesture. What does it mean? What do I want from him? If only I knew myself. Never did I think I would confess my secret to this man. Even though I'd lied about the person who'd committed the act, I wasn't lying about the incident.

I wish you were here, Mum. You were looking after me and you didn't finish. I need you still. Yet maybe I'd asked too much and that's why I lost you.

"I can't promise I won't do something if I see him again but I'll leave it", Thom says, "for now". I nod and take a step back. He is pressing himself against the wall. He takes a side-step towards the stairs but before he can take another, the doorbell rings.

We both look at one another but neither of us moves.

Chapter 26

The Visitor

"Emma", Thom croaks when he opens the door. She isn't smiling but she doesn't look angry either. The wind is making her loosely tied hair dance and she has goose bumps on her arms. He is slow to react and she gives him an impatient narrowing of her eyes. "Oh sorry, come in". He ushers her in and glances outside to see if the stranger is still there, but he is nowhere to be seen. He closes the door.

Sarah is still standing just inside the door. She and Emma are facing one another. They both look as though they are owed an explanation. Thom feels like two opposing forces have met and are pushing against one another but he doesn't know why – no one has moved or spoken.

"Who's this then?" Emma finally asks.

Thom is about to answer but Sarah lifts her hand up and informs her, "I'm Sarah". Emma returns the favour but her mouth slants down to one side as she speaks. After all, she is no clearer on who this strange woman is.

Thom clears his throat and both of them turn to him expectantly. "Sarah, could you leave us please?" he asks, feeling like a traitor.

Sarah just nods quietly and makes her way upstairs (without making the stairs creak, when he still does after walking up them all his life).

Emma turns to him. He remembers her appearance as though it's been years since he last saw her. He recaptures the three-freckle cluster beside her earlobe, the way she twitches her mouth when she feels uncomfortable, her slender fingers that press against his arm now.

"Let's go in the living room", Thom says and leads her by the hand into the darkened room. He turns on a lamp, closes them in and they both settle on the edge of the sofa. Sarah's bed sheets are in a pile by the chair, like dog shit that neither of them wants to acknowledge or clean up. Emma is staring so hard at him that he feels she can see everything he has done in the last few weeks – his obsessive detective work, his tears and depression, his explosions of anger, his taking in of a mysterious woman he knows nothing about. Yet she can't know. She has come here because she doesn't know what he's been doing or what he's been thinking.

"What happened to your hands?" she asks as she lightly traces her fingers over the gauze.

Thom hesitates for a moment, on the verge of confessing but instead says, "I dropped some plates and cut myself a few times". This is the second major lie he has told her. It all started with the note and his first lie. Now, he is lying again to stop her entering the world he has been living in since his first deception.

"You've grown a beard", she comments. She is noting the changes one by one, hoping to get past the surface. Yet Thom hopes she gets lost in unwrapping the bandages and his clump of facial hair.

112

"I just haven't shaved. No reason", Thom tells her, wiping off the small hint of a smile on her lips.

"I've been trying to call you, as you've probably realised..." Emma drops her eyes to her lap, probably not wanting to hear what he has to say about this. What explanation would be a good one?

"I'm sorry. I needed some time... and quiet".

The couple know there is an undertone to the conversation, words and thoughts that are being trapped beneath their tongues and inside their heads. The words and thoughts are cockroaches that struggle to surface in view of others and prefer to scuttle around in the safety of darkness.

"I know you needed time. I've left you for three weeks, wondering how you are every day. I only called because I thought it'd be easier if I made the first move". Emma is leaning closer but Thom shrinks into the arm of the sofa and ignores her.

"You were probably right to think so", Thom agrees blankly.

"Then why didn't you answer one of my calls?"

"I'm sorry. I just had nothing to say". He shrugs. Emma doesn't respond to this, she falls silent. For several minutes, they both find sanctuary in the rhythm of the clock on the mantelpiece. It chugs onwards, regulating their jumpy heartbeats for a small period at least.

"Who is that woman?" Emma finally ventures.

"We met about a week ago. She's having trouble with her rent so Aunty Val invited her to stay".

"Where did you meet?"

"In the front garden, if you must know", Thom answers, realising it sounds completely insane as he hears it. Yet, he has accepted it readily as it happened, as though meeting people in the front garden is a regular occurrence.

"In the front garden?" Emma repeats slowly, like someone who is speaking English as a second language.

"I know it's not ordinary but that's how it happened".

"What was she doing in the front garden?" Emma persists but Thom cuts her down, "Look, I don't have to explain my whole life to you".

"That's not what I'm asking", Emma tells him, folding her arms.

"I'm sorry about this", Thom says quietly after another few minutes of silence. The room feels hot so he goes over to the window and pulls it up. The cold wind hardly affects his bandaged hands. Across the road, he sees the stranger with the photo getting into a car and turning the ignition on. With one last look at the house, seeing Thom, the man pulls off quickly and his lights disappear within a few seconds. Thom almost wonders if he imagined it.

"I think you want to talk to me but you're holding back for some reason. What is it Thom?" Emma can't help but let her affection for him resurface. After all, as far as she is concerned, until about ten minutes ago, nothing had been different between them. Thom's head droops, disgusted that his love for Emma seems to have become buried between all the half-clues and mysteries surrounding Daniel's death. Where have his old feelings gone? All he feels now is curiosity, anger, and infatuation.

"I have things I need to do", Thom reveals, not answering her question. Emma waits for something more and Thom only adds, "I can't go back to my old life now".

"Everyone has to go back sometime. Everyone has to get over losing someone", Emma says, not understanding the situation. Yet, it is not her fault. Thom has kept her separate.

"It's not about that. It's not about losing Daniel. I just have to find answers".

"Have you spoken to the police, Thom? Did they tell you what happened?"

"They haven't even bothered with him. They don't care enough".

"I have no idea why you're isolating yourself, Thom".

Thom watches her approach him in the reflection on the window pane. He doesn't move away, yet doesn't turn to greet her either. He watches her bow her head.

"I'm not. I just can't explain all this to anyone, even if I tried. I need to work on things. I need to learn more myself".

"Have you spoken to Aunty Val about all this *stuff*?"

"Only some. No one would understand it. I have to wait". Thom is being deliberately short, almost relishing the air of mystery he is creating. He imagines he is a renegade detective who will win the case in the end and reveal his amazing discoveries to all those involved! Yet Thom knows real life isn't like this, he is no Sherlock Holmes or the like. He is an ordinary man who is just as lost as anyone else would be given the same facts and clues.

"You sound a little crazy", Emma tosses his way.

"Sarah doesn't think so", he bites back.

"Right, *who* is this woman and what the hell is she doing here?"

In response, Thom does something he himself doesn't understand. He spins round and laughs. After weeks of depression, he finds himself laughing, when there is nothing amusing around him. Emma immediately withdraws a few paces. She is looking at him as if he has just cut his own hand off. He simmers to a chuckle and then only smiles. Still watching him in half-fear and confusion, Thom approaches her, grabs her and kisses her. Emma is rigid in his hold but lets him continue, opening her mouth slightly to allow him in. When he lets her go, she settles on the back of the sofa like someone who has merely tolerated something.

"Who is she Thom?"

"Sarah. She's a nice girl who's been no trouble to us. She needed help and we were there for her. Is it okay to help someone else or not?"

"You know I wouldn't mind that", Emma says, taking a breath and trying to rephrase it, "I'm just not sure you should be welcoming strange people into your life right now. You're the one who needs some help and you need your close family, me – people you can trust". Emma has a good point of course but Thom won't allow her to win.

"I *can* trust Sarah. You don't know her".

"You hardly seem to know her", Emma argues hopefully. Thom can't understand this himself. He feels as though someone has written Emma out of the story of his life and Sarah has been written in instead. Yet he can't tell Emma these things. He can only push her away and hope she realises how deep he has fallen into a white hole where there are endless possibilities and directions he can go.

"I love you", Emma confesses. Thom freezes, taking in her sincere tone. He has flashbacks of them laying in bed at weekends, tangled in the covers, her soft voice whispering those words, the movement of her throat on his shoulder where she is resting it. He is sure the movement and vibration would be exactly the same now. Yet he closes his eyes and the white world recaptures him.

"I'm sorry Emma", Thom manages. He feels certain in his mind, or at least he thinks he is. His body however, seems to be swaying slightly, his eyelid twitching.

"I'll come back, Thom. Just to see how you are", Emma promises, gathering up her handbag and coat. "I didn't realise you would still be in such a state".

"I'm not in a state", Thom sulks. "I'm getting things sorted now".

"If you say so Thom". She nods, unconvinced and makes her way towards the door. Just as she opens it, Thom's legs go soft. He grabs onto the edge of the sofa.

"Emma", he calls out. She peeks back around the door at him, her spark still not diminished. Perhaps this is why he says, "There's nothing going on with Sarah", because she still believes in him.

Emma nods and asks, "So she doesn't know about these 'things' you need to sort out either?"

"No she doesn't. She doesn't know anything".

Thom and Emma both seem comforted by the words, neither knowing quite why. Thom likes to think it is because he is neither together with her, nor together with Sarah so that's some consolation at least. There is a way back for them.

"You know my number", Emma tells him; clearly hoping this isn't the end. Thom nods and lets the door close behind her.

Chapter 27

Red Trail

Who does he think he is? *I know nothing?* How dare he tell that stupid bitch that I know nothing? I've been around him more than she has the last few weeks. He hasn't even phoned her back. But why does he care what she thinks of me anyway? I can tell he was just trying to reassure her, let her know that she's not the only one in the dark. But how can he say that?

I've definitely seen what's been going on: his moods, his obsessive examination of certain strange objects, his comings and goings, his relationship with his aunt. I may not know exactly what he's thinking or doing but I do know more than he told her.

He pretends that I'm not really in his life, yet he seems to want me around. He wants to protect me, as I saw with Michael. He wants to be near me but at the same time is afraid. I know these things, probably more than he does himself! And now, I am only more determined to find out something about Daniel. I will find out how and why Daniel planned for me to push him and that way, I'll prove I know more than Thom thinks. He'll be shocked when I tell him all the things I've found out.

Mum, we'll prove him wrong won't we? Of course, I won't tell him I pushed Daniel; that's our secret.

It had been hard to listen through the living room door but I managed to catch most of it. My skin burnt hearing them together, sharing a connection, her trying to crawl underneath his skin and see the damage. After all, where has she been all this time? I have been the one turning on lights for Thom, leaving him food, watching he and his family day and night, swabbing Thom's slashed skin. I deserve to hear his plans, his need to find things out and discover what things mean.

The first thing I have to do is talk to Thom; perhaps even find out exactly what he's been up to. He might be willing to tell me, everyone likes to halve a burden when they can. And I am the perfect outlet. He doesn't want to hurt Val and Richard isn't interested in anything being harder than it is.

Why can't Thom see me? Why doesn't he tell me about the objects he stares at for hours? Why won't he stop being afraid?

I really thought that Michael might have succeeded in turning Thom against me. Yet fate seems to have saved me. Perhaps because fate knows that this family needs saving and I am the one who can protect them. Yet at this moment, all I want to do is prove I can find out the truth, the plot that led up to the climax as the train bulldozed Daniel out of the family's lives, the reason he led me to them.

When Thom lets Emma out, I am sitting at the top of the stairs again. As he turns back, his face drained, he sees me. He freezes for a millisecond, clearly wondering if, or what, I heard. I smile, writhing inside. Reassured, he returns the gesture and walks slowly towards the kitchen.

Later that night, as he sleeps, I creep into Daniel's room again. Closing the door quietly, I turn the light on.

This is where it begins Mum; the answers…

From the doorway, all the way across the carpet, there is the red trail of blood that Thom left behind. I tiptoe across the trail and arrive at the wardrobe, still gutted. I peel the door away and place it on the ground. The cracked pieces of mirror make a jingling giggle against the carpet. I reach inside the wardrobe and let my fingers dance along the wood inside, each surface, the corners. I find nothing.

Next I open the small drawer at the bottom of the wardrobe. Nothing either. Yet just as it is about to close, I see it. On the left side of the drawer, carved in red pen, is a combination. Underneath that there is a street number and a street name. I wrench the drawer out and it tumbles onto my lap.

Mum – it's here!

Remembering where I am, I sit still for a moment and listen to the movements of the house. Yet there seems to be only ordinary noises, no one has awoken. I give my attention back to the tattooed wood and feel blood rushing to my fingertips that I press against the words. I almost don't have to read them with my eyes because I can feel their shape. If I've ever seen anything more beautiful, I forget then. These carved words are a salvation, a way into a maze that I have only just realised I want to enter.

I memorise those numbers and words. In a few days, I'll follow them to wherever they want to take me. Weeks and months after his death, Daniel is still leading me. This revelation once again is like a set meal, easy and comforting in one sense, yet depressing and controlling in another.

As I am returning the drawer to its place I hear the click of the door handle. The door begins to open as I get to my feet. Although instead of Thom as expected, it is Richard who materializes.

"What's going on?" he pulls at his left ear as though it is helping him wake up.

"Nothing. I thought I heard something in here".

"And is there anything in here?" he persists, looking doubtful.

"No. There's nothing", I say but inside my heart dances with my discovery.

"No ghosts? No poltergeists?" Richard mocks. He is scanning the room, perhaps surprised to see the trail of blood and the carcass of the wardrobe, yet he doesn't mention it.

"Why, have you seen one?" I retort. He has hardly spoken to me. Every time he sees me, he looks at me as though I'm wearing a prison uniform or brandishing a knife.

"No", he answers; his lip and nose curling upwards.

"Well then, let's get back to bed then".

I make to move past him but his hand springs out and grasps my arm. His face is close to mine. His eyes seem to be flickering, like he is staring into fire and the heat is twisting its tongue in the air in front of his face.

"I don't know who you are", he tells me, "but you'd better not hurt my family. They've had enough". He reminds me of a child standing up to a bully for the first time, worried it will result in a heavier beating.

"I don't want to hurt your family", I say truthfully.

"What do you want then?" Richard's hand seems to be trembling slightly. Goose bumps have risen on his bare arm from the cold of the air or the cold of my manner. This must be what keeps him away from me.

"I want to be their friend". *I want to understand your brother Daniel,* I add to myself.

"Okay", Richard whispers, as though I had been asking his permission. As far as I am concerned, he is irrelevant.

"I'm going to bed now", I tell him and without realizing, glance behind at the drawer that contains the secret message I have discovered. When I have left the room, Richard stares in the direction in which I glanced and tries to see something revealing but all he can make out is a broken wardrobe, a door laid out like a body having jumped to its death and the blobs of blood scattered on the carpet like paint splattered without consideration.

Chapter 28

Red m & m's

"I bought you some m & m's", I tell Thom and take the place next to him on the front step. He is open-mouthed for a moment, looking like I have just handed him a bar of gold and then smiles brightly.

"I love m & m's. Thanks". It is pure joy beaming out of him and although I still feel angry with him about last night, it makes me proud in the same instance.

He tears open the packet and unashamedly begins his ritual of eating them in a certain order. I have only watched this from afar several times and I can't help but stare. Now that I am so close to him, I can see the chocolate melting into his fingerprints, the m & m's brand on each sweet, hear the crunching of the shells and nuts under his teeth.

He has eaten four when he offers me the pack. Despite holding it towards me, I see he is biting his lip. I doubt he is being greedy, more concerned that his ritual is being interrupted. I reach carefully into the packet and luckily; my fingers emerge with a red one. I squeal quietly.

"You got your favourite", he notices and after several seconds' hesitation continues; "my favourite is the yellow". He is currently making his way through the blue ones. He hasn't touched any but the brown and blue ones. Next, he will progress to the red, the green and finally his beloved yellow.

"They insist they all taste the same but I've tried them all and I'm happiest when it's the yellow last". He lowers his head as he talks.

I want to tell him I love his quirk and could watch it for hours. Yet, I don't want to scare him so instead I say, "You have to do what you enjoy". He appreciates this, rolling a red sweet around on his tongue and finally biting into it.

"It's nice you didn't laugh at me".

"Has anyone before?"

"I've had some strange looks!"

For the first time in weeks, Thom seems relaxed. His muscles are allowing him to smile. How long will it last though?

"How was Emma last night?" I ask, almost pushing him to lose his smile. He falters slightly but manages to shrug it off.

"Okay, I guess. I just can't be what she wants at the moment".

"And what does she want you to be?"

"My old self". Thom shrugs again, finally moving onto the yellow. He takes each one and holds it in his mouth, letting his tongue absorb the luminous taste.

"What are you like now?" I am desperate to know. Part of me

wishes I'd seen him being his 'old self'. Would I have liked him then?

"I have more in my head", he says but frowns instantly, unsure this is what he wants to say. He opens his mouth again but straight after, closes it and shakes his head.

"What's in your head?"

"Lots of thoughts and questions and ideas".

"Isn't that what everyone's head is filled with?"

Thom appreciates the comment, giving me a small smile. "I guess it depends what all those things are related to".

"And yours are related to Daniel?"

"I guess that's obvious to you, being around me". Thom takes his last sweet and considers it before devouring it like the rest. He crumples the wrapper and stuffs it into his pocket.

"Can I help you with anything?"

"No", Thom says, clasping his hands together. "I think the only one who might be able to help is Daniel". He grimaces, reminding himself of the impossible.

"What's so confusing about it all?" I ask, wondering what it is that Thom knows. Does he know Daniel was pushed? Is he looking for me without realizing it?

"I'm not sure I should be talking to you about this", Thom

begins tapping the step with his clenched fist. "I should've talked to Emma, if anyone. She cares about me but... she's just been so far away". He is toiling with himself in front of my eyes. I know I must act in order to get him to trust me, so I reach across and place my hand on his knee. He looks up sharply.

"I'm here for you Thom", I vow. He doesn't know how much I mean it but even a fraction of it is enough for him. His ignorance over my physical attention is beginning to lose its simplicity. He must acknowledge me soon, either positively or negatively.

"You're right, you have been. And that's what I told Emma..." he reassures me, hoping he won't have to get any closer to me for now. I can't tell if he would like to or not, now or ever...

I wish I could ask you what you think, Mum.

"I do want to talk to someone... but when she asked me last night, I knew it wasn't her I wanted to tell". Thom is thrashing with his conscience, guilt, and the desire inside.

"Who do you want to tell?" I ask; praying *please say me, please say me.*

"I can't be sure of anything anymore". Thom ruffles his own hair as though he is trying to perk himself up. Then unexpectedly, he leans his head onto my shoulder. Like a parent who hasn't been in their child's life for years and suddenly is faced with comforting them, or a person who hates animals and finds themselves having to care for one's wounds, I don't know how to respond initially. I just let his head rest there. Somehow a shoulder is always a perfect pillow.

My heart is thudding heavily – heavier than the moment before

I pushed Daniel onto those tracks? I can't decide. I can only think clearly about the present: Thom's beard poking through my jumper, the dull smell of chocolate on his breath, his increasingly wavy hair squashed against my neck.

"I think Daniel knew he was going to die", Thom mutters, just when I have started to believe my heart can't race any quicker. Or rather instead, stop completely.

The world is swaying slightly, yet the cars continue to chug by, the trees continue to stand motionless in the icy air, and Thom continues to hold his breath.

"What?" I say because it's the easiest thing to say. In a million films and books and useless conversations, people have said 'what' in response to questions for lack of something better. I am disappointed I have joined the masses on this one.

"I've been finding things he left behind..." Thom whispers, keeping it a secret from those cars and those trees. "It all points to him knowing".

A shudder makes my back spasm and I am sure Thom feels it but perhaps he attributes it to the peculiar notion he has just suggested. It is probably how he first reacted when the facts finally crystallized into sense.

"How could he know?" I splutter. Thom reaches his hand across my stomach and grabs onto my rib. I wonder if this is the moment when he will reveal he knows, when he will squeeze me so hard that my heart will suffocate and die. Yet he doesn't move after the initial movement, just grasps onto the place where he has seized initially.

"He left a letter, a note, notebooks and clues and rubbish. I don't know what I'm supposed to do with it all". Thom isn't crying but his fingers are beginning to clutch so fiercely that they are settling into the structure of my rib bones. It's as though he wants to dig a way in and hide himself.

"What did he write?" I almost plead. Thom doesn't notice that I am asking the wrong question. He accepts it because he doesn't know what to ask either.

"He wrote terrible things or maybe I did, I still don't know". Thom sinks into my shoulder further, a rock sinking in quicksand. "He knew when he was going to die", Thom adds so quietly I almost don't hear it, or maybe I just wish I hadn't.

I'm glad that Thom is on my shoulder because although he thinks it's for his benefit, to hide his face, I am relieved he can't see mine. If he could, he would see my curls shivering and my eyelashes flicking in unison. He would see guilt screaming out of my pores and features like a spontaneous eruption.

"Did he know how?" I ask, realising that Daniel did but trying to gauge what Thom knows.

"He wrote down the train station", Thom answers and begins digging into his pocket. This causes him pain, as his palms are still raw underneath the bandages. Finally he drags a piece of paper out, as wrinkled and as ragged as his beard. He hands it to me and I can barely move my fingers to open it. Before me are words, words that would seem irrelevant to someone else, someone who didn't know Daniel, someone who didn't push him.

Highbury and Islington station. 15:30 Sunday.

I stare at the words until they seem as hard as brick, as though Daniel is head butting me. And I have only one thought: it says the wrong time; it should say 15:32.

Chapter 29

Disclosure

Once Thom shows Sarah the note, and tells her about his beliefs, his investigation seems to spill out of him. One tiny incision and Sarah has unleashed a waterfall. Unknown to him, Sarah has struck at exactly the right time and will easily gain the knowledge she thought she would have to work much harder to attain.

From the front step, Thom takes Sarah upstairs and shows her the notebook (but doesn't let her read it), he shows her the collection of items he took from the lock up, he tells her about the lock up and how Daniel left it specifically for him, he tells her he met someone who has proof Daniel knew about his own death in advance.

Despite Thom's disclosures, Sarah doesn't reveal her own clues; such as the combination she discovered last night. She makes the noises of someone who is surprised to learn about Daniel and the prior knowledge of his own death. Yet there are some surprises. After all, Sarah has no idea there were such a multitude of clues and taunting items that had been left behind.

Thom can't help drawing parallels between Sarah and Emma, in particular the way he has responded to both asking the same questions. What does that mean for him and Emma? What does it mean for him and Sarah? Thom feels he might already know the answer but he shrugs his thoughts away.

Sarah seems fascinated by his discoveries. He imagines he is a detective again, revealing all the answers to a less superior counterpart, and he delights in showing her some of his findings and delights equally in holding parts back.

He lets Sarah touch the objects from the lock up but it physically pains him. With each fingerprint she leaves on them, he feels his muscles tensing. Eventually he has to collect them up and put them away again without explanation. She begins moving towards the notebook but Thom snatches it up.

"I'd rather you didn't", he says and shoves it into a drawer. Sarah tosses her hair, unconcerned and runs her hand over the note, which is still on the bed in front of her.

"So this was your first clue?" Sarah questions, not looking up.

"Yes. I found it in Daniel's room just before his funeral".

"I thought nobody was supposed to go in there?" Sarah half-mocks him but he doesn't appreciate it.

"Well I have more of a right than you do", Thom snaps and throws himself down on the end of the bed. Sarah instantly apologises. Silence fills the room like a flood and Thom closes his eyes, letting it conquer him.

"Have you told Val or Richard about this?" Sarah asks after a few minutes. Thom reluctantly reopens his eyes and turns towards her.

"Would you?"

"It would be pretty devastating for them".

"Do you think I should tell them?"

"*No*", Sarah answers harshly, and then coughs gently, "I mean… it probably wouldn't help anyone if you did". Thom nods gratefully but doesn't realise Sarah is only protecting herself. Yet, Thom also knows he is running on a stopwatch, sooner or later Aunty Val or Richard will start asking questions about his behaviour and actions. If the positions were reversed, he would've asked ages ago.

"It feels good to share some of this", Thom tells Sarah, who smiles whilst wrapping her hair around one of her fingers. It does feel good but, equally, Thom feels as though it's been easier than it should've been. How can the words slip off the tongue like soft butter, yet have such a heavy impact like a bludgeoning? Thom feels betrayed by his secrets.

"I'm so happy you decided to tell me what you've been thinking".

This troubles Thom. Has he really told her what he's 'thinking'? No, he has shown her some physical things that he's been consumed with. Has he told her how he feels isolated? Has he told her how he feels guilty and sad about Daniel? Has he told her he can't stop thinking about her red underwear and her black curls? No to all the above. She thinks she has submerged her head in his mind but she has only dipped a finger in.

"What are you going to do now?" Sarah persists.

What a question. Thom thinks and thinks more. He imagines he is in an interview and tries to think of an answer rapidly but it's not possible. After several minutes of bending his fingers backwards and forwards he says, "I'm going to keep trying. I don't know how but I'll keep trying".

As Thom speaks, he studies Sarah. At his words, he notices an odd flick of her head, a jut or a tick. Her chest is rising rapidly. Her forehead looks clammy. If he saw her in a lift now, he would guess she is having a panic attack. Yet she isn't in a lift, she's sitting on his bed having a quiet discussion. What is happening?

"Are you okay?"

"Yes, I'm fine", Sarah answers hastily. She gives Thom a wide eyed look, pleading for him not to assault her and suddenly he thinks of her being attacked by the man in the street. He doesn't want to make her feel afraid. Why is he always so suspicious? Perhaps she is just hot or feeling a little ill, what business is it of his?

"Sarah, tell me about your family". Thom changes the subject, hoping this will relax her. Instead her face goes through several expressions in succession and Thom wants to kick himself. Her family were probably killed in some freak accident, he sighs inside.

"What do you want to know?" Sarah attempts a smile and Thom gets a sense she is stalling. More paranoia? Probably.

"Anything. I don't mind".

"Okay". Sarah pretends to be selecting information or memories but really she is constructing lies. Thom waits patiently, allowing her more time than he should.

"I have a brother called Peter who's three years older. He lives in Scotland now", she pauses and hastily adds, "my Mum and Dad live in the country so I don't see them much either".

"When is the last time you saw them?"

"Probably one of their birthdays, I can't remember exactly".

"Do you all get on?" Thom is getting nothing from the questions. What he wants to ask is; did the stranger tell the truth about you? Why haven't you mentioned your family before?

"Yes, mostly. All families have their problems sometimes", Sarah dismisses him confidently; anyone would've believed her.

"When you were having problems with your rent, couldn't you have asked them for help?"

"I was embarrassed really". She shrugs. It's moments like these she's had recently, when Sarah has begun to feel like a 'normal' person who can have a conversation, who can answer unpredictable questions. Other times, she regresses and implicates herself without even trying.

"I understand. Sometimes it's hard to ask for help, especially from those closest to you".

"I'm glad I didn't ask them because I wouldn't have met you otherwise", Sarah says quietly, bowing her head as though she has just told him the most humiliating thing that has ever happened to her. She is a frightened innocent in this moment and her hushed confession makes Thom's obsession with Daniel thaw, for a few moments at least.

135

Thom gets up and moves next to her. She doesn't look up as he scratches her cheek with his thumbnail. He wishes he didn't have these bandages on anymore. He wants to press his palm against her warm cheek. Thom moves his thumb over her lips and she opens her mouth slightly, still keeping her eyes down. Thom wonders if she is only complying with his touch out of fear. Should he stop?

He can hear her swallowing, frozen except for her tongue brushing a layer of moisture over her lips. Thom touches the wetness with his thumb and imagines it is his tongue instead. Sarah hasn't met his gaze yet and Thom worries briefly, she is staring at his erection. Yet with most thoughts in this area, the worry quickly disperses.

Thom is about to boil over with tension, her icy ignorance acting in reverse. Hoping she won't scream, he kisses her. She finally meets his eyes, wide but not afraid, and grabs onto him. They kiss like they are grappling; it is hard, oddly diamagnetic. He finds, although she tries so hard to seem cold, her skin is as warm as other women's.

Thom isn't sure who pushes back first; he is still kissing her in his mind. His unfounded obsession with her has been partly indulged; he has felt those lips again and crushed her bouncy curls between his fingers. Strangely he also feels the desire to do it again turning his stomach like a violent urge to vomit.

They stare at each other for a few seconds, perhaps unsure that what they have done is 'right', perhaps still shocked that it has occurred, perhaps wanting more. Sarah stands up, smoothing her top as she does. As she passes Thom, she grazes the side of his neck with her fingers. Thom closes his eyes and a second later hears the door being closed with the same tenderness.

Chapter 30

The Red Lock

I don't leave the house until the next day; bathing in the moment Thom removed the gap between us, holding our desire and curiosity in a violent whirlpool. He has calmed the waters with his soothing kiss and transferred the whirlpool into my stomach and my bouncing heartbeat.

I spent the evening sitting across from him whilst the family watched TV together, remembering the tough bristle of his stubble making my chin grow a rash and go slightly pink. Later, I stared at the rash and only felt happy. In the living room as I sat across from him, he looked over only once, neither smiling nor frowning, perhaps winking at me without moving at all.

I have forgiven him for telling Emma I know nothing, as he has now confided in me. He has let me get closer to him. She is irrelevant now. He can't want her if he kissed me can he? He must think about me too. He must want me to help him like I always thought I needed to.

Yet I am still following up the address I found. Daniel must have left it there for me. I have an obligation to go to the address and see what is there waiting. Perhaps it is just something to tease me, perhaps there will be nothing there at all, or perhaps there will be something important there like I fear.

I can easily give this up, I tell myself. I can easily go back to the house and take Thom to bed with me, make him forget about Daniel too. I'm sure if I try I can dominate his attention and make Daniel release his talons on Thom's mind.

More than half of me wants to take this option. More than half of me wants to jump on a new train and leave Daniel's one behind where it belongs. Yet like the blood will always remain in traces on that tunnel wall, on the platform, underneath its chugging feet – similarly, he will chew on the corner of my mind until I do as he wants. He has left this message for me, as he'd left the note for Thom and we are pathetic to his remains. We are both like animals picking at his carcass.

This is why I am standing outside a post office with an address written in my mind. This is why I am reeling it off and checking it against the street sign on the corner. This is why.

But, Mum, I'm so afraid of what I might find. Will you stay with me?

The post office is a discreet looking building. There is nothing spectacular about it. As the clock had spoken to me on the day I pushed Daniel, the post office is tipping his hat to me. He is open-ing the door repeatedly, asking me inside. He is poking his tongue out.

I finally grab hold of his tongue and enter the post office. It's much more spacious inside than I expect, it is as wide as a concert hall. There are people queuing with their parcels, letters, and bill payments. I am searching for where the address intends to lead me, panic swelling up my throat. Finally, the sign floats into vision that reads 'Lockers'. An arrow points towards the back of the building.

This way, Mum…

I skip towards it; past the lines of people sending things to those they love or know, to the place where I think someone might have cared enough to leave something for me. Although what could Daniel possibly have left here? And do I really want to see it? The point is he knew I'd find the clue. Thom missed it because he couldn't see things properly; it may as well have been invisible. This clue is definitely mine.

I greet the lockers with an ecstatic cry, as though I am meeting old friends. I reach out and touch their metal bodies, checking they aren't apparitions. They are definitely real. They are cold and smooth and beautiful. Dancing around the locker room, I count up the numbers until I finally reach my beloved – locker 11.

I chuckle to myself at the sight of the red lock securing it. He really has thought of everything and then with that thought, I frown. He has planned so much. He knew more about me than I seem to. How did he know I love the colour red? He has used it several times to speak to me. How did this stranger know all about me? And be certain that I would push him to his death?

I shake the thoughts away and instantly begin to turn the dials to the four numbers from the drawer, not shocked by it; I line them up like perfect soldiers to combination *1530*. Again, I want to correct it. Perhaps I should reset it to the correct time and afterwards go home and change the time on Thom's note with a red pen.

That would be irony for Daniel, wouldn't it? Correcting his note like a schoolteacher, with the only colour appropriate for such tasks.

The lock gapes open in my grip, allowing me to twist it sideways and rip it away from the body it has hung from like a piercing. The locker is now unlocked, ready to be opened, ready... *Go!* I tell myself and fling it open, expecting ghouls to fly out or a hammer to swing towards me and crunch every bone in my face.

Yet everything is still. Nothing comes towards me out of the locker. Nothing is hiding in there to bite my fingers off, one by one. Inside there are only a few small objects. A red scarf, origami shapes made from red paper, a brown file and a few letters with the name Daniel written on the front. The handwriting looks familiar yet I can't place it. The red shapes mean nothing to me, the scarf seemingly useless when I am wearing one exactly like it. The file is fat and bulging, squashed together with two fat elastic bands, holding its secrets inside.

Mum, what do you think it all is? I wonder if you'd tell me to just shut the locker door and leave it all here. But how can I do that?

Checking nobody is watching, I empty all of the contents into my bag. The fat file is a monster, its corners pressing against the closed zip, bursting to spill its contents. A few strands of the scarf get caught in the zip but I stuff them back inside and hastily pull the bag onto my shoulder. I close the locker and hang the lock back in its place, locking it without thinking.

I hug my bag as I pass through the crowds, anxious someone

will try to steal it or that some undercover policeman, who has been following me without my knowledge, will suddenly reveal himself and demand I hand it to him. I wouldn't be able to hand it over though, not even Thom could prise the bag handles from my bloodless fist.

Chapter 31

The Intervention

As Sarah is searching for a safe place to examine her items, Thom is on the living room sofa, staring at a family picture. It is a photo from about four years ago when Aunty Val and the three of them took a day trip to a theme park. They are all smiling in the photo, all the outward 'signs' point to a happy family but Thom wants to rip it apart now. Underneath Daniel's shy smile there is only hate and the desire to destroy others, to destroy all of them.

Thom is so engrossed in his dark interpretation of the photo that he only notices the others when their shadows drift over it. He lifts his head up reluctantly, yet is still undeservedly warmed by Aunty Val's smile as she lowers herself beside him. Richard enters the room behind her and before taking a seat in his usual armchair opposite, empties his pockets of a screwdriver and some nails. For some reason, he thinks carrying these things will keep him prepared or something. Yet, can he fix us all with some nails and a screwdriver?

Aunty Val notices the photo he is holding and runs her hand over it, her mouth stuck like a cross, a smile overlapped with a frown. Her fingers linger over Daniel for a split second and then fall into her lap. She wraps her other arm around Thom and squeezes him to her. Part of him melts into her familiar form, the part that also wants to find Sarah and melt into her warm moist mouth. Another part doesn't want to be squeezed in case all his dark thoughts and questions and anger gush out.

"Can we talk to you Thom?" Aunty Val asks gently, like someone approaching an addict who needs rescuing. Thom smiles weakly and nods. He glances over at Richard, who has his hands clasped together in front of him, seeming like a doctor or a CEO delivering bad news. Thom has an urge to simply jump up and run.

"Richard saw what happened to Daniel's room", Aunty Val begins warily and continues gently as though Thom is a landmine, "and your hands have been injured recently. So we put two and two together..."

"If you want to ask me about something, why don't you just do it?" Thom says flatly, staring her directly in the face until she blinks rapidly and looks down.

"Thom, did you smash up Daniel's room?" she asks quietly.

Thom casts a glance in Richard's direction and announces, "Yes, I did".

With his omission, the air in the room tightens. "Why would you do that darling?" Aunty Val's expression is that of Thom having peed all over her favourite possessions. A storm is churning inside Thom, and he can't look at Richard or Aunty Val for the next few moments or he fears he will detonate. One sight of them will split him in two and he doesn't know if he will be able to fuse the nuclei back together and exist as before.

"Did you look around in there, Aunty?" Thom doesn't want to do this but she is forcing him. It's her own fault if she wants to find out this way.

"No. I just stood in the doorway and looked in. I still can't do that".

"And you Rich, did you check anywhere?" Thom persists.

He hears Richard shuffling in his chair. "No, I just saw the wardrobe", he pauses, and even from the corner of his eye, Thom sees him tugging at his ear lobe. "What are you getting at?"

"I didn't want to tell you", Thom moans.

"Tell us what?" Aunty Val whispers but her voice is so tight Thom can see she wants to cork her ears. She still feels like a pane of glass without a frame. She has lost one child and another of her 'children' has become consumed by something ever since. What can she do to save the one who still lives?

"It's all empty". Thom shrugs, almost bored with the revelation. He and Sarah have both seen this revelation through each phase and they have reached the surface again, not wanting to go back for those still struggling below.

Richard sits forward in his chair. "What's empty? Stop talking in riddles, Thom", Richard chides.

"When have I ever spoken in riddles?"

"We spoke to Emma. She's worried about you", Aunty Val adds, trying to quell the rising argument, not realising she is only sparking more anger in Thom.

"She's just trying to get back at me because she got knocked back".

"You shouldn't be so rude about her", Richard says.

"Do *you* always act the way you're supposed to Rich?" Thom snarls.

Richard shrinks back in his chair and gives him a shocked smile. "Of course not, but what does that have to do with anything?"

"You've both come in here to judge me, haven't you? Because you don't agree with how I've been acting, because you think I wrote those horrible things in that notebook, because I haven't acted the same as *you*". Thom spits each sound. Aunty Val begins to breathe shortly beside him and he has to use all his strength to scream at his body not to attend to her.

"We just want to know what's going on". Richard stands up and waves his hands around in the air, someone drowning or waving to a boat pulling away from him. Thom leans forward, rubbing his eyes into his palms.

"I tried to tell you about his room, didn't I?"

"*What*, that it's empty? What does that mean?" Richard stares at Thom.

"Exactly what I said!" Thom barks back.

"Why would his room be empty? He was living in there, Thom. The day before he died, he slept in there". Richard is pacing the space in front of the sofa, as if he is a coach trying to decide what to tell his team at half time. Thom hates to see Richard troubled, he hates to see him pulling at his ear again like the day they first discussed Daniel and smoked together in Thom's room. Yet, this is what they are both asking him for – discomfort, awkwardness, and revelations.

"I don't know, Richard. But...the drawers are empty, the wardrobe is empty, there's not a scrap of anything in there. Believe me, *I've looked*". Thom is jerking in his seat, so much that Aunty Val reaches over and presses down on his leg. Thom tries to regulate his breathing, in the same instance wondering why Aunty Val seems so composed.

"How could there be nothing Thom?" Aunty Val asks quietly.

"You think I know? I've thought and thought and thought again about all this and I have no answers. If you were expecting me to help you out, I'm afraid I'll have to let you down".

"Why are you being so aggressive about this?" Richard is leaning towards Thom, his hands stretched towards him, yet he doesn't touch Thom. "Does this have something to do with Sarah?"

"What have you got against her Rich? Leave her alone", Thom cautions him and continues angrily, "I've been dealing with all this for weeks and suddenly *you're* interested. Oh woe betides me, I've known this fact for about five minutes and I want all the fucking answers!"

"Thom, please don't swear", Aunty Val says. Thom is about to say something biting when he looks into her eyes and changes his mind.

"Who cares if he swears Mum? Have you heard what he's been saying?" Richard kicks the carpet. All his muscles and veins are Braille on the surface of his skin. "He says Daniel emptied his room somehow, without our knowledge! He's been really rude about his girlfriend and he's started hanging around with some strange woman. And when we ask him to help us understand something, he completely turns on us like a stupid dog. You have to get him to talk normally Mum, *please*".

Richard slumps into the armchair and stares at the ceiling. Perhaps he is praying and, if he is, Thom wants to tell him that God doesn't exist. Like he told Sarah, he's a fabrication. He's a lifeboat that people search for in a violent sea but one that deflated itself for him after his parents died.

"Richard, would you mind leaving us alone for a moment?" Aunty Val asks as softly as ever, seemingly oblivious to the last ten minutes. She sits next to Thom with a straight back and with her hands placed by either leg. Thom remembers in that pose why he respects her so much. Why has he been pushing her away?

Richard stares at her, yet after a few seconds, he pushes himself to his feet. He gives them both a concerned frown and leaves the room with a few large strides. As he slams the door, Aunty Val swivels her body round to face Thom and makes him do the same. Thom hears the clock again and with the slam of the door, the hands instantly get down onto their knees and begin to crawl around the clock face.

"Aunty, I'm..." She puts her hand up and Thom closes his lips immediately.

147

"Thom, I want to speak". She massages her forehead briefly. "Darling, I'm so worried about you. And I have to tell you…" Aunty Val's lips are choking on shapes. Thom reaches up, sweeping her cheek with his fingers briefly, meeting her gaze. "I have to tell you something…" she resumes, "I'm afraid Thom. More afraid than I've ever been". Aunty Val has weighed down the life-raft and must empty the excess out before she sinks. Thom isn't sure he wants to hold all her excess though.

"Aunty, I don't…"

"I'm not finished Thom", she warns. Thom bows his head.

"What I'm trying to say to you is… well, you know how important you are to me, don't you darling?" Thom nods quietly. "Well, when your parents died, I felt so worried about you. I didn't know if I could help you…" Thom doesn't know why they always seem to be talking about this subject lately. Why does she want to keep returning to this? Why does she want to poke and infect the wound? He wants to tell her that their deaths are necrotic tissue that he would be happy to surgically remove.

"You are so important to me. I love you so much darling. And I'm so proud of you, do you know? Well, I'm sure you do. I'm just saying that I'm proud of you for everything but most of all, for how you dealt with it. How you rebuilt your life and let us be your family…"

"Aunty Val, this isn't helping anyone", Thom pleads; tempted to gouge his eyeballs out and stuff them in his ears.

"Thom please, I've always been so amazed by your strength. I know you can get yourself back on track". Aunty Val grabs one of

Thom's hands between hers. It is a clamp, Thom can only dream of escaping it. All the while, he is chuckling inside his mind at her use of the word 'track'. He is on a track that's true, just not the one she hopes he is on.

"What's been worrying you? Why have you been so angry?"

"My cousin dying isn't enough?" Thom challenges. Aunty Val squints and looks away as though he has squirted lemon juice in her eye.

"Of course it's enough... But I asked you about more than that".

"I told you about his room Aunty Val. If you don't believe me, check for yourself!" Thom tosses her hand back to her. She stares at it, an invisible gash leaking blood down her arm.

"But you haven't said why you think it happened. Was he moving out? What do you know about it Thom?"

"I'm trying to protect you". Thom grinds his teeth with each vibration of his tongue. Aunty Val is putting her organs on a stick and ramming them into a fire. Why is she asking him to hurt her?

"Sometimes you look so much like him", Aunty Val whispers.

"*What?*" Thom feels his brain splitting in two. "Don't say that ever again".

"Why?"

"I don't want to look like him or be like him or remind anyone of him *ever*. Do you understand that?" Thom speaks the sentence slowly and she doesn't appreciate it.

149

"Fine, forget that". She bites her lip. "But what are you hiding about Daniel? If you're sad about losing him, we can understand. We've felt all the emotions too". Aunty Val grabs him by both shoulders and holds him steady. Thom curls his hands into balls and stabs his own skin.

"He's the one who hid things Aunty".

"Is this my fault?" Aunty Val asks suddenly.

"I'm not saying you're a bad parent. This isn't about you".

"Have I been there for you Thom?" Aunty Val pulls him closer. Her breath makes his cheek moist.

"Yes Aunty, yes", he stutters, trying to regain a distance between them. "But I have to tell you something".

"You're frightening me, Thom".

"I'm frightened too". Thom is shaking to emphasise his point.

"Just tell me. You *can* tell me". She is gritting her teeth. Her mouth is twitching. He is worried what he will do to her. He might as well stone her to death. This way he is instead throwing her overboard into an unsure sea that could drive her anywhere and even make her lungs so heavy she might sink.

"He knew, Aunty Val", Thom manages to say. Again, he has failed to articulate the whole sentence he intended. Speech has floated away from him once again.

"What did he know?" Aunty Val shudders, her voice shrill. Thom gets the sense she already knows something, she seems too quick to panic. Yet she hasn't given any hints before. Is he being paranoid yet again?

"That he was going to die", Thom surrenders.

Her eyes instantly roll and she collapses.

Chapter 32

Red Gifts

I scurry through the city, a fugitive, a dirty rat trying not to get stamped on, and finally settle underneath a tree in a small green. I spend twenty minutes scanning the surrounding area for spies. I even focus on several nearby bushes and monitor them for irregular movement and stare up into the branches above, watching the sway until I feel I can trust it.

I'm so glad I have you with me. I can't face this alone, Mum.

Unzipping my bag, my chest grows increasingly hollow the wider the mouth opens. I wonder what will happen when I reach inside, whether I will fall in and keep sinking. Trembling, I close my eyes and plunge my hand within. I let my fingers drift around the items, trying to feel Daniel's presence pulsating from them. Yet there is nothing and I fear I have lost him, my pulse racing for someone else instead.

I pluck out the red origami first and examine each one. One has been made into a swan, another a flower, another looks like a horse. There are six altogether. Someone has obviously taken time making these, each fold is precise, each structure complex. I place them in a line next to me, assembling an army.

I take up the scarf; hold it to my nose as I did with his scarf after the push. It doesn't smell of him. I am even more disappointed because he has faded from the original scarf too. Slowly I am losing him and I can't weave him back into the threads. I toss the scarf aside, making sure it doesn't mix with my original scarf that at least has some sentimental value.

I decide to tackle the letters next. I stare at his name on the front trying to decipher the author, yet I am blank. Something is familiar in the way the capital D is slanted, aggressively sharp and with a slight dip in the top half. I know who wrote this, why can't I place them?

I lose patience and turn the envelope over. The seal has already been broken, the lip is cracked and tattered, the adhesive clumped together and dried. With tremors still echoing through me, I fumble with the opening until it slowly gives in. Inside I see white paper folded into three. Holding my breath, I snatch the paper from inside, the swiping sound of its exit like a guillotine rushing towards a helpless neck.

I unfold the paper and find a letter. Looking at the first word it stops me dead: *Daniel*. I feel like I have been hurtled into a brick wall, not just because of what the first word is but because I finally connect the writing with the owner. Like my shadow finally catching up with me, I realise the author is me.

Mum, mum, why is my writing on this page?

After stalling on the first word, I eventually manage to break through the current and begin to take in the rest of the letter:

153

I can't stop thinking about you. I love the gifts you sent me, as always. I take them out when everyone is asleep and stare them. I like to imagine your hands when you were making them, how you wanted to make me smile, how you snuck them in for me without the others seeing.

I have to hide your gifts under one of the floorboards so at night I feel like I am freeing them. I wish I could show everyone how thoughtful and loving you are. I really don't deserve to have you giving me attention but I thrive on it, it keeps me positive every day I am in this prison.

The doctors have been asking about you but I won't tell them anything. They just want to catch us out. They don't want me to be happy or connect with anyone, and they want to keep me in here forever.

I will never forget when I first met you, how you kept trying to make me smile because I looked so sad. I hadn't spoken properly to anyone in months but you managed to connect with me. I actually feel like you care for me. I haven't felt that since my Mum and before that, the only person I thought loved me ended up hurting me in the worst way.

I know you won't hurt me. I can't wait to get out of here and spend time with you in the real world, among the birds, the wind that thrashes in the trees, the coldness of the lake outside the window I can never touch.

I particularly love the bird you made me. It gives me hope that I will escape one day. I can't wait to see you again; I'm waiting for you here.

There is no signature. Yet the letter needs none. This is written by me, there are no doubts. If I needed clues, I could even authenticate my identity by underlining the references to not having you around anymore and someone who I cared about hurting me 'in the worst way'.

154

You know all about it, don't you, Mum? We can't deny that it's me in this letter.

This is my handwriting. This is a letter written in a hospital. This is a letter to the man I pushed in front of a train. All the details point to me being the author yet I can't understand this. I am submerged in water; my fingertips are burnt to numbness, my nose clogged with blood. What do these combinations of black marks really mean?

This letter is a classic example of a yearning lover writing to her beloved. Even when I reread it several times, I have a notion it must be a prank or something that Daniel wrote to torture me. Yet the handwriting is undoubtedly mine. I can't deny it more than I can deny my own reflection.

I drop the letter and tear open another envelope. This letter contains much of the same musings. I toss this one down and grab the next one, shivering as I read yet more similar expressions of adoration. I almost scream when I get to the bottom where in shaky writing, I see: *I think I love you Daniel.*

I screw the paper up and hurl it aside. I jump up and stamp on the origami army beside me before they can lead a mutiny against me. I start beating my fists against the tree behind me and kicking it until my toes bruise and groan in my shoes.

How could I have written these things? I have no recollection of any of these words, their combinations, or even the thought of picking up a pen to scratch them out. It is as if I am staring at a pile of vomit confined to a page, I have no idea where to start picking it apart to make sense.

Is it true that I cared for Daniel, Mum? And if I did know him at the hospital and had all these feelings for him, how did it result in my pushing him in front of a train? I wish you were here to help me understand this. I wish you were here to hold me and stop me shivering.

I slump next to the tree again, my breath a rag that seems as filled with holes as my memory. Trying to refocus my heartbeat and sensing the water layer over my eyes blistering, I drag the file towards me. I figure things can't get much worse.

I fight off the elastic bands around the file, imagining I am a child prodding my fingers into a mousetrap. I have to succumb though. I have no choice but to continue with my journey into the darkness of my unknown past. The file opens easily and I prepare myself for a shotgun to annihilate my dizzy head.

The first page is nothing alarming. It is my admission record to the hospital, all the standard details: age, name, gender, date of admission, current drug treatment, notes on special requirements, the reason I'd been sectioned.

There are several dull pages of this. Then something different; some handwritten pages making notes on some of my counselling sessions with Doctor Rosey. None of this is particularly new to me either. I can't recall the memory of actually talking to Doctor Rosey but the subjects seem familiar. The subjects are those I discussed even just before I left the hospital. The guilt over losing you, the helplessness of being taken advantage of, the confusion over why you left me, the anger and fear of living a day-to-day life. I have no idea why they let me out of there…

Still pondering the failures of the system, I come across another strange document. On the header it has the address of the hospital and the word 'memo' written in large red letters. Underneath are the words 'Attention: Serious Issue Reported'. I continue reading. The memo describes an incident of a staff member being caught acting inappropriately with one of the patients. Apparently, the reported staff member was suspended (pending investigation), but the memo also notes that several witnesses had come forward saying the staff member and patient were definitely having an inappropriate relationship. Furthermore, the staff members had stepped up their vigilance on this particular patient, a certain patient named Alice...

The evidence is a mountain that towers above me. The branches are waving at me. I watch them stretching higher in the sky or maybe I am sinking into the mud or the tectonic plates of the earth have hiccupped underneath me.

Chapter 33

The Awakening

As Thom cradles Aunty Val on the sofa, the door blasts open. Richard rushes over to Aunty Val and wrestles her out of Thom's arms. "What have you done to her?" he asks, shaking her gently. She is already stirring but keeps her eyes closed. Richard is staring at Thom like he is holding a knife covered with blood.

"We were just talking. She's fine".

"She doesn't look fine", Richard screeches.

"I didn't hurt her Richard", Thom says, yet swallows heavily. Is he sure about that? He just told her about her recently deceased son knowing he was going to die? Surely that is hurting her, not physically, but nonetheless…

"I can't believe the way you're acting. You're being exactly like him before he died". Richard is stroking Aunty Val's hair. She is mumbling but Thom can't understand a word.

"What?" Thom sits on the edge of the sofa, trying to look open for negotiations.

"He hurt her too", Richard tells him, shaking his head as if he should have known this would happen. Thom can't believe Richard could draw these comparisons between him and Daniel. How long has he been thinking these things? Why hasn't he said something before?

"How did he hurt her?" Thom asks, not bothering to defend himself again. He doesn't think Richard wants to hear it; he is convinced he is Aunty Val's protector and Thom the attacker.

"He hit her", Richard answers flatly.

"What? When?" Thom lurches towards them, making Richard hug Aunty Val even closer to his chest. Thom settles back again, not wanting to frighten Richard's information away.

"About two months before". Richard's answers are curt; his lips so tight Thom can't see even a minute fraction of his usual smile. Thom can't remember seeing Richard this angry. In a way, Thom is proud to see him stand up for something, yet he wishes he didn't have to be the receiver.

"Why Rich?"

"She wouldn't say". Richard gestures to the awakening Aunty Val. "I just came home to see this horrible purple bruise on her face. She tried to lie but I could tell straight away. Something had been going on with them for months".

"Why didn't you mention this before?" Thom jumps to his feet. "Maybe it would've helped with everything, with finding out..."

"Shut up!" Richard shouts, so bloodthirsty that Thom halts instantly. "This has nothing to do with your stupid quest or whatever it is. This is about him and now you, hurting *my* mum".

159

Aunty Val opens her eyes and stares up at her devoted son. I envy her for having someone whose job it is to protect her, who will always love her no matter what. Even though Thom has pretended he can play that role too, he isn't her real son and he isn't doing a good job of protecting anyone, even himself.

"I love her. I wouldn't hurt her on purpose", Thom insists, squeezing his bandaged hands until they begin to ache. He deserves the pain so he increases the pressure the more they throb.

"But you still did!", Richard shouts.

Thom feels like someone has stabbed a needle into his lung and is letting all the air rush out of him. He remembers the day he received the phone call from Richard, the tears in Richard's voice. He has failed them.

"I'm sorry Richard... Aunty. I haven't meant to do anything bad".

"I should smack you in the face like I did him", Richard swears but Aunty Val grabs his clenched fist and holds it against her cheek. He slackens the tension but gives Thom a dark look, warning him that he is still capable.

"He didn't do anything, Richard", Aunty Val says, letting him help her to sit up. He holds onto her torso like a human stabiliser.

"Why were you unconscious then?" Richard persists, feeling like a child being lied to. He is certain he has missed something and wants to be included.

"We were just talking, weren't we Thom?" She reaches a long way in order to touch Thom's knee again, nodding in a discreet way only he understands. She doesn't want him to tell Richard what he told her. Why? Yet, Thom nods quietly anyway.

"I just felt a bit woozy". She waves into the air and proceeds to gently peel away Richard's hold from her chest. Richard stares at his rejected hands.

"What were you talking about mum?"

"It's nothing darling". Aunty Val gives him a broad smile. Thom's stomach spins at the sight of it. He can't help feeling she is a mother protecting her last innocent child from the world. Thom is already lost, Daniel already dead, she only has Richard now. He wants to hold out his hands and beg her *save me too; I need you to keep me from falling apart.* Yet Thom can't make his muscles tense to speak, they are tumours impeding function and he doesn't know if they will ever be granted freedom.

"I think you should leave, Thom. At least for a few days", Richard suggests coldly. Thom doesn't hesitate; he ejects himself from the sofa and attempts to eject himself from their lives. Feeling he is now the tumour, he decides to hack himself out as quickly as possible.

"No Thom", Aunty Val chases and grabs him by the hand. "We need you here".

Thom shakes her off. "He's right, I think we all need some space". Aunty Val grabs tighter so Thom pulls away more roughly. He may as well have kicked her to the floor. In the next moment she sinks to her knees anyway.

"I need you Thom".

"Aunty Val *please*..." Thom dismisses her, with a desire to stab himself in the heart instead of watching this sad display. Richard stands up behind her and presses her against him. She is still on her knees so she holds onto him through his legs. He is staring at Thom, a solemn lip clashing with his furrowed eyes.

"You have to come back", Richard tells him firmly. Thom nods, fascinated by the words. Come back to where? To the house? To his old self? To them?

Thom turns sharply and shuts them in, pausing in the hallway. He glances up the stairs, expecting to see Sarah on the top step or hoping to visualise his way back. He takes the few small steps to the front door and leaves the house. The wind whispers to him outside *come back, come back.* He doesn't see Aunty Val peering out of the front window, her face raining on the inside.

Chapter 34

The Nose Bleed

I run all the way back to the Mansen house, doubled over with breathlessness and sickness by the time I arrive. Crouching in the middle of the road for several minutes, I gasp and suck in air, not concerned if a car were to speed around the corner and bulldoze me into the asphalt.

My bag feels like it's swelling with rocks but I haven't been able to let go of it. I don't want to lose the evidence or let my past escape from my memory ever again. I want to be able to say I have knowledge of something, even if it's something bad.

Mum, it's time to get the past back. It's time for me to realise you can't help anymore.

I think about going back to the house but my feet don't want to go that way. They walk down the middle of the road, slowly and even leisurely, until I reach the part where the ascending road begins to roll downhill again. I reach my hands into the air and begin saying 'Michael', louder and louder until I am screaming and sobbing.

I am sobbing heavily when the figure appears out of the darkness. He presses me against him like he wants to seep into my body, trying to calm my moaning. His familiar smell wraps around me like his embrace and I run through several memories in my mind of a time when we were happier, when we didn't stand on two opposite ends of a scale that are never level.

"Oh Alice…" He coos and kisses my forehead. "Are you okay?" he asks and I wonder why I have been running away from him for so long. He does love me. He didn't mean to disappoint me by deserting us. I can tell by his digging fingernails that he is sorry.

"I'm not okay", I snort, burying myself into his clump of curls. I feel like I am reacquainting with myself, his hair so similar to mine, his bony nose the mirror of my own. I'm returning to the life I thought I lost and it is easier than I imagined. I can talk to him. I can act human. There is hope for me.

"Whatever it is, I'll help you", Michael promises, holding my face between his hands like people do when they are being earnest. I rest my forehead against his, reminding myself of his clammy blemished skin. "I love you Alice, I'm so sorry about everything. I won't let you down again".

For some unknown reason, I believe him. I have been trying to escape him for weeks but hearing his voice now, it is as strong and honest as a piece of steel. I need him anyway. I can't deal with these new revelations alone.

"Will you tell me the truth Michael?"

"I will if I can". He stares into my eyes, not shaken by the increasingly cold wind thrashing all around us. I feel like we are in a bubble that nothing can touch, everything is frozen except the two of us.

164

"Tell me about a man named Daniel, then", I say. Michael's eyes protrude in response. There is no attempt at disguise.

"How do you know…" Michael rolls silence around his tongue for a moment but finally finishes, "…about him?"

My insides instantly sink. He has confirmed it. It's true. I don't even need to ask any more questions, the file is a hub of answers. Yet to keep our interaction going, I say, "I found a file from the hospital".

"I wish you hadn't found out about this". He lowers his head.

"Why didn't anyone tell me?"

"We thought it would make things worse". Michael pouts. "But if you want to know more, maybe we should take you to see Doctor Rosey".

I instantly pull out of his hold. He stiffens up and reaches his hands out towards me. "Please, don't run". He is standing like he is ready to chase me.

I shake my head and reassure him, "I'm sick of running".

"Thank goodness", he sighs happily and brings his feet back together. I want to throw my arms up in victory at this small gesture. It seems that suddenly Michael and I are communicating.

"I don't trust that Doctor. She wants to take me back to the hospital".

"I won't let her", Michael slants his head, "…not again. You can come and stay with me".

"But your family…"

"My family will get to know you and support you". He nods seriously. My chest is threatening to rupture with elation. Another small part of me wonders if Michael is merely trying to trick me. It has happened before. What makes this situation different?

Reading my mind, Michael adds, "you can trust me this time Alice. I won't let you down again. I've realised…" he inhales deeply, "I should've been there".

"I want to believe you". I begin pulling at my hair and letting the curls spring back. Michael watches, a smile rising on his lips.

"It's so good to talk with you like this again".

"I'm still ill Michael". My admission makes him smile even wider.

"That's a good step". He takes me by the shoulders, a brother praising his little sister. It's obvious but I enjoy every moment. I've done nothing for him to praise the last few years.

"Come and see the Doctor now, we'll talk to her together".

Michael starts leading me towards his car but suddenly he is wrenched backwards. I spin round and see Thom standing there. He is shaking like an infected dog, salivating as he stares at Michael.

"Get your hands off her", Thom snarls, his jaws crunching loudly.

166

Michael instantly remembers Thom and doesn't take him seriously. "What business is it of yours?" Michael stares Thom down. What Michael doesn't realise is that Thom thinks he's a rapist, that Thom has just been accused by his cousin of hurting his Aunty, and that Thom would love to skin someone alive.

"She told me about you". Thom jabs him.

I jump in front of Michael and raise my hands. "Thom, you don't understand".

"No, I do Sarah", he growls. "And I won't let him scare you anymore".

"You have the wrong idea", I appeal to him again.

Thom's nose is hooked upwards with disgust, his nostrils flaring like tunnels. I want to pull him close to me to make him settle but equally I can't stand to see his face, taunting me with the living vision of the man who has made me sick with obsession and perhaps even love?

"The wrong idea?" Thom cries. "This bastard raped you". Thom jabs Michael over my shoulder. Behind me, Michael lurches forward like a spring and I am pushed aside.

"What did *he* say?" Michael shouts, turning white. "Are you crazy?"

"You have the nerve to call *me* crazy you fucking pervert!" Thom shrieks and grabs Michael by the throat. I hear Michael cough and grunt, trying to claw at Thom's hand. I pull on Thom's arm but he shoves me backwards, making me stumble over. I can only watch

Thom pushing Michael against a car, throwing his fist into Michael's face. Whilst I try to hoist myself up, my legs suddenly numb.

Michael is attempting to push Thom off him, his face swelling with desperation and blood. When Thom finally releases him, I am holding myself up at the end of the car, blowing out the air I have been holding. Yet my relief is short as in the next instant, Thom begins punching the still recovering Michael, as if he is a piece of meat he needs to tenderise.

As Michael slumps down the car, with blood exploding from his nose like a dam battered by flood, I squeeze myself between them. Thom narrowly misses striking me with yet another punch intended for my brother. He leaps away from me. I think about saying something to him, then shake my head and turn away.

Michael is lying face up on the floor, leaning his head as far back as he can, staring up at me drowsily. He is probably thinking about what a terrible person I am, or what a terrible person Thom is, or why he is being called a rapist when he is not.

I kneel next to him, bowing my head close to his body, atoning for my lie and its bloody offshoots that pierced him like shrapnel. He grabs my hand. I stroke his sweaty forehead and press my scarf against his bloodied nose until he squints and groans. This scarf is no longer a bind; it is a bandage.

"What the hell are you doing?" Thom yelps from behind me.

"You have no right to hurt him".

"But he hurt you!" Thom cries as I help Michael sit up, and then turn to face him.

"I told you it was fine and you ignored me anyway. Why didn't you listen?" I hit at his chest, hoping to bruise him.

"But you told me he hurt you. I don't understand". Thom holds his head with clawed fingers, backing away from the source of his throbbing confusion.

"Why did you tell him that, Alice?" Michael coughs, equally as perplexed.

"Don't call her Alice". Thom snarls and kicks Michael in the ribs, who yelps sadly and slouches sideways. I drive forward and shove Thom into the middle of the road. He stumbles as if he is standing on one leg. He holds his hands up, to help him balance and to reach out.

"Stop hurting my brother", I spit. A current of shock mixed with awareness thrashes over his expression. He drops his arms, his body a balloon wailing into a slump.

"Your brother?" Thom squeaks, glancing at Michael on the floor, who is pushing himself up with a half press up.

"This is Michael", I say blankly.

"But you told me..."

"I know what I told you", I interject before he can repeat my poisonous lie. "I told you that because I didn't want you to listen to Michael". I step closer to him but he immediately backs away the same distance, afraid I have a disease that is airborne.

"Why Sarah?" Thom's words seem to froth from his mouth. "Or Alice or *whatever* your name is", he sulks.

"I've been ill for a long time and I haven't been ready to face up to that. I didn't want Michael to disturb my life".

"You were ill?" Thom repeats, his tone lacking surprise.

"I have had some issues… well, I still do". I hear the words and feel them clear and bold in my mind. There is no static or interference. I see the truth like a fact in an encyclopaedia. "I've been running away from dealing with them for ages. Even though they let me out of the hospital, I'm really not better".

"The hospital?" Thom shouts out. His mouth moves like he is a dummy being manipulated by somebody else. He isn't thinking about talking, he is merely performing it.

"I spent time in a hospital Thom. And just for the record, I *was* raped".

"Why should I believe you now?" he mumbles dejectedly.

"Would I really want to tell you all these bad things about myself if they weren't true?" I move towards him again and manage to sweep my hand across his.

"Well, you told me your brother was the one who raped you", he reminds me and I bow my head.

"I shouldn't have done that", I pause and look into his face again. "I was afraid that he would tell you all these bad things about me and you would hate me. But I should've realised it would have been the best thing to get this all out, to realise how sick I've been".

170

Thom shakes himself out and begins to turn away, then snaps back, kicking the floor between us. "This is all crazy. You've been lying to me this whole time".

"You didn't actually ask that much about my past. And when I told you anything, you just accepted it". I don't mean to criticise but Thom has no other way to hear this.

"You're blaming me?" he cries, his mouth hanging open. I want to reach over and press it closed, fix one of the growing holes in his life.

"No, I'm sorry".

"I can't believe this Sarah". Thom screws up his face. In this moment I feel superior because he is falling apart. I decide to close the gap between us and take him by the hands, as Michael had done with me only ten minutes before.

"It's not your fault. I shouldn't have lied". I want to hug him but his bruised knuckles stop me. Thom's legs are wobbling, his face a piece of paper gradually crumpling, creating passages for his tears.

"I can't deal with this right now. I need *you*..." he whimpers.

"You're okay Thom, I know you are", I say but I am lying again. Yet this is a lie that is needed, an exit clause and a scaffold.

"But Richard thinks I'm trying to hurt Aunty Val". Thom pulls me towards him and grabs onto me. I have to push him away. "He told me to leave and now... now you hate me too". He tries grabbing me again for a few seconds, I instinctively squeeze him but remember to urge him away again. Thom's posture drops and he shuffles backwards.

171

"What did you do Thom? Why did he tell you to leave?"

"They don't understand Daniel", Thom sighs and looks ready to lie on the ground and wait for the tyres to crush him into a pile of slush and chunks. Although Thom thinks he has nothing left, his words actually repair the smallest thread of our relationship. It is a microscopic fragment on a large tapestry. If anyone can empathise with the damage Daniel has done, I can.

"You can stay at my place. It's a horrible bedsit but at least it's somewhere", I say, giving him the address and the key. Thom nods at the gesture and holds the key tightly in his hand, a hook and line keeping him attached to the shore, no matter how weakly.

I force myself to turn my back on Thom and finally help my brother to stand. Michael leans against me and we walk towards the car. I hurriedly help Michael into the passenger's seat and he reluctantly hands over the keys when I fasten myself in the driver's seat.

In the mirror, I struggle to pick Thom out in the darkness of the street. He is a thin line amongst trees and lamp-posts and the buildings. I shake the dull smudge of him out of sight and start the car, knowing I have to get to my bedsit before he does.

Chapter 35

The Copper Smell

After we leave Thom in the road, merging into blackness; we stop by the bedsit. I tell Michael to wait in the car, his blood drying and cracked, and make my way inside.

I have to knock on the landlord's door and ask him to let me in, saying I have lost my key. Thankfully he is so drunk he can't even climb the stairs, so he is forced to lend me his keys and leave me grope-free on this occasion. He asks me to return them when I've finished.

The lock opens with a crack, adding sound effects to my desertion. *If I'd had the choice, I'd never have come back so count yourself lucky,* I chide the door. Then I toss the thought away with a quick shimmy of my head. It's exactly that kind of thought that made me crazy in the first place…

The room is dark inside, so to avoid surprises I switch on the light and shut the door behind me. *So I'm back,* I tell myself, pursing my lips. The plants are much further into their decomposing process, the rat and insects are still motionless on the floor with several additions, and it still smells of damp and emptiness.

I instantly see some of the incriminating pointers that I must remove before Thom arrives. The paper from the day of the murder is buried in the duvet, thankfully folded so I don't have to see the photo of Daniel again, the menacing photo that now looks even more eerie with the knowledge I now have. I thought he had been speaking to me when I first saw it and I was right. Yet I still have no idea how he made me kill him.

I think about keeping the paper but decide it's too much of a risk. Thom could easily look through my things and find it. Why would I have kept this paper and no others? I go to the kitchen cabinet and collect a plastic bag, dumping the paper inside. I use a dustpan to collect the dead insects and rat, and pour them inside too; sadly adding the deceased plant. Everything here is dead.

This place always seemed like a desperate and dank environment but looking around now, when I feel like each breath is clearer and deeper, it appears much worse. How could I have ever lived here? How had I not grown diseased or died out of solidarity with the fading plants and insects?

I can't see anything else in the bedsit that can alarm Thom. The other links to Daniel are the scarf, which Michael has, and the contents of my bag, that are safe in the car at present. In fact there is little in this room that reveals much about me. There is the bare amount of clothes, a few books and tapes, basic living provisions. This place has never been my home and for a while the concept of 'home' hasn't been as prevalent as it should have been, too focussed on my stalking Daniel.

Yet I want a home now. I want to have somewhere that isn't full of decay and sucks the breath from any living object forced to live within its walls.

More contented, I tie the bag up. I don't bother to say goodbye to the bedsit or take the vision of it away inside my mind. Instead I have an urge to close my eyes whilst I walk to the door, not wanting to risk accidentally memorising the details. I fling the door open to leave, turning the light off with my back to the room. I feel for the handle and pull the door up against my back, sighing into the hallway.

I post the keys through the landlord's door and deposit the bag of rubbish into the bins at the front of the building. As I close the gate, I glance back at the building and can't help thinking this is the second prison I have managed to escape in a matter of months.

The car is alight where I have left Michael. I skip towards it and jump in. Michael opens his eyes at the noise. He looks like he has been dosing. The stench of dried blood smothers me, and I imagine sheets of copper nailed all around the car, blockading us inside.

"All sorted?" he mumbles.

"Yes, I needed to do that".

"Where are your clothes?" Michael asks, noticing my hands are empty. I stare at them for a moment, remembering I had told Michael I needed to collect some clothes to take to his house.

"Oh, I decided to make a new start". I shrug.

"Okay then", Michael agrees, closing his eyes again. "Let's get to the house. I think I need a shower and my bed".

He does need a shower; he looks like he has eaten a messy hot dog and is now smothered with ketchup. The loss of blood and the trauma has left him sagging.

175

I start the engine, pulling away quickly. I have to take my brother home. I have to be the one to carry him back to his haven. As I cast a quick look into the wing mirror, I think I see a dark shape standing by the space the car had just occupied. Yet before I can begin to add detail to it, a car flashes its lights at me in the road ahead and I focus on that instead.

Chapter 36

The Bedsit

Thom watches Sarah pull away from him and can only stand in the space that the car has departed from, not wanting another car to take its place. Perhaps if he keeps the space empty she will definitely come back to fill it once again. Can she just leave him like this? Can she completely forget him?

Thom resists the plan to simply sit down on the ground and wait for her return. He makes himself turn towards the house behind him, a towering cracked form that seems to sway. Although if it falls down whilst he is asleep tonight, he isn't sure he will care. It certainly won't be something to deter him.

He has kept the key safely in the inside pocket of his coat, where he will return it once he is inside her bedsit. He doesn't want anyone to see what she has given him, a small token of rescue, a passage carved out after an avalanche. She has lied to him sure, but he stills needs her, still wants to call her by any name she wants him to. Sarah has watched him bruise and break her brother's skin and she nonetheless has offered him somewhere to rest his equally broken body and mind for the night.

Thom tiptoes up the stairs, thinking how dark this stairway is, not like the lightened and warm passage to upstairs at Aunty Val's. There is no carpet on the steps so each positioning of his feet, despite him being on tiptoe, makes a loud tapping sound. He can hear someone's TV talking behind the wall next to him and hopes the bedsit will be quieter. He fears one whisper will throw his fragile mind against the floor, smashing it into tiny shards that he won't be able to reassemble.

Thom finally reaches the door, his feet aching as though he has walked for days. He even imagines the tight squelching of blisters rubbing against his shoes. Shaking the thoughts away, he unlocks her front door and closes himself in. For a moment, he lets himself be immersed in the rush of darkness, glad to forget his physicality.

As his eyes begin to adjust, he sadly flicks the top light on and sweeps the room with a squint. He can see why Sarah would refer to it as 'horrible' but he accepts it for what it is – a refuge and a decent bed where he can bury himself for the night.

As he thinks what to do next, he hears a beeping noise and looks down at his pocket. It is only then he remembers his mobile, a distant friend he hasn't connected with for weeks, and wonders how it even got into his pocket. He has no recollection of shoving it in there, but here it is, telling him he has a message. He presses open and reads:

I spoke to your family. Are you okay? Did you find somewhere to stay? Em x

Thom throws himself onto the bed. He stares at the words. He feels his heart slowing down for the first time in days and lets himself fall back on the bed. He wonders why he feels so alone when there are all these people talking about him – Richard, Aunty Val, and Emma. Can someone really be alone when others are talking about them?

Thom releases the phone and lets his hands plunge into the bedclothes. They are used, soft, and Thom is sure he can detect a faded whisper of Sarah. She has slept in these sheets; she has thrashed in them during nightmares. Sarah has let him borrow her sheets for the same purposes.

What kind of things has Sarah been through the last few years? How can Thom ever understand them? He may not ever comprehend her experience of being raped or even her mental illness but what he does understand is her fear. Fear of being judged, fear of alienating those you care about, fear of being discovered, and fear of facing up to yourself.

He doesn't hate her for lying to him but he wishes she could've been honest. He is just so tired, his senses and perceptions fuzzy clouds that used to be sharp shapes that fit correctly into specific holes. Now he keeps pushing everything into holes that are too small or the wrong shape or holes that appear out of nowhere and extend for miles without a visible conclusion.

Thom remembers his phone and picks it up, rereading the message. He is nearly warmed by it but feels like a shard of ice slithers between him and this extension of concern. His eyes glaze over and he can hardly look at the screen. From memory of where the keys are, he types a message and when he finishes, turns over and falls asleep almost instantly.

Somewhere in another part of London, Emma receives a reply to her message and can only guess at what Thom might have been trying to tell her:

4 am mk. Stazing with a eriemd. Uhbnks 4 gettimg 4n tovch. I mis7 u + I'n rorry. H wish I 2ovld gn ba2k btt its ton late. Notiinh makes sdnsf. Tjom

Chapter 37

Red Recollections

Walking around Michael's house after my first night as a guest, I touch the objects he sees and uses everyday (the blender, the kettle, the radiator, the taps), and I feel I am returning to life with each sensation. I can use these things. Maybe I can even live how I did before all of this.

You believe me, don't you, Mum?

When we lived together, we owned all these things too. Touching them, I remember their sounds, their texture against my skin. I also remember you; standing in the kitchen in the early morning, waiting for the kettle to boil for your tea, smiling and tapping your spoon against the side.

I wish you were here now, the kettle's boiled…

I am still busy thinking of you when Michael calls me into the living room. I am forced to leave you before the kettle has stopped spluttering. Yet I freeze in the doorway to the living room when I see Doctor Rosey, sitting with her clipboard, her legs crossed, pen poised for action. I expect her to click her fingers and have me dragged away or to press a button and have a cage drop down around me. Yet, she merely smiles. A-tiny-line-on-a-large-piece-of-paper smile.

"Alice. It's so good to see you again", she tells me as I sit opposite her. Her tone couldn't have been more stretched. It is a tired balloon that has been inflated too many times. She bites her lip as she takes me in. She is probably wondering just how insane I still am. I come incredibly close to making a strange screeching sound and rolling around the floor but looking up at Michael standing between us, for once, I don't want to fail him.

"Doctor Rosey", I spit. She notices my tone and immediately scratches something onto her board.

"I think it's time you put that down and answered some of *my* questions", I tell her firmly. Doctor Rosey's face drops at the suggestion but Michael repeats the same request, translating it for her. She then does as she is told and places the clipboard beside her. I want to laugh as her fingers claw into the sofa and unconsciously spread towards her treasured sidekick.

"Tell me about Daniel Mansen", I say. Thinking I have already drained her face of colour, she surprises me by turning even paler.

"Don't lie to her", Michael adds; crossing his arms and taking a seat on the arm of the chair I am sitting in. Doctor Rosey looks instantly betrayed and straightens herself up.

"I presume you've already discussed it with Alice", the Doctor addresses Michael.

"You can talk directly to me". I wrestle into her attention and she is forced to meet my gaze, nodding rigidly.

She takes a deep breath. "What do you know?"

"Why don't we start with what *you* know for once?" I challenge her again.

"Okay, I'll tell you what I can, if you promise one thing…"

"And that would be?" I lean forward.

"Not to take any action against the hospital". She squashes her lips together and waits for my reply. I glance at Michael who half-smiles and raises one shoulder in a sign of passivity.

"Okay, I promise. And Michael can be your witness".

"Good". She nods sternly, recovering her authority for a few minor seconds. Yet she doesn't speak immediately, she rolls her tongue around in her mouth and repositions her body several times.

Finally she says, "Daniel originally worked as an administrator at the hospital but, over time, he demonstrated his ability to create a rapport with several of the patients. Some even showed a marked improvement with his support". Doctor Rosey gazes into the air above our heads, recalling a star pupil. Although, she quickly scolds this admiration with a downturned mouth.

"We decided to increase his duties, make him a mentor to some of the patients who had taken to him. He had shown himself to be trustworthy, or so we thought…" She sighs here. "What we didn't know was that he had designs on one of our patients".

"I'm guessing you mean me", I predict flatly.

"Yes…" She shakes her head as though she is faintly trying to escape a net. "You made no progress for months after you arrived and only began to speak when Daniel made an effort with you. We were happy to see you talking, at least, but we had no idea what price it came with. You understand that, don't you?"

Doctor Rosey is on the edge of her seat. I fear she might attempt to touch me so I sink further into the chair. Yet she doesn't move; her soggy eyes work on her behalf to show me an extended hand.

"Don't you monitor things in there?"

"We do Alice but on this occasion, we just missed it..." Doctor Rosey has transformed before us. I am the one asking questions, she is the one smashed to pieces by the bludgeon of guilt and shame. "And to our miniscule credit, we don't think anything physical took place between the two of you before he got caught".

"*Your credit?*" I laugh. "*You* let some strange man take advantage of me. You have no credit!" I am ready to leap from my chair but Michael pats on my shoulder softly and this is sufficient. Yet, it doesn't stop my eyes from tearing Doctor Rosey into strips across the room.

"You're right. We failed you", she agrees, glancing aside at her clipboard for comfort, but it doesn't move. "He was immediately fired of course", she adds.

"Oh that makes me feel *so* much better". My mouth is oozing.

"I can only apologise and explain this to you".

"How could you have let it happen? He groomed me... influenced me. How could you not see it happening?" Michael grabs my hand and squeezes it. Glancing up, I see the purple

184

bruises smudged underneath his eyes like tribal face paint. It reminds me of all the casualties Daniel has triggered, directly or indirectly. He is the first wave that pushed us all into each other, with numerous reactions spinning and colliding like sparks wrestling in flames.

"He was a clever man. Like you said, he groomed you so he didn't have to worry about you telling on him. As for the staff, they trusted him and as for me... I just didn't see it. I couldn't get through to you and he did".

"So he's better at your job than you are?"

"There's no need to be so cutting. After all, I did help you in the end, didn't I?"

"I wasn't well enough to leave", I whimper, covering my face with my hands.

"We decided you were well enough, with supervision of course". Doctor Rosey defends her decision. She can't face the idea of failing me twice.

"But I know now I wasn't well enough", I insist, sagging into the chair. Michael puts his hands on my shoulders and attempts to lift me back up again. I try my best on his behalf. "Why don't I remember what happened?" I ask, resting my head in Michael's lap. He doesn't move at first, staring down at me, and only after a long pause does he massage my neck with his thumb.

"You were very ill and when we caught Daniel, you were still *very* ill. As soon as he left, you seemed to forget about him and only after a few more months did you start to talk about anything at all", the Doctor explains.

"We thought you had enough to deal with, Alice", Michael adds from above and I cast one eye onto him, which is enough to make him turn his head away.

"I'm sorry", Michael whispers.

"You all lied to me".

I move myself out of Michael's lap and shake my head. My head is filled with helium, all I want to do is cut the cord and let it float away.

Mum, I know I shouldn't talk to you anymore but I think I need you still. All these people, they've lied and let me down but you never did.

"We didn't lie Alice, we just didn't discuss this with you", the Doctor claims but Michael betrays her with his clammy hands that leave sweat marks on the side of the chair.

"You don't know what this has done to me". My voice is a metal beam bending under the weight of tonnes of rubble.

"What has it done to you Alice? What does that mean?"

"You let him get inside me. You let him lead me. You let him influence me to…" I feel as if I might be sick and stumble out of the chair. "You let him mould me… how could you?" I hold onto the arm for support as the room swirls like paints being blended into one. "You don't know what you've done", I squeak as my throat closes up.

The train is coming towards me. The lights knock me to the ground as I try to scramble away from it. Yet the train is skulking closer, the reversed stalker. Daniel's lips are moving again but I can't hear or guess the words he is trying to say. The cold fingers of the track have locked me in place and I wait for the monster to churn me into pulp. I scream and call for help but the blurry figures on the platform don't respond or move.

Mum! Mum! Help me please!

The only figure is Daniel and he is beside me, then inside me, then I hear his voice in my brain, *right on time right on time* to the pulse of the monster, to the pulse of his heart, to the pulse of my own organ scratching against my rib cage. The raspy breath of the train louder now a scream a flood of light...

Chapter 38

The Hospital Visit

Thom wakes up in a strange room. It takes him several minutes to realise where he is. He rolls over and finds his phone stuck within the covers. It is 9:42am.

His neck is aching and his left arm is numb from the way he has been sleeping. He can't remember closing his eyes last night. He hasn't even switched the main light off and he is surprised that he'd been able to sleep with it on.

Thom familiarises himself with the room. He decides that it looks even more tragic in the daylight and opts to leave the place as soon as he can. He takes a fast shower in the bathroom down the hall, dries himself off with a stained towel, and throws on the same rags he came in with. He hopes the spots of Michael's blood on his sleeve aren't noticeable to anyone else. The grey swelling on his fists only underlines his shame further.

When he has his hand on the front door, Thom realises he has no idea where he is going. He slumps back onto the bed and considers his options. First, he could go back to the house and face Aunty Val and Richard. Second, he could go and look for Sarah and talk over the revelations of yesterday night. Or third, he could try to discover more about Daniel and why he died.

Out of fear and perhaps tiredness, Thom chooses the most familiar. He will keep investigating Daniel. He can't talk to his family yet, and finding out more about Sarah's lies can wait. Just because everything in his life has changed so much, it doesn't mean he can forget his task. He has to find out about Daniel.

But where should he go now? The lock up? Mrs Tray's? Yet Thom feels like these are places he has already been, places which make up the past and are not to be revisited. Where or what is he missing?

Thom thinks back to when he met Mrs Tray and the way she played solitaire. What did she say to him? *'Sometimes all it takes is a fresh eye'*. And Thom remembers how the phrase slithered into his ear and solidified there. He has been caught in a whirlpool for weeks or months now and he needs to break out. As he always hears them say on the news, he needs 'fresh leads'.

So what places or people has he left out? Well there's the station where it all began of course, but Thom isn't sure he's ready for that. He hasn't even been in a tube station at all since Daniel died, let alone the one where he was smashed to pieces.

The only other 'lead' he can think of is the hospital. Thom has never known enough about Daniel's time there, and Mrs Tray made the link to it when they had talked. Therefore, this seems a sensible plan to Thom and he finally feels able to turn the door handle and leave the frowning room behind.

Outside the air is cold and instantly stings Thom's cheeks. He zips up his coat and makes his way towards somewhere where he hopes he can catch a bus in the vague direction of the hospital. He knows little about this hospital but he at least knows which one it is.

Two long bus rides later, he is standing somewhere in South London, in front of an unassuming building which is actually a hospital. People walk by without even looking at the building, which Thom finds troubling as it is a grand and stony character. There is a large wall guarding it and only a small entrance at one of the sides, guarded by one man sitting in a booth, as though no one ever tries to gain entry to it. Or perhaps no one ever comes out?

Thom hesitates as he stands on the pavement scrutinising the entrance. Standing here, the normality of the crowd threading past reassures him. At least here, his 'madness' of late is concentrated by all the other bodies and their sanity. But inside that hospital, his 'madness' will be spiked by all the insanity of the patients. In there, will he finally fall apart and reveal his strange thoughts? Will he finally tell someone he isn't sure whether he can ever rejoin the life he left behind?

Thom forces himself to approach the guard. He explains he is considering placing a relative into the hospital and wants to discuss his options with the managing director. The man reluctantly replaces his cigarette with the phone receiver and makes a hushed call to someone. When he replaces the phone, he nods towards the hospital and mutters, "see reception". Thom does as he has been instructed; walking gradually towards the hospital he fears can undress him.

Thom takes on the stairs like a warrior certain he is climbing to his death. The door of the hospital grows with each step, a mouth that will swallow him. Yet when Thom finally grasps the handle, he feels reassured by its cold stillness, and manages to navigate his trembling legs through it.

Inside, he is buzzed through another door and is greeted by a young woman. She tells him the director would be happy to see him and discuss admissions, perhaps even give him a tour should he want one. She asks him to take a seat but Thom barely grazes the chair when he jumps up again.

"I don't have a sick relative", Thom confesses. The receptionist freezes and for a strange moment Thom believes he has stabbed her in the spine and she is paralysed. Yet after a few moments of silence, she turns to face him again.

"So what is it you want exactly?" the woman asks, her hand creeping towards the edge of the desk. Thom suspects there is an alarm there and he doesn't blame her for reassuring herself with it. If the position were reversed, and he was the one looking at a clammy faced man with his clothes stretched to all sides and hanging off his shoulders, he would press the alarm instantly.

"I want to ask about my cousin". Thom attempts to straighten his clothes, as if this will help the situation greatly.

"Who is your cousin?" She doesn't take her eyes off Thom.

"Daniel Mansen". Thom is watching the woman equally as closely as he says the two words. These two words seem to spit glass in all directions whenever they are mentioned. These two words make Thom want to duck down after he's said them and wait for the screams.

"Daniel", the woman repeats, letting her arm move back towards her body. She lets go of the physical alarm in response to the alarm in her mind.

"You knew him", Thom states.

The woman slowly nods and takes a step towards Thom. "Why are you here?"

"Daniel is dead", Thom tells her. The woman bites her lip and looks down.

"I'm sorry", she mumbles, drawing even closer to Thom. "But why have you come here *now*?"

"I know he left his job here but I don't know why".

Thom is standing next to the woman now; they are huddled beside the reception desk, speaking in quiet tones. Thom guesses the woman can feel his pinched sticky desperation and he can see her guilty curiosity that made her let go of the alarm.

"He didn't tell you?" she sighs.

"I feel like I'm really missing something here", Thom admits. He has just summarised his feelings throughout the whole investigation. Yet Thom guesses this is the nature of an investigation: always being in a state of lack.

"I am sorry Daniel's dead but I don't think I should tell you anything".

"I'm sorry to ask this but I need…" Thom rubs his hands over his face, "I need to know what happened. I know it's something bad, so you don't have to worry".

"But the hospital…"

"This is about people, *not* about this hospital", Thom wrestles in. "Look, I promise you I won't say anything to anyone. I just want to know, *for me*". Thom pronounces each word precisely.

"I understand how you feel and I'm sorry…" she persists, shaking her head.

"No, don't say that again. You have to help me, no one else can. I need to find this out, to help me understand him. I can't ask him, can I?" Thom knows this is unfair but he is grasping at anything, showing only traces of his once noble self.

"What is your name anyway?"

"Thom", he answers and holds his hand out.

"Kelly", she nods, taking his hand. Thom is glad he took the bandages off this morning. After all, they had been covered in Michael's blood. "You know, Daniel and I were friends. I was shocked when I heard he'd been fired…" Kelly pauses, expelling air loudly, "and the reason, it made me sick…"

"Daniel was fired", he repeats. It is meant to be a question but it comes out as a fact, a brick wall suddenly complete. Thom can't believe he hasn't thought of this already. He should've figured this out by the fact that no one in the family ever discussed it, yet at the same time it hadn't seemed crucial when it happened. But now, everything is vital, everything is a grain that gathers together to form a giant textile. Thom wishes he didn't have to collect all of the parts so slowly.

"He was caught with a patient", Kelly adds, after a few minutes of cold silence.

"What?" Thom snaps his neck up, too fast, and massages the ache that mushrooms across the back of it. It takes about thirty seconds for it to fade.

"He was caught kissing a patient".

"Oh fuck". Thom punches the desk. Although he is ninety percent sure Aunty Val might've known about Daniel being forced to leave his job, he bets she doesn't know the reason.

"How could he do that?" Thom covers his face.

Kelly hovers next to Thom, her fingers twitching beside his arm but not making a connection. Thom doesn't notice this and when he uncovers his face a minute later, she has moved her fingers away.

"I can't tell you anything else Thom, I'm sorry". Kelly shrugs. "And I wish I hadn't had to tell you that". She smiles gently.

"I don't know why I'm surprised. I've been finding out so many things about him and most of them not good". Thom is tired, he wants to hang himself over the desk and close his eyes. How much more can he take? Was Daniel a bad person, or a good person who'd made some bad mistakes? Had Daniel felt so bad about himself that he threw himself in front of that train?

"Daniel seemed like a good person, but he really abused that patient's trust, the hospital's trust". Kelly seems almost as broken as Thom. Yet he doubts the cracks extend as deep as his.

"What happened to the patient?"

"She got better". Kelly smiles.

"That's good".

"I can't believe Daniel's dead…" Kelly shakes her head.

"Me neither".

"I'm sorry Thom but I have to get back… to work".

"Okay". Thom takes her hand and relishes in the warmth for a few seconds. Kelly smiles again and takes her hand with her, when she returns to her seat behind the desk. Everything is as it should be again, she behind the desk and he in front of it like a visitor. Their moments of sharing have finished.

Thom reaches the door, still rolling the new information around in his mind and his heart. As he stands in the doorway looking out, his feet seem to curl up into balls, making his balance uneven. He holds onto the door frame to stop himself from falling. Taking a few breaths, Thom suddenly thinks of Sarah. He thinks about the revelations she shared with him yesterday night and before he has even considered this properly, he swings round and says, "Kelly, what was the name of that patient?"

"I don't think that's relevant", she dismisses.

"I'd just like to know, out of curiosity…"

"Okay". Kelly leans across the desk on her elbows, like a little girl unloading a secret to her best friend. "The patient's name was Alice".

Chapter 39

Red Bruises

I wake up in Michael's guest room. The sheets are moist and my curls are pasted to my forehead. As soon as I attempt to push myself up, Michael appears at my side.

"Don't move", he says quietly, stroking my sweaty curls. He lowers me back onto the pillow. I don't want to do as he says but I feel weak and my body doesn't have the same determination to defy him. I wonder how long I have been unconscious.

"Alice, I'm so sorry", he whispers, bowing his head. "We've really hurt you by keeping this secret. I mean… just look how your body reacted". Michael's eyes are glistening in the semi-darkness of the room. "You just flopped on the floor and…" he breathes in shakily, "and I was *so* scared. I feel so responsible". He grabs hold of my hands and squeezes them between his. "I threw Doctor Rosey out by the way", he adds and I can't help smiling slightly. Michael lifts his lips to one side, knowing I would appreciate this.

"I understand why you lied", I confess; pushing myself upwards so I can sit against the headboard. Michael waits for me to continue. "It's just that I think he influenced me and it's affecting me… now". Michael brings his eyebrows together in a slanted V at my words.

"How has he influenced you now?" Michael asks. This is my cue, the moment I could reveal my nasty deed to him; the moment I tell him I am a murderer. Yet, I can't bear to have him let go of my hands in shock, or have him look at me with the same confusion as he did a few days ago.

"I saw an article in the paper, saying he had died", I venture, not sure where I am leading myself.

"I saw that too". Michael nods. "I hoped you wouldn't or if you did, you wouldn't remember".

"I didn't remember that I knew him", I say, my chest seemingly filling up with air that is blocking movement and function. Yet, here it is: another lie. "But I felt curious for some reason. So I ended up going to his house".

"What?" Michael jolts in his chair.

"I know, it's crazy but I just felt some unconscious need to go there", I pause, "and now I know why I found myself drawn there". *Drawn to him,* I add to myself. Finding out about me and Daniel being together at the hospital probably did explain my fascination with him, the decision to follow him, perhaps even the decision to kill him. He'd been leading me for months before the push and he wanted me to know with those horrible words: *right on time.*

"I just needed to look at the house, for reasons I couldn't place. But as I stood there looking at it, one of his family came out and started talking to me..."

"You left didn't you?" Michael interjects hopefully.

"No Michael, I stayed. We talked and he invited me in".

"It was that Thom guy, wasn't it?" Michael asks, running his fingers over his still swollen nose. I nod faintly, anticipating his anger or disappointment. Yet, Michael lowers his head and shows me his bald patch, mumbling, "If I'd been there for you, maybe you wouldn't have gone to him".

"I don't know. I clearly felt some link to Daniel".

"Does he know you knew Daniel? And how are they related?"

"They're cousins. And no", I emphasise with my eyes, "he doesn't know I knew Daniel". I grimace appropriately.

"You're *not* going to tell him?" Michael places his hand on my arm.

"I don't want to and I'm not sure it matters".

"Is he a decent person, Ali?" Michael continues, calling me by a name he hasn't used since before you died. I relish its familiarity for a few seconds and give my brother a warm smile.

"He's not a bad person Michael. I know he hurt you but he just thought he was protecting me". I lift my hand up and brush his cheek, trying to dull the red-grey stain that has blossomed there.

"And you two... are an item?" He winces.

"No", I say, convinced this is what he wants to hear, "we're just friends". As I use one of the clichés people always use, *just friends,* I wonder what Thom and I actually are. Yes, we kissed the other day, but does it mean anything? I've supported him for a few weeks, he'd invited me to stay when he thought I had nowhere to sleep, but isn't that merely friendship? Only that one violent kiss hints at anything more and now after all the lies, what does he think of me now?

"I think you should be careful with him Alice". Michael grapples with my eye contact in order to stress his point. "I've only met him twice but he seems unsteady... I think he's capable of something..." Michael scrunches his mouth up and looks aside, imagining what Thom is 'capable' of while staring at the wallpaper. I sit up and take his hand.

"What might he be capable of?" I ask, all the time thinking of what Michael is unaware of. He doesn't know his own sister is capable of murder. He doesn't know his sister is also a liar, a manipulator, still fascinated with the colour red. The whole time the two of us have been talking, I have been imagining his nose gushing with blood again and thinking of the scarf soaking it all into its body, a parasite sucking on my brother's lifeblood.

"I wish I could tell you. I mean; we've already seen he can hurt people. I just don't know..." Michael stares at the wallpaper again and finishes, "just how far he could go". Michael is unconsciously running his fingers over his bruises again. I think whenever he sees Thom, even weeks from now; he will stroke the areas on his face where Thom struck him.

"He's a good person", I say, shaking my head.

"Good people can still do bad things". He frowns and suddenly pulls me towards him. He hugs me tight and continues to hold me for several minutes, his uneven breath humidifying my neck.

As I am in my brother's arms, I think about good people and bad people, good actions and bad actions. I consider how they are all interchangeable and question which way the scales tip for me: am I a bad person who commits bad actions? Or am I a good person who commits bad actions?

Chapter 40

Alice

Thom doesn't remember what happens for a certain amount of time after he hears that name again. It seems to crack against his head and make him lose consciousness, although he somehow manages to still walk and breathe. He next finds himself back at the bedsit, standing in the doorway. The clock above the kitchen sink says 1:27pm.

He doesn't remember how he'd slumped against the wall at the hospital, or how the receptionist shook him, or how he'd sworn and muttered incoherently about things even he couldn't have made sense of, how he'd pushed the woman off him and sped out of the door into the street, into the city, into more unknown things and more unknown people. Even the people he thought he knew have become false.

Standing in the doorway of the bedsit, the room seems to pulsate and all the objects in it begin to contort. Thom rubs his eyes and shakes his head. Yet the phenomenon continues and he slowly lowers himself onto the bed, pressing against the mattress to steady himself. Thom fears he is about to vomit when a voice distracts him.

"Thom". A happy tone but tight. A familiar voice but distant.

"It's you", he says, not using either of her names. He doesn't know which one fits her anymore. Like the objects, the names warp at the thought of attaching to her.

She smiles and takes a seat beside him. She doesn't move to touch him. Instead, she stares at his still purple and grey knuckles. He wonders how long this will be the case and, at the same time, wonders how much he cares. He is in the middle of a field with space stretching in every direction with nothing else in even the farthest sight. Which direction should he choose? Which might lead him to somewhere familiar that won't implode?

"How are you, Thom?" She takes a strained breath, clutching onto her left arm with her other hand.

"I don't know what to call you anymore", Thom says, not answering on purpose. She meets his gaze, trying to remind him of the exact colour of her metallic blue eyes.

"Call me Sarah..." she says and adds hopefully, "if you can".

"If Sarah's what you want". Thom shrugs. She nods happily, reaching across and clutching his fist in her hand. "How is Michael?"

"He's okay, still a bit bruised".

"You shouldn't have lied to me". Thom's face crumples. He snatches his hand out of hers and massages it. He doesn't want her poison seeping through his skin. All he can think about, as he looks at her, is her kissing Daniel. Had she enjoyed it? Which one did she prefer? How can she have kissed them both?

"I'm so sorry", she says quietly. As Thom listens to her words, he realises how human she sounds. When he first met her outside Aunty Val's house, she spoke in a methodical way, every word considered. Now, she seems to speak more impulsively; perhaps more honestly. After all, what is there to consider when you're telling the truth?

"You understand why I did it, don't you? I'm ill Thom, and felt completely ashamed and afraid that you would push me away if you knew". Sarah bows her head knowingly. "I didn't realise my lies were hurting people…"

"You told me you had a different name, a different history, you told me your brother raped you. You didn't think *that* would hurt anyone?" Thom enunciates each word, his saliva thick with distaste.

"I didn't think you would hurt him". She kneads her forehead.

"I was just trying to defend you", Thom snarls.

"Let's not go over all this again. It's not helping either of us", Sarah says, turning to face him and lifting her head up with effort. "I came to tell you about everything".

"*Everything* as in…?" Thom leans towards her expectantly.

"Why I was in the hospital", she tells him solemnly. He wonders if she will include the part where she met Daniel and then somehow ended up living with his family after his death. *Doubtful*, he decides.

"Okay. I'm listening". Thom pushes himself back and leans against the wall. Sarah copies him, smiling at him gently as she settles. It feels like they are two children sharing secrets. Thom is tempted then to reach towards her and press his hand over hers that is squashed against the bed.

"Right, well... I guess I should start... I guess... the start is..." Sarah trails off. Thom is mesmerised by her fumbling. When he'd found out she had been lying to him and he'd found out about her knowing Daniel, he felt sure he would only hate her. Yet as he watches her lips struggling to form words, he feels an explosion of warmth rising inside. This unexplained warmth is what troubles him, not the hate.

"I was raped", she finally begins, holding her breath, as though she is the one who has been told something difficult by him. He merely waits for her to continue. "I didn't lie about that Thom; I promise you on my life". She meets his eyes, water flooding them, as she pulls desperately at his sleeve. He nods gently and she lets go of his clothes. "It ruined everything. I dropped out of uni, I couldn't go out, I was afraid of men... I couldn't trust people". She shakes her head, still unable to comprehend all these facts even now.

"Is that when you ended up in the hospital?" Thom asks, trying to rescue her. She seems to be sinking into the mattress, her past suspended over her like a noose.

"No", she sighs. "I wish". She chuckles sadly. "My Mum... she really helped me get through it, or she did until..." Sarah rolls her eyes upwards, wishing she can shoot through the ceiling, away from him, away from the truth, "she died", she exhales quietly.

"She died", Thom repeats. He can't tell if he is unconvinced. If someone can lie about rape, can they lie about death? Yet Thom can't imagine she would lie to him about this. It seems too large a lie to slide out of her small delicate mouth.

"I came home one day and she was lying there, her slippers were… she was cold, and there was blood and she didn't move…" Sarah looks like she is lost in the middle of a supermarket, beginning to cry loudly and crush her curls until Thom thinks they will flatten permanently. Perhaps to stop her from losing her curls, he gathers her up and presses her against him.

Thom cradles her but, at the same time, has an urge to crack her neck. Just one sharp pull like the snap of a Christmas cracker…

Her words are now tiny injections stabbing at him through a waterfall of tears. "Her skin… so pale… a line of blood… twisted legs and bruises and… she didn't move…" Thom feels her words have physically penetrated him and he checks his arms for puncture wounds. He worries that when she moves away from him again; she will uncover holes she has made in his chest and allow the blood to ooze out like uncontrollable foam blistering from a champagne bottle.

She pushes back from him. Her eyes are swollen and bloodshot, her eyelashes clumped together in a moist huddle, her hair glued to the sides of her face as though she has dipped her face in a sink full of water. Thom feels nauseated by the display of raw emotion. Much like Aunty Val, he feels like he is being forced to hold Sarah up.

"So *that's* when you ended up in the hospital?" Thom asks again but is greeted by Sarah's shaking head.

206

"I didn't understand, Thom". She squashes her lips together, trying to stop them from trembling further. "I think I've only just fully accepted it".

"What do you mean?" Thom snaps, slightly impatiently.

"I stayed in the house with her, for weeks... I still didn't know when they took me to the hospital and even months after... I don't think I knew properly until recently".

"That your mum had died?" Thom clarifies. Sarah closes her eyes and takes a few deep breaths. Her eye twitches gently, her muscles stubborn and wavering at the same time.

"Yes, she's dead", she nods weakly.

"Wait, you kept her in the house... when she was dead?"

"Yes", Sarah admits tight-lipped. "I told you... I was ill".

"That's terrible. That's so sad", Thom spurts breathlessly.

"I was already distraught and I guess her dying just shoved me over the edge". Sarah holds her hands out in front of her and stares at them intently. Thom stares at them too, watching the veins swell and throb, watching the skin swirling as if he is looking at them through a kaleidoscope.

"Do you feel better now?" Thom inquires hopefully. Sarah faces him, her eyebrows creasing together in the middle of her head, thinking.

"I'm sorry Thom but I don't know yet", she smiles meekly. Thom's posture drops in response.

"You still feel like you're ill?"

"I've only just realised properly so yes, I'm still ill, whatever that means…" she trails off, still considering this. Thom puts his hand on her knee, his hand that continues to ache; his hand that looks like someone has drawn lines on it with a red biro.

"So that's everything? Everything you lied about?" Thom verifies, pressing down on her knee, staring into her eyes. She doesn't twitch, blink or look away.

"That's everything", she says. All Thom's ribs seem to crumble apart in one rapid moment. All the air in his chest sucks downwards, to where he can't tell, but all he is concerned with is the fact that he can't feel his own heart.

"Everything huh?" Thom echoes, taking his hand off her knee and burying it in the duvet. He crushes the duvet with both his hands to stop himself from crushing her neck between his fingers.

"Thom I think I should go now. We've said enough for today". Sarah stands up. Thom jumps up after her and feels his muscles locking, except for his facial muscles that keep rolling into different expressions.

"There's nothing else Sarah?" Thom persists, almost desperately. His tone is strained. He is a man asking for the truth, for the piece of information that is the hook to pluck him from the angry sea he has been battling in for weeks.

"No Thom", Sarah says firmly. She bends her head sideways, with an expression of confusion, a trace of anxiety? She pushes her shoulders back as he stares at her, a hard stare that hammers into her.

"You're *really* sure?" Thom offers her a last chance.

"Nothing else", she reiterates hollowly. She is insistent but unconsciously falls back slightly, hiding in daylight. Thom can't help the chuckle that vibrates feebly in his throat. Sarah's mouth quivers momentarily.

"So you don't want to tell me about the hospital?" Thom moves closer. Sarah has to force herself not to move back, Thom sees it in her shaky legs that are set apart like someone about to burst into a sprint.

"What do you mean Thom?"

"What do I *mean* Sarah?" Thom's words are clouded by the thunder of his heartbeat. "What-do-I-mean?" he shouts. Sarah gives a distasteful glance at the spit that jumps from his mouth onto her body. She doesn't say anything. What can she say except to tell the truth? And apparently she doesn't know how to do that, despite her attempts to prove otherwise.

"Were you ever going to tell me you met Daniel at the hospital?" Thom snarls, the blood thrashing at his cheeks and tears assembling in the corners of his eyes, preparing for an assault.

Sarah doesn't react initially. She watches him, his arched back and his teeth sharpening, her expression unchanged. For a moment, she reverts to the woman he met in the front garden of Aunty Val's house with mechanical movements, thoughts and functions.

Then a full minute later, the signs of shock set in. Her eyes widen as though he has jumped out on them, her body stiffens like an exclamation mark and she suddenly spins towards the door.

Taking a few desperate leaps, she reaches the door and scrambles with the handle. Before she can manage to make her fingers function properly, Thom pounces on her and slams her against the door. She groans as though he has punched her in the stomach and sags in his hold.

"You'd better tell me Sarah. I'm tired of your fucking lies", Thom spits as they both fall back onto the floor. She looks exhausted, as though he has clubbed her with a blunt object. He feels a moist patch on the back of her head and worries it might be blood but gratefully realises it is only sweat. Thom wrenches her up to a sitting position and pushes her against the door.

"If you lie to me again, I think I'll go insane", Thom whimpers. Sarah nods and tucking her curls behind her ears, she opens her mouth.

Chapter 41

The Red Secret

"I promise you, I only found out a few days ago", I tell him, grabbing onto his arms.

He is on his knees before me, a man pleading for honesty.

"What?" he growls. His dark expression makes him look strangely attractive but I don't think this is the time for sharing these types of thoughts.

"I didn't know I'd known him", I swear, tightening my fingers around his arms like a clamp. He doesn't move. Perhaps I am holding him up or perhaps he is too weak to move away.

"How could you not know?" Thom shakes his head hopelessly. If he's ever been certain of anything, I think he's finally lost his last ties to it. He seems to have no comprehension of the divide between certainty and uncertainty anymore.

"I don't remember a lot of things from that time. I guess... I guess I blocked it out or something. But I only found out when I read the letters".

"The letters?" Thom's neck snaps up. His eyes are burnt wood still lit with a tiny ember.

"I found a combination and an address in Daniel's room", I admit quietly. How could I have trespassed on their grief the way I have?

"You were in his room…" Thom broods but instantly shrugs it away and adds, "how did you find anything in there? I searched *everywhere*". His mouth is slightly open, with an expression of minor admiration at someone doing better at investigating than he has.

"It was inside the closet drawer written in red pen. It wasn't easy to find".

"But *you* found it", he says sulkily.

"I think it was meant for me to find". I smile gently, hoping he will accept this. He shrugs. A moment later he reaches up and pulls at one of my curls, making it spring back at my face. After he does this several times, he moves his fingers over my lips, dabbing them as though he is pressing against tacky glue.

"So the letters…" he reminds me, squashing my lips down with his thumb.

"They were in a locker", I mumble incoherently, due to his probing. He takes his thumb away for a moment and waits for me to continue. "There were letters inside. They were written by me", I reveal, still unconvinced by them. I cradle my head in one hand, remembering the handwriting that looked so familiar. *Of course it was familiar – it was yours!* I hadn't seen my handwriting for so long; it is no wonder I didn't recognise it. And the things my own hand created!

"They said horrible things about… about me… and Daniel". I feel the nausea solidify and mushroom up my throat. I have to close my eyes and concentrate on trying not to vomit on Thom. When I open my eyes, Thom is staring at me. He moves his arms so he is holding onto me instead. I blink and nod my head in gratitude.

"They sounded like love letters, Thom", I moan, kneading my eyelids until the threatening tears are squashed out. With my eyes closed, I jolt slightly when I feel his warm skin clashing with my clammy cheek. I reopen my eyes and gaze into his.

"Do you think I loved him Thom?" His hand drops.

"I hope not", he mumbles.

"I can't believe I don't remember meeting him".

"Is this the truth Sarah? Is this really the *truth*?"

"Yes Thom", I vow.

"But why did you end up at the house? You can't tell me it's just coincidence?" I shrug his hold off and move away. Thom scrambles after me. I watch his movements, a lost infant chasing a parent, and my heart feels like someone has plunged a skewer through it. Although I want to tell him the truth about everything, this is the blockade in the road.

"I saw the article in the paper and I don't know what happened… I just found myself…" I pause, "…at the house". I stand by the window looking out at the street. I imagine myself walking along the pavement, under the quivering trees, inhaling the fumes and the sharp air. Thom hovers behind me, hanging on the silence. "I didn't know you would talk to me", I stress.

"If I hadn't found out", Thom moves to stand beside me, "would you have ever told me?" I don't look in his direction but I feel his awkward stance contorting in my peripheral vision.

"I can't tell you that".

"At least that's honest", Thom says. He is silent but I feel he isn't finished. This is clarified when he grabs my arm and pulls me in his direction. "Can you tell me Sarah?" He stammers for a few seconds. "Was it nice... to kiss him?"

This isn't the question I expected. I fall back on myself. The bind between our gazes seems unbreakable. I think about the question and wonder if I even know where to begin. Do I really remember kissing Daniel? Since reading the letters and talking to Michael and Doctor Rosey about it, there had been vague flashes about the hospital and Daniel. Yet, I can't be sure I actually remember anything. After all, I could've invented recollections now I have the information.

I haven't spoken for several minutes. I only realise when I see the colour draining from Thom's face. His body begins to quiver quietly, but he pushes his shoulders back and tries to maintain the gaze we are sharing.

"I'm sorry Thom but I don't remember..."

"But you must have some recollection now", Thom insists.

"I wouldn't trust any memories that came to me anyway". Thom slumps at my words and finally snaps our stare. He turns away. I reach out and touch his back gently, feeling his back muscles tensing and bulging.

"I love your curls", he says suddenly. I move closer, circling him with my arms. I think he will flinch but he leans back into my body. He smells of sweat, as though he has been running for days without stopping. I am so close I can see his broken strands of hair, the loops that have formed at the back like an army waiting to conquer the rest.

"Since I first saw you, I couldn't stop thinking about them", he confesses. I can't see his face but I imagine his cheeks have rashes of blood rising on them.

"I didn't want to kiss him, Thom", I say. His body shudders in my hold but he quickly recovers himself, knowing I can feel each movement. "But I wanted you". My whisper claws its way through his beard and up to his ear. Some of my hair is stuck to his beard as though it is Velcro and when he pulls out of my hold, it clings on until it has to accept defeat.

I am sad that we are apart. Yet as soon as I think this, Thom takes hold of me by the hips. Unlike the first time when we wrestled, this time there is an awkward approach. There is a slow draw between us, the clash of breath, and the replacement pressure of his thumb with his lips.

I pull back after several seconds and gush, "Michael says I should be careful with you". Thom smiles briefly, glancing to one side for a long moment before he gradually turns back to me. He opens and closes his mouth like a goldfish that never intends to speak. Then another cheeky grin later, he pushes me into his lips and fills his silence.

Chapter 42

The Red Slippers Revisited

Getting into the car outside my bedsit, I avoid looking up at the window where I know Thom is standing. I am certain my lips are flashing or my cheeks are still flushed, yet when Michael nods 'hello', he shows no signs of suspecting anything. He starts the car and with a glance in the mirrors, pulls away.

"Is he okay?" Michael asks, although I'm not sure he is actually interested.

"He's okay", I say, staring at the world rolling by outside like a continuous rapid slideshow. Michael fiddles with the radio and after several options, settles on one station. I don't recognise any of the songs they play. It feels like years since I listened to music, either religiously or just as background music. What kind of music am I actually interested in anyway? I can't remember.

"What did you talk about? You were in there a long time". Michael says after two songs have passed.

I look over at him, fiddling with my hands in my lap and tell him, "We talked about lots of things. Thom had questions too". Michael nods at my words and stops at some traffic lights.

"Did he get angry?" He glances over.

"Why would he?" I snap.

"It's not that unreasonable an assumption". He narrows his gaze at me, making sure I have to look at his bruises once again. I sigh, knowing he is right.

"Well, he's fine". I shrug. Michael keeps looking at me but I don't acknowledge him. Finally, he sees the lights have changed and is forced to concentrate on driving again.

"I thought we could go to the house", he says quietly. Jumping in my seat, I look at my brother, trying to decide if he's being serious. Only I would understand which house he means. To anyone else, it could be any house in the whole city. But to me, it's *your* house.

"You didn't sell it?"

"No Alice". He appears he is pouring petroleum onto a fire and is waiting for the backlash. "I thought you might want to see it again", he mentions it as though he is talking about buying some milk. "I just told you I did, because I thought it would be easier, for the time being..."

"I don't know Michael..." I splutter, wringing my hands and leaning forward in my seat. My chest is tightening. I have to focus on dragging the air into my lungs and letting it slide back out easily. I hold onto the dashboard, steadying myself slowly. All I can think about is the staircase, your crooked legs, the unnatural paleness of your skin, those slippers...

Mum, can I go back? Will it still feel like you're there?

"It's okay Alice, we don't have to go", Michael says, taking his hand off the handbrake and patting my leg quickly. His obvious lack of surprise angers me though.

"No, we'll go", I blurt.

Michael looks over again, almost forgetting he is driving and nods gently, "If you're sure…"

We arrive outside the house twenty minutes later. The closer we have travelled to the house, the more my throat has swollen up and my breathing has grown raspier. Michael has said nothing.

The car stops and is silent but I can't make my hand rise up and grab the handle. Michael leans across me and swings the door open for me. I throw him a look as though he has just smacked me in the face. He sits back in his seat and stares ahead, waiting for me to move first.

"I don't think I can do it Mike", I confess, pressing my back into the seat so hard that it begins to ache across my shoulder blades. Michael grabs my hand, hearing my wavering tone, and hearing me calling him by the name I barely use when addressing him.

"You can Alice. *You can*". He squeezes my hand.

"Michael, can you call me Sarah?" I glance at him. His forehead burrows in a sudden avalanche of skin.

"Your name is Alice", he tells me, as though I have forgotten.

"But I really prefer Sarah".

"Okay", he mumbles. "I'll try Al—*Sarah*", he adds, pronouncing Sarah as though in a foreign tongue. He shakes his mistake away.

"Thanks", I tell him and swing my legs out of the car. "I should be able to do this", I inform myself out loud.

When I am standing outside, my legs seem to dissolve and I grab onto the car. A second later, Michael is propping me up. Even though I want to let him hold me up, I push away and tell my legs to work properly. The least I can do for you is stand up by myself.

That is all you'd wanted for me especially, Mum, before you died.

"Do you have the key Michael?" My voice is as shaky as the hand that I extend towards him. I hear him fumbling in his pocket and he places the key in my palm. It feels light and cold. It is a small object but when I use it to open the front door, a waterfall will thrash into me, submerge me with the emotions and memories I have locked away since the day I found you there.

The walk towards the door is quick and easy, when I feel it should be a harrowing journey through mountains and rough currents. I don't look back but I know Michael is behind me. Just a few days ago, I wouldn't have trusted him to be there, but I have a different sense of him now. Even the air around him seems firmer, a commanding building looming over a skyline.

"Okay", I say to the door and jam the key into the lock. It feels stiff as I turn it and the door sticks as I try to push it open. After a brief struggle, the hallway opens up to me. I sway slightly, Michael's hands instantly steadying me.

"That's where I found her", I reveal quietly, stepping across the threshold. I point to a spot on the carpet, unremarkable to others' eyes, and circle it, hunting the memory. Michael stays in the doorway, watching me in the throes of interest and guilt, gnawing at his bottom lip.

"She was on her front, her face bent towards the door, her legs bent in weird directions, her slippers..." I move towards the stairs, "One was here. I put it back on her". I can see you like you are before me now. I can feel the rubber texture of your skin; see the chalky tone of your face. When I had picked you up, it felt like there was an anchor attached, dragging you away from me.

Don't worry; I haven't forgotten you, Mum.

"Did you know..." Michael holds his sentence hostage again, "she was dead?" He speaks quietly, so quietly I'm not convinced he wants to hear the answer.

"I don't think I did. I think I just really 'lost' my mind..." I give him a pleading look. "Can you understand, Michael? It was like someone flicked a switch and I just couldn't figure things out anymore..."

Michael stares at me. I begin to think he will regress into his old judgemental self and get me locked up again. Yet after a few minutes, he drops his stare to the space on the carpet. "I can't imagine what it must've been like for you", he says, surprising me. "After what happened to you with Harry, I don't blame you for taking Mum's death badly".

"I don't want to talk about him", I spit.

"I know, I know". Michael holds his hands up and moves closer. I study his steps as he walks over your outline. I cringe, imagining your floppy limbs being trodden on. Michael skips a few steps when he realises what he has done. "I should've realised at the time", he continues, taking my hands, "it's just hard *Sarah*. I can't ever completely understand it. It still confuses me how…" Michael shakes his head, "look, it doesn't matter. I'm just trying to say I'm here for you now, even if I can't understand it all".

"Thanks", I mumble, taking my hands back. "Michael, I'm going to look in Mum's room now and I'd like to go alone". Michael steps back on himself, grasping at his thinning hair.

"Must you?" He croaks.

"Yes", I answer simply and turn away.

Leaving Michael behind, I'm instantly lost in the soft padding sound my feet make against the carpet. I remember the sound of you, Mum. Outside my room; your slippers flashing underneath the door, the slice of light as you checked on me whilst you thought I was asleep. The truth is; I could never sleep until I heard you check on me. Even now, it's a struggle to drift off without imagining the flash of light and the click of the door.

The door to your room is shut. When I touch the handle, it feels as cold as you did when I touched your cheek several days after the fall. I pause, nausea swirling in the pit of my stomach. How had I been so deluded about you?

I push the door open. The first thing that strikes me is that your bed is missing. I step inside and close the door, taking in the space. Examining the floor, I see the darker square of carpet where the bed used to be. Where has it gone? Why has it been taken? The bed is the last place I saw you and now it's gone. This absence physically stabs me all over my body like pins and needles.

I enter the empty space and try to conjure you back into existence. If I concentrate, I even believe I can smell the scent of your soap but then the sense is overrun by the last smell of you, when your body had started to radiate the stench of death. Tempted to vomit, I go over to the window and wrench it up, putting my face next to the gap and sucking in air.

I sag to the floor. Sitting in the room now, years later, I can't see it how I did then. I can't imagine what steered me to take the actions I did. How could I have brought you up here, talked to you, cooked you food, tucked you in and propped you back up? Yet all these things were done when you were quite clearly cold, unresponsive, dead.

Although I realised the fact long ago, and have since become more familiar with it, this is the moment when I really understand that you are dead. The absence of the bed proves the absence of you. The clear lines on the carpet that are less faded by the sunlight seem to make the realisation sharper inside my mind. It has been lost in there for years and I have finally pinned it down. I feel its cold body, the overwhelming taste of salt, the sound of screaming and sobbing, the smell in my nostrils of stale furnishings.

Forgive me, Mum. I've held on too long…

I don't hear the door open or Michael softly crossing the room, avoiding the space where the bed is no longer, and kneeling beside his rupturing sister. The first thing I am aware of is his voice. "You shouldn't have come in here", he says, tucking my curls behind my ears and pressing his hands against my sodden cheeks.

"No Michael, I'm glad", I say, muffled by the onslaught of tears. "She's dead. She's really dead", I tell him firmly, as if he doesn't know.

Michael frowns, bowing his head, his bald spot baring itself to me again. It is only after several seconds that I realise he is crying too. I instantly pull him towards me. I think he might resist, yet he tumbles into my messy hold and allows me to comfort him.

"You're so much better", he says, a sad smile on his lips. I am too busy staring at his wet skin. I haven't seen him act this way since we were much younger. I almost think he has just come out of the sea and is wearing a skin coloured wet suit and when he takes it off, he will show me he hasn't been crying at all.

"Everything's much clearer now". I lean back, gazing through the still open window. I think about how I haven't been able to let you go, thinking that keeping you in the house back then somehow meant I would never lose you. Yet looking out at the sky now, I know that although you are dead, I will always have you in some sense.

Mum, I'll look after Michael, I promise. And even though I know you're dead, I'll still talk to you sometimes. Yet it's not the same. I have to talk to real people now – like Michael, and Thom, people at the shops and people in the street.

Mum, you're dead and we both have to let go.

If only I had been able to see that a couple of years ago, perhaps I wouldn't have pushed that man onto the tracks.

Chapter 43

The Secret

Thom still has the taste of Sarah on his lips when he retraces his route back to Aunty Val's house in the numb darkness of early evening. He feels like he has been absent for so long; the paint on the door looks more cracked, the weeds droopier and extending their talons closer to the gate.

Is he ready to go back in there? Is he ready to face Aunty Val and Richard?

He stands at the front gate as though it is an obstacle to his entry and runs his tongue over his lips, closing his eyes and imagining he is back in the bedsit with Sarah. He doesn't understand why she left or why he'd been abandoned in the cold damp room immersed in the memory of her warm kiss.

It is only a few hours later, after Thom decides he needs some fresh boxers, that he makes his way across the city and back to the house he ran away from only days before. After all that has happened, he feels like he is an explorer who has returned after months of rough expeditions that have taken him to the brink of death.

He finally slinks through the gate, tiptoeing around the cracked paving, wondering how broken his family are inside the house. He reaches the door and somewhere in the depths of his pockets, rediscovers his keys. It takes him several seconds to direct the key into the lock at first; then he turns it in the wrong direction.

Eventually, Thom pushes the door open. The hallway is a murky crossing. All the lights are off, the darkness huddling in the corners and threatening to smother him. Thom takes a step inside, the soft pad of his feet on the carpet sounding like a stick clashing against a gong. Thom winches and closes himself inside gently, the lock making only a whisper as he guides it into the frame.

Thom stops and listens to the house, hearing nothing but the central heating humming and the natural creaks of the structure, like bones cracking spontaneously. Thom sighs loudly, adding to these sounds, becoming a human instrument. Thom closes his eyes and enjoys the way his breathing is in harmony with the moaning of the house. Is it sad? Like all three of them?

Thom still has his eyes closed when he realises that someone else is in the hallway. The music in Thom's mind is interrupted by the ragged breathing of another person; sounding as though they are catching their breath after inhaling smoke into their lungs. Thom opens his eyes and sees Aunty Val standing in the doorway to the kitchen. She slowly tiptoes her way towards him. She stops in front of him, giving him half a look before staring at the wall. After her tearful pleas the other night, Thom isn't expecting this.

"I didn't know if you were coming back", she says quietly. Thom has to strain to hear.

"Of course I would", he insists. He considers reaching out and taking her hand but decides not to. The only person he wants to touch in any capacity at the moment is Sarah. His hands have hurt too many people lately. His hands have been prying into things blindly with serious consequences.

"What happened to us?" she asks, locking her fingers together and twisting them. Again, Thom expects her to cry but she seems calmer. Perhaps she has finally accepted that Daniel is dead.

"We lost someone", he tells her, "and we found out more than we wanted to".

"Do you wish you hadn't found out that he knew about his death?"

"Sometimes I do". Thom shrugs. "But at other times I'm glad I can finally understand Daniel more than I did when he was alive". Aunty Val gives him a tight smile, not sure how she feels about this comment. Perhaps she has similar thoughts but, as Daniel's mother, can't justify vocalising them.

"Shall we sit down Thom? We can't talk properly here".

He nods and follows her to the kitchen where they both take a seat around the table. The table; where numerous family arguments, dinners, birthday parties, board games and bingo have taken place. What is this occasion? And will it restore the family that has been deteriorating revelation by revelation?

"You were right about Daniel's room", she starts quietly. Thom simply nods. "Where do you think it all went?" she continues.

"I have no idea". Thom answers and he really doesn't know. Perhaps Daniel burnt everything, or donated it to charity, or it is all stored in another lock up somewhere. They will probably never find out.

"How did you find out that Daniel knew about his death?" Aunty Val thrusts at him, nearly giving Thom a head rush. Thom thinks about how this all started – *the note* on the day of Daniel's funeral. An ending and a beginning in such close proximity. Why hadn't he just told them all there and then?

"I found a note in his room", Thom confesses, relief hissing out of his mouth.

"A note", she repeats slowly and continues, "what does it say Thom?"

"It has the time and place that he died". At his words, she slams her hands down on the table, the thud echoing through the groaning house. Thom stiffens in his chair, regressing for a moment, and then tells himself to sit forward again.

"Nothing else?" Her voice creaks.

"No Aunty", Thom insists, his face flushing with heat, despite telling the truth.

"Why would that be in his room?" She grabs his sleeve and shakes his arm violently a few times. It is as though he is the one who wrote it.

"I don't know. I just found it", Thom pleads, pulling his sleeve out of her hold.

"Why didn't you say? Where is it?" She barks, shoving the table towards him so it crunches into his ribs. Thom sags over the table and massages his chest, winded. Aunty Val immediately sprints to his side and pulls his chair back. She rubs his chest in an attempt to apologise but he pushes her off.

"You just had to ask". Thom jumps to his feet and digs into his pocket. He drags out the crumpled note that he has carried everywhere since he found it. It looks worn and faded, a shadow of the pristine clue it had once been. It seems as overused as Thom's thoughts that have circled around him like a whirlpool, sucking him down and vomiting him back out.

Aunty Val hesitates. It takes her several seconds of staring into Thom's face to reach towards the note. She flattens it down with her palm and bends towards it as though she is peering over the edge of a cliff. Thom watches her expression twitching and contorting as she reads the words, her eyes rolling from side to side as she reads. It seems like she is reading a long book, not a one-line note.

Thom thinks about comforting her, placing a hand on her shoulder, but he doesn't. He waits beside her, arms crossed, ribs sore. Aunty Val begins smoothing out the paper again, scratching out the creases with her fingernails but it hardly makes any difference.

"Does this mean he did it?" she finally asks quietly, a tear slipping beyond her control and crawling down her cheek.

"Did what?"

"Killed himself?" She nearly chokes on the words.

"I think he did". Thom swallows hard.

228

"The police called and said that", she whispers, wrapping her own hands around herself, "but somehow I thought, maybe he didn't... But I guess there's too much proof now". Her teeth chatter, although the room is boiling.

"The police called?"

"Yes. They just said it's an open and shut case".

"It figures..." Thom shakes his head at the police's tendency to take the easy way out. "You know, I kept thinking that perhaps he just knew someone was trying to kill him, as crazy as that sounds... But I met that lady who came to the reading, Mrs Tray, and she showed me a letter from Daniel asking her to come to the reading in advance".

"Why did you go and see *that* woman?" she asks, her voice shaking on her body's behalf. She is looking at him as though he has done something wrong. Much like the note, him keeping it from her is a betrayal.

"I wanted to know why she attended the reading. I thought it might help me understand more about Daniel and why he died". Aunty Val grabs his hand and wrings it between hers. Thom wants to cry out but he holds it inside, the screaming roaring until he feels his head begin to throb.

"I know why", she says noiselessly but he only understands because he is staring into her face and sees the movement of her lips. The throbbing intensifies, yet Thom only hears the silent words in his mind "*I know*"... "*I know why*". Thom thinks he understands what the words mean; he thinks he remembers the definitions he learnt for them. Yet they don't seem to make sense, in any order, in any context he has known before.

"What?" Thom eventually murmurs. Aunty Val grips his hands harder until they begin to numb. She is trying to push him against the table, make him take a seat but he resists and pushes back. She lifts her hand up, pressing her clammy palm against his facial hair. Her sweat soaks into his beard.

"I know why he killed himself", she tells him again, louder, but she is looking at the floor.

"I can hear you but I don't understand", Thom confesses, grabbing her by the shoulders and shaking her gently as if the meaning will fall out of her. "If you knew something all this time, why wouldn't you have said?" Thom persists, grabbing the note from the table and wagging it in her face. "You can tell I've been going crazy with it all, tearing myself in pieces... *Why* didn't you save me?"

"That's all I've tried to do", she insists; grabbing him by the face and making him look into her eyes. Thom shoves her backwards, the blood throbbing through his veins so fiercely he feels dizzy.

"You were *saving* me? How exactly were you doing that?" he snarls.

"I'm sure he would've told you himself, if he hadn't died..." Aunty Val's chin crumbles as she fights her tears. "But then he died and I didn't think it was important... But I guess it was the reason". She stares into the distance, and Thom has to jab her in the arm in order to attract her attention again. She almost looks surprised that he is still there.

"He was dying anyway", she explains, a sob stabbing at her body so that she folds for a second, holding onto the table for support. Thom stares, wide mouthed, waiting to receive the words. Why do they sound so distant? Why does it sound like a language he has never heard before?

"Daniel was ill", she adds, sucking in air continuously but with little effect. She is bent over the table, as though she is about to give birth.

"What are you talking about?" Thom spits. "Daniel wasn't ill. I would've known. Richard would have known... we *all* would have..." Thom stumbles over words like he is jumping hurdles with his legs tied together.

"I'm sorry", Aunty Val moans, pressing against her eyelids to force the tears back into her eyes but they gather under her eyelashes anyway. "I'm so sorry Thom. I've been a terrible mum". She sobs harder, bending further towards the table as though an invisible force is pushing her down.

"What are you talking about?" Thom pulls at his hair. Aunty Val turns and pulls him towards her, her nails digging into his arms until he is certain the skin will break.

"Daniel was dying", she repeats. "I should have told you but I just didn't know how to. After he died... I didn't think it mattered anymore".

"Of course it matters". Thom shoots his words at her, causing her to cower away from him slightly. "Do you understand what you're saying?" Thom screeches. "Do you understand?" He screams louder. Aunty Val bows her head, her tears now dropping straight from her eyes onto the wooden floor with a loud splat.

"I wanted to tell you but Daniel got so angry when we talked…" she trails off, closing her eyes, remembering. Her eyes are clenched like tiny fists. "I know he didn't mean it, he just got so angry…" She lifts her hands up, still holding onto him by the wrists, and presses his tensed hands against her cheeks. She is performing his actions for him.

"Is that when he hit you?"

"How do you…?" Aunty Val begins but loses her words in her stuttering.

"*Know*?" Thom finishes for her, taking his hands back. "Richard told me the other day when you fainted". Aunty Val's face plummets instantly.

"You shouldn't think he was a bad person. *Please Thom*. You believe me, don't you?" She raises her arms again to reach out to him but she drops them at his flat expression.

"He must've been upset. He just found out he was ill, maybe dying". Thom shakes his head, some of the puzzle he has been twisting and turning around for weeks finally making sense. "I guess he just thought jumping would be quicker".

"I don't think that's why he jumped", she says. This time her words are clear, like bells echoing in his ears for minutes afterwards. Thom stares at her, feeling faint.

"I think you need to explain that".

Chapter 44

The Donor

Initially, Aunty Val doesn't say anything. For a moment, Thom wonders if she remembers what she has just said, how she has just ripped his feet from his legs so he can barely stand. She gives a short exhale, pulls out a chair and seats herself. Thom watches her, clasping her hands together in front of her, staring straight ahead. Thom finally takes the seat opposite her.

"You know why he jumped?" Thom asks sternly. Aunty Val blinks for several seconds, her lips taut and dry. It is so silent Thom can hear her swallowing; it is the loud and elongated sound of fluid squeezing through a tight pipe.

"Yes", she whispers, not wanting to reveal the secret she has been keeping from him for months. Thom feels livid and guilty, because although he should be mad for Daniel's sake, he mainly feels angry for himself. How can she have lied to him? How can she have let him comfort her when she knew the truth?

"I'm sorry Thom", she mutters.

"I'm not interested in that, just tell me", Thom says viciously.

"Okay", she agrees. Thom is staring at her, wondering how the person he has always trusted and respected can look so hazy and stained across the table.

"About nine months before he died, Daniel asked to talk to me. Well you know how he never liked to talk much... so I sat down straight away to listen", she pauses, each letter an obstacle course from her brain to the atmosphere. "He said he was ill, he said he'd been to the doctors because he'd been feeling really tired. He thought nothing of it... but they called him back in and told him; he had leukaemia".

"How could that be?" Thom leans forward, the word 'leukaemia' striking him in the face. There hadn't been an inkling of this or even the hint of an inkling.

"I know Thom... *leukaemia*. I had no idea about it. I always imagined children got it, not young men..." She keeps gulping in the middle of words, chewing on their sounds and leaving them ragged. "I didn't take it very well Thom. After all these years just the four of us, it felt like part of myself was torn away". She hopes Thom will say something, perhaps sympathise with her, but he remains silent. "For one of only a few times, he looked scared, Thom. He was nearly crying. He *even* let me hold him".

"Did they say they could help him?" Thom asks quietly, imagining the scene at this very table as she describes it. He can't see Daniel though; he can't see Daniel in the pose she describes.

"A few weeks later, Daniel went to hospital. They told him he would have to have chemotherapy and after that, might need to get a bone marrow transplant", she explains sharply. The end of the sentence is pronounced but Thom thinks there is a lot more she should be divulging here. She can't end the conversation here, although she seems to want to.

"So what happened?"

"Well, Daniel wanted to be prepared for everything involved with the treatment". She pauses, taking a few deep breaths. "Do you know what that means, Thom? About the bone marrow?" Aunty Val takes his hand. She seems to be tugging on it gently as though she is trying to stay afloat. Thom ignores this but when he looks into her face, finds it harder to ignore the sweat that has swollen up underneath her fringe.

"How does it work? I might think I know but I probably don't".

"Full siblings are usually the best match. Their healthy marrow is meant to encourage the growth of blood cells or something like that. I asked a friend to look it up online but I don't remember everything now".

"I did hear some things like that", Thom agrees. She nods and begins rolling her head, rolling her thoughts around. They splash out in her expression like water slamming against the sides of a deck.

"I have something else to tell you Thom but… I'm scared".

"Why he did it?" Thom tries to pull it out of her. At his words, she lets out a quiet whimper. Her secret seems to be fighting its way out.

"I have wanted to tell you for months, well – for years".

"What the hell is it, Aunty?" Thom snaps. She reaches out, letting her hand hover near his face but instantly takes it back. The conversation has been plagued by half-gestures and withdrawals.

"Daniel wanted to ask Richard if he would be a donor", she says, every sentence seeming like the start of a novel.

"Did Richard say no?"

"No", Aunty Val answers quickly. "Daniel never asked him".

"Why not?" Thom yelps.

"When Daniel told me he was ill, he asked me if I thought Richard would help him", she pauses, her breaths growing shallow and rapid, "but I told him that Richard couldn't help him, even if he wanted to".

"Are you saying what I think you are?" Thom finally believes he understands something, in the whole scheme of facts that have been eluding him.

"They weren't full siblings". She lets out a muffled sob. Thom gets up and moves to her side. After some hesitation, he puts his arms around her. She leans back into him.

"How could you have never said something before?"

"I don't know..."

"So there's no chance Richard could have helped?"

"Not *no* chance", she admits, tightening her grip on his arms.

"So what happened? Why didn't Daniel talk to Richard? Why didn't *you*?" Thom feels like he is accusing her of something but he doesn't know what. He tightens his grip around her but not in need of affection, instead possessed by anger.

"It was too hard to talk about". She shrugs.

"Don't you know who their fathers are?" Thom taunts her unfairly. She instantly throws his arms off.

"Of course I do", she spits.

"Well which one of them has a different dad to Uncle Peter?" Thom leans against the table, looking at her sideways. She tears at her hair, which has become unloved and clumped together.

"Daniel", she confesses in a whisper.

"Shit", Thom twitches. "Can you imagine how heartbroken he must've been? He probably thought he might be saved and then he finds out that they weren't real brothers". Thom shakes his head. "And more than that, it meant life and death for him".

Thinking about Daniel, he wants to sob on his behalf. Thom wants to tear the cupboards from the walls, pull out the pipes and let the water spray out like punctured vessels.

"Did you tell him who his dad was?" Thom asks, not able to look at her. He turns and stares outside the window into the garden. He sees the chair where he sat after finding the notebook, the notebook that said terrible things and claimed he wrote them.

"I told him".

"And how did he react?"

"He went crazy", she whimpers, "but I didn't expect any less. I deserved it..." she trails off, too traumatised to cry. She locks her eyes on an indistinguishable spot on the wallpaper and begins to sway.

"You should've told him but it's not your fault for being with someone else". Thom tries to comfort her but his words feel like wood being eaten from the inside, ready to crumble at the slightest touch. Thom slides into the chair next to her, feeling slightly dizzy.

"I wish it was that simple". She finally turns to look at him. With a small toss of her head, her whole appearance seems to have changed. Her face is still and not wet with tears for one of the first times in weeks.

"There's still something else, isn't there?" Thom narrows his eyes. "I can't even fathom what it might be, but there's definitely *something*..." Thom ventures. He wonders if Daniel's father is violent or a murderer or some obscure relative of Aunty Val's.

"You're such a clever boy". She smiles, forgetting the situation for a brief reflex. Similarly, Thom bathes in it for the millisecond it lasts.

"Daniel's dad, well it's complicated... he and I weren't in a relationship".

"That's not that complicated".

"No Thom", she stops him. "This is important for you too". She is staring so violently that Thom has to look away.

"How is Daniel's dad important to me?"

"Daniel's dad is important... to you... because..." Her voice shows her weakness again. It sounds like a radio losing reception. "You have the same father".

Chapter 45

The Red Threads

The house is sinking. To everyone else, it looks the same as it always has but I know the truth. Its insides are rotting and crumbling. The imploding ceilings are striking them all on the heads so they leave the house feeling dazed and detached from everyday life. Soon perhaps they will be stuck inside because all the doors will be blocked and the stairs a pile of dust, shaved down by pressure.

When I'd been falling apart, I didn't see this all clearly. I saw their grief painted on their sullen faces, their ragged clothes and ragged skin, in their diminishing forms. Yet with the house, only the edges of the wallpaper had begun to peel and fall off. The red paint on the front door had begun to crack, the grass in the front garden grown wild and unshaven.

Looking at the house now, even in settling darkness of night, it looks like a person slumped over. How can it be saved? How can I push the bricks and windows back up so they are standing as they should be once again?

I wonder if Thom is in there now, what they are saying to each other, whether they will ever understand each other post-Daniel's death. Will Daniel's ghost ever release the house? He has removed himself from that room but the house won't forget. The people inside are connected to him with an invisible thread that will follow them for years, through their daily lives, in relationships with others, during sleep. Just as the scarf has never quite released me, they are trapped forever.

The vain part of me thought I could save them. Yet I am the one who needed saving and still do. I have managed to get a hand above the ground but I am still buried in the past and all the things I have done. If I stay near them too, I will never get away from Daniel and what he made me do.

But Thom... I think I love him. I can't help thinking about him, letting him press his lips against mine, letting his madness fester in front of my eyes. It must be real love if you can still love someone when they are losing themselves. Or is it blindness? Can you really love someone if they don't know their own feelings?

The questions are infinite now. Before this, I have no recollection of what I thought about all day. What flashed through my mind as I walked down the street? Or whilst sitting in my bedsit? What did I dream about?

It seems when you died; my life was severed. And now, I have been severed from the life I have been leading since then. I'm no longer who I was the last few years, but I'm no longer who I was before you died either.

If I just tell Thom the truth... Maybe he can understand? No. He does understand what Daniel can do to a person but murder... why should he understand that? Either way, whether coerced or voluntarily, I killed that man.

If I tell them all, will it really help any of them anyway? It isn't the fact that he is dead that pains them the most; it is the confusion and the unanswered questions. Thom looks so helpless sometimes, when all he wants is someone to tell him why Daniel left all these things behind. They don't want to know how he died, but why. Maybe it would help if I could tell them why he made me push him. But I don't know that. And if I did, could I put myself on the line for them? Would Michael put me back in the hospital and never trust me again?

All the questions make me wish I could recede into my madness, yet madness makes no sense to me now. I see it flaring up in Thom and I don't know what to do to rescue him from its grip. I hope his family will do that for me, as Michael rescued me. When I met Thom, I asked myself how I could've hurt this man for no reason. Now, I ask how could Daniel hurt his own cousin and why and why and why and why?

Chapter 46

Reverberations

Thom doesn't know how it happens but the next time he is aware, he is sitting on the kitchen floor. His elbow is throbbing. A chair is lying beside him. Aunty Val is peering over the table at him but doesn't move to help.

"Did you hear me Thom?"

"I'm not sure", Thom mumbles, cradling his elbow with his other hand. He wants a sling so everyone can see there is something wrong with him. How will people be able to tell that he has been split in half when there are no signs on the outside?

"You and Daniel have the same father", she repeats. Her voice keeps slicing through him like a glacier.

"But that would mean he and I were..." Thom can't even say that word, though it is only two syllables.

"Yes, brothers", she finishes.

"But that doesn't make any sense". Thom heaves himself to his feet, supporting himself with the table. He retakes his seat.

"It makes sense if you know the details", she tells him and pushes her chair back, the scraping of the chair rupturing his insides further. She walks past him, her familiar smell touching him in the way she can't now, and opens a cupboard behind him. She places a set of papers on the table and steps back.

"What is this?" Thom demands, focussing on her lips, hoping they will lie.

"Read it Thom".

Thom reluctantly obeys but it takes him several seconds to focus on the words at the top. Finally, Thom sees them: *Contract of Surrogacy.* As soon as his eyes absorb these words, his eyes instantly blur again. "What the fuck..." Thom mumbles, the word 'surrogacy' repeatedly crashing against his forehead.

"Your mother and father couldn't have kids together", Aunty Val says quietly, as she sits opposite him again. The table sits between them like a mediator. "After years of trying, they finally got tested and found out your mother was infertile".

"What the hell are you talking about?" Thom snarls.

"The truth, Thom".

"How could my mother be infertile? And what the fuck does this have to do with me and Daniel having the same dad?" Thom thinks he should faint but instead, he feels like he has seized up, ready to attack.

"They came to me one day and they asked me if I would consider being a surrogate for them", she says, a brief smile passing over her lips. Yet, they quickly darken with a guilty frown. "After thinking about it for a while, I decided I would do it. I just wanted to help my sister, *that's all*".

"So you're some saint are you?"

"If I were a saint, I would've told you years ago". She bows her head.

"What exactly are you telling me?" Thom slams his hand against the table and winces as discreetly as he can when it begins to throb. Aunty Val grabs it, squeezing it hard to enforce the words that follow; "I carried you. You were twins".

Thom rips his hand away from her and jumps from his seat, wrenching the table upwards and launching it across the kitchen. Aunty Val stays in her seat, as though she is expecting the table to return and she can once again lean her elbows on it. Thom doesn't move again. Inside his mind, moments and words are gathering together like a puddle at the bottom of a gutter.

When he entered the room after the wake and Aunty Val turned white...

The way Sarah seemed so fascinated by him instantly and kissed him...

How Daniel left him clues to make him question everything and everyone...

The number 11 on the lock up door...

Why hasn't Thom realised? Daniel has been trying to lead him here from the moment he died. In the face of leukaemia, Daniel discovered something so hurtful that he didn't want to live anyway. And through these clues and his departure, he wanted to show Thom how similar they are, so similar because of a genetic bond neither of them knew about for most of their lives.

Thom shakes himself. "So who is the woman?"

"What woman?" Aunty Val says, sticking to the chair. Thom paces around her as though he might swing an axe and behead her.

"The woman who gave her egg for my dad… you know, to put in you". Thom feels like a child again.

"Thom I thought you understood", she says in a high-pitched tone. Thom stops in front of her.

"Understood what?"

"Your mother asked me to do it, so it wouldn't be some stranger. I'm the one", she tells Thom, cowering, shaking. Thom sags into nothing. He once again finds himself being looked down on, staring up at her from miles away, her face shivering behind a curtain of tears.

"You are not… you're not…" Thom splutters and crawls away backwards. "How can you say you are, when I already have a mother? You're just sick and lonely and you want to keep me here because Daniel's dead." Thom pushes up against the wall. "Well, I'm *not* staying here with you, no matter what lies you tell me". Thom doesn't take his eyes from her as he heaves himself up near the kitchen sink.

She edges closer. Thom glances at the back door, trying to gauge how far away it is. He also stares at the hallway behind her, wishing it would chew her up. Yet nothing happens and he doesn't escape. In the few seconds he has been thinking, she is only inches away and when he realises this, she has already grabbed him.

"I *am* your mother", she declares. "I've tried to tell you so many times but it's been so hard. Your parents kept promising they'd tell you and then they died and I didn't know if you'd be able to cope with it. I didn't want to take their memory away from you... I'm so sorry Thom".

"Say this is true..." Thom begins, nauseated by the mere notion, "If you gave birth to us, why did we get separated?" Thom feels smug; sure he has discovered the minute snag in her claims. Yet she remains in the same position, with the same expression and his hopes begin to plummet.

"If you read the contract, you'll see. We changed it after you were both born. We only found out it was twins much later in the pregnancy and when I gave birth, I just couldn't let you both go..." She is sobbing.

"Your parents weren't happy and it took a lot of talking and thinking but we decided – well *they* agreed, to let me have one of you", she pauses, a sour smile on her lips. "It's scary and terrible and I don't think either of us were truly happy with it but thankfully, they understood how terrible it would be to have to give up two babies at once".

"I can't believe this. You said I was early, that's why we were both born then..." Thom shakes his head violently. Then his attention turns, "How did you decide anyway? Did you flip a coin? Did you play highest card draw? How exactly did you choose a baby to give away?"

Her shoulders are slumped, her eyes red and soggy, her mouth a drooping flower that cannot be revived. "You don't understand Thom", she cries, sobbing and moaning, "If you knew what it's like to give up a child, let alone two…" Thom swivels his arms and grabs hold of her by the arms, shaking her.

"And you think being lied to your whole fucking life isn't hard?" he screams, his spit jumping out and clinging to her skin. "How could you do it, Aunty…?" Thom demands and instantly feels like a fool. "Or whatever the hell you are", he adds, starting to sink once again but she holds him up.

"I didn't want to give either of you up but we'd agreed, Thom. I couldn't back out because even if I'd tried to take them to court, the lawyers said I would've lost".

"Daniel and I deserved to know".

"I couldn't tell him without you being told too and your parents kept saying 'when the time is right' but then they weren't around anymore".

"You're blaming them? I guess that's convenient for you now they're dead". Thom feels like his blood is boiling in his veins. He looks at the back of his hands to check bubbles aren't rising underneath his skin. However, his skin retains the normality he can no longer see in this kitchen, in his 'Aunty', his whole stupid lie of a life.

"I think your mother felt very hurt she couldn't even provide an egg. I think she couldn't bear to tell you she wasn't your biological mother".

"You won't take her away from me", Thom tells her firmly.

"I never wanted to, especially after they died. I didn't want to take those memories away from you, you'd lost everything else". She tries to pull him into a hug but he pushes her back.

"I hadn't lost everything then, but I have now". Thom drops her arms. He moves away from her towards the door but before he can reach it, he bends over and vomits. His body convulses violently as it forces its way out of his throat. Thom can't fight it, he lets it overpower him and watches it elongating on the floor below him.

When his stomach is empty, he pushes himself up and swallows several times, the sour taste of vomit lingering. He remembers having the same reaction after finding the note. He remembers the guilty sick stain on his sleeve that he stared at throughout the funeral.

"You haven't lost me Thom", Aunty Val says, placing her hand on his back without looking at his indiscretion on the kitchen floor.

"What am I supposed to do Aunty? Start calling you *mum*?"

"No, Thom. Not at all. But we can sort this out".

"Daniel didn't think so".

"I hoped I wouldn't lose both of you because of this". She shakes her head sadly. Thom can't help looking at her now. When he considers her features properly, he can see the truth. He can see the shape of her mouth that he and Daniel shared, and he remembers the shade of her natural hair that matches his unkempt mop. He has never seen her properly before. He has spent his life with foggy eyesight, his beloved Aunt elevated so high that he could never see the frightening similarities.

"Why didn't you tell me?" Thom's face crumples. He looks down; ashamed to show her how she has torn him apart. "Why has everyone been lying to me?"

"Who else lied darling?" She cuddles him. He is tempted to resist her again but he is too weak. He lets her hold him up, like he did for her on the day of the funeral. Somehow telling the truth has made her stronger, for the both of them.

"Sarah. You. The only people that matter", Thom muffles into her shoulder.

"Sarah matters to you? What about Emma?"

Thom pushes back. "Is it really your place to be grilling me?"

"No, of course not. I just didn't know". She touches his un-shaven cheek and scratches his beard playfully. "I miss talking to you Thom".

"I've missed you too", Thom admits, "but we can't just go back".

"I love you Thom. Please work at this with me". She leans her forehead against his. He stares into her eyes, his heart clunking. He wants to ask her thousands of questions, he recounts times when she started telling him something but then changed her mind. Why hadn't she ever finished the sentence?

In the next moment he thinks about the last time he was here. He thinks about how he told her that Daniel knew he was going to die and how she collapsed. Had she been afraid he'd found out about the leukaemia? Or had she been afraid he had found out they were brothers?

"How *did* you choose Aunty? How did you pick?" Thom presses his head into hers until he thinks he hears the bones crack. The words poke her in the eye. She blinks several times.

"There was no decision, I took one baby and your parents took the other".

Thom shoves her away. "That's it? A lottery to choose which child you take?"

"It would be more horrible if we'd had some criteria, don't you think?"

"That's why he hated me", Thom says suddenly.

"What?"

"The night I arrived, I took over his bedroom. And you were always giving me all this special attention. He must've sensed it all along and when he found out... no wonder he left me all this shit to figure out". Thom crushes his hair in his fists, his brain unfreezing.

"What stuff did he leave?" Aunty Val asks.

"Nothing, nothing..." Thom dismisses her. "He must've always known something but I guess he didn't really believe it. He just couldn't deal with it".

"Stop it Thom. We couldn't have changed things. People take things how they want to", she says, resigned.

"You're actually blaming *him* now?" Thom advances on her.

"I'm not blaming him".

"You've ruined us". Thom starts to sob. He moans and attempts to bury himself in the wall. Yet he can't push himself inside and hide. She can still see him; she can still claw at him and try to comfort him.

"I love you Thom. I love you so much", she cries. Her sobbing and her words seem fake to him. She is a lying bitch who has torn his heart out, who has watched them grow up in her lie, who has taken away his parents forever.

Before he can stop himself, he swings around. The first thing he knows about what he has done, she is leaning against the worktop holding her lip. The blood doesn't appear until a few seconds later. Thom watches it swell out between her fingers.

Thom tries to speak but all he can do is howl.

"It's okay Thom. I know you didn't mean it". She lowers her hand, the blood spotting her hand and lip. Yet she doesn't wipe it away. He stares at it until it appears to spread across her face, turning her entire face into a red mess. This is the blood that made him. This is the blood that runs through his DNA.

"I'm so confused. I can't work out... I don't know how... Please tell me..." The words get lost inside the avalanche steadily blocking exit points through his synapses, his mouth.

"It can be different this time", she says hopefully.

Thom hears her words but can only think of how everything isn't different at all. Like Daniel, no one really understands him anymore. Like Daniel, he feels angry and betrayed. Like Daniel, he has found out his whole life has been a lie. He has hurt her too. He has kissed the same woman Daniel had.

Thom begins to back away into the darkness of the hallway. She reaches out, tries to speak but realises it is useless. Her lip quivers hopefully, like a person still clinging onto the faith that after everything, it can't possibly be over. Yet Thom feels like a full stop has been stamped on his heart.

He is swallowed by the darkness, becomes an outline and flashes briefly in the light from the streetlights outside, before disappearing completely.

Chapter 47

The Bloodied Scarf

The air covers me like a hot flannel. My skin feels numb so I can't feel the sweat dribbling down my face. I only feel it when it gathers above my eyebrows and I have to wipe it away with my sleeve.

I guess I knew I would end up here at some point. After all the confrontations with my past lately, it seems apt and only fitting that I face up to the location of my crime. Yet, it doesn't stop me shivering in the muggy cavern.

After sitting outside the Mansen house yesterday, I realised that I had to come back. This station, the trains, the smells, those over-sized posters and the silence of death – they have all been haunting me since that day. I can't run forever.

The scarf trails behind me, darkened with my brother's blood. I slowly approach the place where I stood on that day. It seems wrong when I see the clock says 13:45. I am early. Yet I won't be meeting anyone here. No one knows where I am and the people around me are all strangers, with no inkling that I'm a murderer returning to the scene.

I wonder if any of the others on this platform were here that day. If as they watched helplessly; they screamed in horror, had been unable to tear their gaze away from the broken body crushed and flung by the train, the spray of blood marking them forever. Am I the only one who walked out of the station on that day unable to remove the image of that falling man caught by the train in mid-air?

I am standing on the spot. Nothing about it distinguishes it from the rest of the platform. There are no marks, no blood, and no red tape prohibiting others from stamping all over it. It sickens me how life continues so easily. How many people have stood here since that day? How many trains have passed through the tunnel? How many people have seen the clock at 15:32?

I look down at the tracks and see nothing but dirty metal and a few pieces of rubbish. When I try to imagine Daniel's face, I can't even remember how he looked. All I see now is Thom. I wish then that Thom could be here, holding my hand tightly to stop me jumping into the escalating wind. Yet how could I explain to him why I need him here in this spot?

The wind begins to thrash against me until I nearly topple, the scarf fluttering madly beside me. Others begin moving forward and I look back at them, wondering if one of them will push me in front of the train. It would be fitting after all. The tunnel is lightening, the spotlight approaching, honing in on me – the culprit.

I am sure I am a beacon, a firework spinning in circles. I am certain I am screaming out loud but it is only inside my mind. This is the scream I didn't give Daniel on that day. I killed him without surprise, without emotion, without my eyes rolling in water. I believed that I knew exactly what I'd been doing but I'd been miles from reality, standing in a bubble where the only thing that could reach me was Daniel.

The air seems clogged with dirt, thick with the sweat pouring from me. I try to breathe but the opening seems blocked. The train's nose is poking out of the tunnel and within moments, rushes past me, without hesitation. I realise how quick the transition is, how I must have taken the precise split second to kill him. He must've been proud of his work. He must've loved saying those words to me. *Right on time...*

I suddenly realise I am standing in the way of the doors and people are barging their way past me. I move aside. When the last person has exited, a man waves me to go ahead of him, but I shake my head and tell him, "I'm in the wrong place". He frowns gently but I turn away and make my way off the platform.

It is only when I reach the surface that I feel I can breathe again. I gulp in so much air that I feel dizzy. At the same time, I feel so alive. Although I believed killing Daniel brought me to life, I know now that facing up to everything has made me alive again. No matter how hard this all is, I am living a normal emotional and complicated life. My feelings are more realistic now.

I am aware now that I am connected to only some things in this giant maze of a city, not connected to everything. I can't see emotions in the air anymore. I can't save that family from implosion. I can't make up for the murder by joining their lives. I can't blame anyone but myself.

In a sense, I am limiting my world again but it feels good. By realising my limitations, I am setting myself free again. I am putting the objects and people and thoughts back in the 'right' places. When I look at the street now, I am fascinated by the shop signs, the signs telling people what to do and what not to do, the traffic lights, the paving slabs set in lines – how controlled everything is and how everything is there to warn and instruct.

This is the world I left behind several years ago. It is coming back to me like a lover I rejected, still enthralled by me. I am remembering its beauty, the way it merges together and functions. Having imagined my own messages for so long, I realise they are naturally here all around me. Yet, I have ignored them. Now their messages are like kind words sent to a recovering relative.

I can never rewind time and take back my actions. It is too late to save Daniel but I can save myself. I can feel regret. I could go as far as to report myself to the police but I am not brave enough and I can't see the benefit. After all, what I did is exactly what Daniel planned. Can you be a real murderer if someone led you to do it?

Beginning to shiver, I'm suddenly aware there is a sharp wind whipping at my face. I pull my coat around myself and begin to walk away from the station. Looking back a few times, I see the cars continuing to jam and crawl and argue. I see the people passing but not noticing one another. I decide that life is continuing for them so it should continue for me. He is gone. Not even the platform remembers him.

Chapter 48

The Beginning

Thom misses Sarah by only moments. He may not have seen her anyway, as he is in a trance, his feet leading him to the one place he hasn't allowed himself to investigate.

The first time he is aware of anything, he is standing in front of the barriers, which won't open. Thom thinks for a moment and decides it's money he needs. Digging a few coins from his pocket, he slots them into the machine, buying the first option he sees. He hasn't come here to travel; he's come to see the place where his 'brother' died. The brother he never owned, the brother he has lost before he even had him. Can this all be true? Can the woman who saved him after his parents death really be half of what made him?

Thom feels nauseated whenever he even tries to think about it. He had spent the entire night walking through the city, darting through the backstreets, believing he could hide from himself.

He shakes the thought of his 'Aunty' away and gets through the barrier. The world can't get through though. In the station, it is only he and Daniel. This is what Daniel wanted, to show him the truth, to punish them all for their lies.

He follows the signs for the platform. He remembers reading the platform direction in the paper and thinking it an odd addition. It was probably just to explain to everyone why the tube service was disrupted that day...

As Thom takes each step, he begins to shiver. He thinks it's the wind but he realises it's his legs softening and failing him. He feels humiliated, letting some people pass while he recovers himself. Was Daniel afraid? Did he clutch onto the banister with sweaty hands? Did he consider changing his mind?

Thom decides that he must move quickly or he won't get there at all. He almost runs down the last ten steps and lands on the platform he has been running from since the day of Daniel's funeral. He hasn't been in a station for a long time. Yet it looks the same as most others. There are people dotted along it, a countdown machine reporting on the train destinations and times, large posters faded by dust and soot, an empty track.

The track is a snake that can sliver to life at any moment. It can take him into its dark mouth. It seems to wrap its chain-like body around his chest and leave him gulping for air. He leans against the wall and tells himself to breathe. When he finally feels calmer, his hand comes back to him covered in dirt. Like the lock up, he will leave dirtier and more damaged than when he came.

"Are you okay?" a woman, who is standing several feet away, asks. Thom nods hastily and moves hurriedly past her, further down the platform. Thom realises then that he doesn't have a clue where Daniel jumped. Was it that end nearer the entrance? Or this end nearer where the train comes from? Thom wishes there is some kind of marking, or a sign: *This is where he jumped!* Yet, there is nothing that can tell him anything about that day.

This is useless, he spits in his mind. He stamps his foot so hard that some people give him a sideways look, too afraid to stare in case he becomes vicious.

The wind begins to increase and Thom hears a faint roar. If he really concentrates, he can already feel the platform vibrating. The increasing rush revives the crowded air. He closes his eyes and thinks about the lights of the train, the people inside who don't know what awaits them, the driver thinking about his dinner plans, and Daniel.

The roar gathers momentum, the sound making Thom's heart bang to its rhythm. He is no longer a person; he is a beat, a heart standing alone with its scars and holes. The train is speaking to him in a language that only he can hear.

Thom is hypnotised by the train. Thom is captured by the track. He doesn't realise how enthralled he is until he feels the train whip just past his nose, a fraction of a millimetre away. He is being dragged back by something. He tries to pull forward but he can't escape. He has a knot in the middle of his back and it won't release him.

"What are you doing?" a voice cries out by his ear. As the doors of the train slide open, Thom finds himself sagged against some-one. The other people on the platform stare at him; the passengers coming off the train step over him and look back.

Thom pushes away from the person he is lying on and sits up. He turns to see a man, breathless and still clutching onto him. He is wearing a luminous waistcoat and Thom recognises the London

Underground uniform beneath it. His face is wet with sweat. Thom is sweating himself, his t-shirt clinging to his body.

"What are you doing?" he cries again. The crowd of people who have got off the train have gone away, but some linger to watch the two men tangled on the floor; unaware they have just avoided screeching breaks and chaos. The doors of the train have snapped shut and the train is now moving off.

"I'm sorry", Thom mumbles to the man. He can't force himself to stand up. The man finally lets go of Thom's coat, satisfied he can no longer harm himself, and gives him an encouraging pat instead.

"I'm Sam", the man tells Thom and offers his clammy hand.

Thom thinks about refusing but decides he is just as sweaty, "Thom".

"Let's get you out of here", Sam says, pulling Thom up. Thom leans on him, like an injured footballer limping from the pitch. Thom leans on this stranger because he feels like he hasn't got anyone else.

Sam takes Thom to a door along the platform. Thom has never really noticed these doors before, or not properly anyway and experiences an odd stab of adrenaline thinking about what could be behind it. Yet when Sam struggles with the key and heaves it open, there seems to be nothing spectacular there. There is only a harshly lit corridor that Thom can't quite see the end of. Sam carries Thom inside and locks them in.

Thom can now see the doorways lining the corridor. There is the sound of a television or a radio coming from one room, the smell of burning toast and the faint hint of smoke hanging in the air. Sam directs Thom to the second door on the left and deposits him on a rundown looking sofa. Thom feels quite comfortable on this, as though a new sofa would offend his state of mind.

"Tea?" Sam asks. Thom nods and watches the man disappear out of the room. Thom leans into the chair and seems to breathe for the first time since he entered the station. Perhaps for the first time today.

His whole life is irreversibly changed. There is no way to retrace the steps and go back, no sense in which his existence isn't different. Everything he thought he was, he is now not. He is not a nephew, not a cousin, not a boyfriend, not an employee, not a detective, not a victim…

"Here". Sam appears beside him and hands him a mug. Thom accepts it and wraps his hands around it, letting the warmth of the mug attempt to melt the icicle speared through his heart. Thom knows it is meant to be tea but he can't taste anything. It could be blood or poison and he wouldn't be able to distinguish it.

"Don't people usually say thanks for saving their life?" Sam jokes, sitting on the arm of the chair. Thom looks up at him, almost amused, wondering why he doesn't feel thankful.

"I guess they usually do". Thom shrugs and rethinks, "thanks for doing that".

"So were you going to do it?" Sam says quietly. Thom considers the question for a long time, staring into his tea.

"I don't know", Thom admits. "I didn't even realise what I was doing".

"Someone was hit by a train not long ago".

"You saw it?" Thom jumps, spilling a few drops of his drink on his trousers.

Sam sits upright in his chair. "You sound like you know something about it".

"It was my... brother". Thom exercises the term. He has been an only child all his life, an orphan since twelve. Now he has a brother, a mother, and a half-brother. If only it didn't all come from lies, he could feel happy about it all. Yet he only feels betrayed and lost. He didn't even know about he and Daniel being twins until it was too late...

"Your brother?" Sam gasps. "And what were you doing? Going to join him or something?" Sam's heroic act is now undermined. Has he merely saved someone who is ready to die?

"I just came to see where he died. I didn't plan on anything... like that".

"But you were about to do it. You were about a millimetre away!" Sam wriggles, biting his lip hard.

"I'm a bit of a mess. I have no idea what I was doing".

"But what if you'd died?"

"Then I guess we wouldn't be here". Thom shrugs. He even smiles, although it isn't funny. Sam's mouth also curls into a small smile in response, not knowing how else to put his face. They fall silent for a few minutes, the trains rumbling on the platforms, the smell of burnt toast weakening.

"Did you see him die? Were you on the platform?" Thom finally asks after the silence nags him into speech.

"I was in the surveillance room that day", Sam tells him. The full stop on his sentence seems so final that Thom's suspicions instantly swell out of him like a scab forming, forcing him to scratch.

"So you saw it happen?" Thom looks up at Sam, who is staring into his mug, with an expression as though he is falling into a black pit.

"I saw it, yes. That's why I've been watching people even more", Sam confesses. "I don't want it to happen again".

"What did you see, Sam?" Thom asks desperately, appealing to the stranger like he is an old friend. Yet, this man owes him nothing. And equally Thom knows nothing about this man except what he can see: a broad shouldered man with a hint of a Jamaican accent, wearing a loose fitting London Underground uniform, with a wedding ring that clatters against his mug. Does this add up to disclosure?

"I can't believe I'm talking to that guy's brother". Sam shakes his head.

"His name was Daniel", Thom tells him, hoping the personification will appeal to him. Sam nods and exhales heavily.

"What do you know, Thom?"

"I know he's dead, that's all". Thom doesn't tell the entire truth, that Daniel knew about his own death, that he left behind clues to let Thom know. It will only confuse this man if Thom tries to explain.

264

"I think I need to show you something". Sam stands, scratching at his short afro. He puts his mug down on the table. Thom does the same. "Come on", Sam gestures and leaves the room. Thom scrambles after him.

He takes Thom further down the corridor, stopping in front of a door. The sign says *surveillance room*. Sam enters and Thom slowly follows him, the room seeming like a tunnel leading into a deep cavern. Even if he physically exits the room, will he ever be able to really take himself out of here?

"Do you really want to see this?" Sam asks as he takes a seat in front of a screen. On the screen, people are standing on the escalator, staring ahead or playing on their phones for the last time before they are cut off. Thom meets Sam's eyes and nods weakly. Does he want this? Does he need this?

"I didn't think about a video", Thom mutters inaudibly, shrinking into himself.

"I'm sorry", Sam says, digging under the desk and retrieving a DVD. He checks the date on it as though he is checking which film he recorded from the TV, nodding to himself in agreement. "I may have held onto it for a few days afterwards". He flashes Thom a guilty look, bowing his head as he pushes the DVD into the machine. "But I gave it to the police last week. Didn't they call you?"

Thom guesses that it explains why Aunty Val has only just heard from the police, simply to be brushed off with the words 'open and shut case' and 'suicide'. Thom begins to speak but, as the fuzzy screen flicks on, Thom's head feels just as fuzzy.

265

The platform appears on the screen, a time and date tattooed on the edge of the screen. It says 15:29. It is nearly time. Thom guesses Sam has looked through the footage and recorded only this part. Perhaps he has watched it several times, wondering why Daniel jumped too.

The camera must be at the far end of the platform, near where the train will soon shoot out of the tunnel. The platform looks crowded. Lots of the people seem to be wearing scarves, hats or a football shirt. If Thom didn't know better, there would be nothing remarkable about this scene. In fact, it wouldn't even be worth his attention.

However, he is searching for Daniel in the crowd. The people look blurry and Thom has to concentrate hard to distinguish them. Yet eventually, he manages to recognise Daniel. Thom finds it strange seeing him again: moving, breathing. Thom has the urge to touch the screen so maybe he can feel Daniel's life once again. This is his brother, minutes before death. This is his brother, and he hadn't known.

Thom focuses hard on Daniel. At a few points, Daniel's head seems to turn as his curly hair flashes in the camera. As Thom locks his gaze on Daniel, Sam stares at Thom. Strangely, Thom feels safer knowing someone is watching him.

Thom can hardly understand what he is watching. The clock is rolling ruthlessly fast, indifferent to the fact it is counting down to the moment that Thom will lose Daniel forever. Thom wonders what Daniel had been thinking at this moment. Thom wonders if his legs had ceased up as he waited. Thom wonders if Daniel hesitated. Thom wonders how much longer Daniel would have lived otherwise. Thom wonders and thinks until his mind is a vacuum.

Thom doesn't realise he is sitting on the edge of his seat. He is gripping the sides so hard that his hands are turning numb. Yet all he can do is stare at the screen, helpless, wanting to climb inside and pull Daniel back. Why hadn't he wanted to be Thom's brother? Why was this a better alternative?

Then Thom sees it. Some people's hair has started to move, their clothes flapping from a wind that Thom cannot fully understand. He can't feel it, and he wants to, more than anything. He wants to have the air rushing towards him as Daniel felt it in those few seconds. The only way he could relate was standing on that platform before, hoping he could connect to Daniel, too late.

Then the train is there. 15:32 – his note is two minutes early. And Daniel is falling. In a snap second, Daniel disappears and the train keeps rocketing through the picture. Thom screeches, rocking in his chair but unable to let go. Sam jumps up and switches the screen off. He grabs Thom by the shoulders and tries to look into his eyes. "I'm sorry", he whines breathlessly.

"Put it back on", Thom orders. Sam stands up, his forehead furrowed, putting himself between Thom and the screen.

"I really don't think..."

"Put it on!" Thom shrieks, jumping up and pushing Sam out of the way. He jabs the 'stop' button and then 'play' again. It's 15:29 and Daniel is still alive.

Thom watches it all again. Thom counts down the longest three minutes. Thom grabs the sides of the screen and is so close his nose is touching. It is almost time when he sees something. Behind Daniel: a person. This is not spectacular at all, being a crowded platform, but Thom knows this person.

Thom has been fascinated by this person; her strange mechanical voice, her dark curls, her evasive love. The only woman who has kissed them both. She is there. Thom turns and grabs Sam, pointing at her.

"Do you see her?" he asks desperately, pushing Sam's head close to the screen.

"Who?" Sam asks; trying to push back but Thom holds him there.

"The woman with the black curly hair. Do you see her?" Thom wheezes.

"Yes", Sam nods. "I see her".

Thom releases Sam. *So he isn't imagining her...* She is standing right behind his brother on the day he died. She is there and now she is in Thom's life. How did she get from this platform to his lips?

Thom is gawping at Sarah. Daniel is now a secondary character in this short film. The crowd sways and swells as the train approaches. He loses her several times but keeps his eyes on the space where he thinks she is. He barely notices Daniel is gone until the train shoots through the left-hand side of the screen.

The crowd are moving back like they are being showered with glass. Their faces are contorted with shock. The doors remain shut as the whole platform seems to freeze. Thom has to look at the clock to see that time is still moving.

He is searching the spot where she'd been standing. And then he sees it. As the people continue to move back, he sees a hand outstretched, holding a piece of material. This could mean nothing, but Thom knows inside, that it is her. He also knows that despite the fuzziness of the screen, the material is a scarf. And although it is a black and white picture, Thom is also certain the scarf is red. It is Daniel's.

Chapter 49

The Video

Thom presses the eject button and snatches the DVD. Sam immediately tries to block Thom's exit but his body is slumped slightly, showing that he isn't convinced he has the right to.

"Are you going to stop me, Sam?" Thom dares him. "Are you going to stop me having the video showing my own brother's death?" Thom shakes it in Sam's face. "Would it be better to leave it here so it can collect dust?" Thom spits.

"I shouldn't have even shown you it". Sam shuffles on his feet. "And you seem to be obsessed with that woman in it. Are you going to try and find her?"

"I don't need to. I already know her", Thom tells him, smugly.

"Are you going to hurt her?"

"Did you show this to the police?"

"Yes I did, last week – *I promise*". Sam nods vigorously, emphasising to Thom that he has completed all the 'right' actions, although delayed.

"And they didn't see that he was pushed?" Thom's limbs are flailing beyond his control. Sam is pressed against the door, looking as though he wishes he were on the other side of it. "They said it just looked like a jumper", Sam repeats and winces as he speaks, waiting for the repercussions he doesn't personally deserve.

"A jumper?" Thom laughs bitterly. "A fucking jumper? Are they blind?" Thom screeches. "She's standing right behind him. She's holding onto his scarf".

"I don't think they saw what you saw", Sam argues, holding his hands up.

"No one seems to". Thom is feverish, his clothes drenched, the sweat from his hair dripping onto the dusty floor. "No one can see what I see. That you're all liars, that you all betrayed us, that he only wanted to show us the truth".

"Take it. But please don't hurt anyone". Sam moves away from the door.

Thom holds out his hand. "I need your keys".

"Did you hear me tell you not to hurt anyone?" Sam lets his hand linger above Thom's as he gives up his keys.

"I heard you", Thom says, snatching them and flinging the door open. "But I don't think I can promise that", Thom calls back as he runs towards the exit. He unlocks the door hastily and throws the keys on the floor.

As Thom bursts out onto the platform, he knocks out a man with the door. The man sags to the ground, cradling his head. Some

271

people quickly gather around the man, and one of them bends down, trying to look at the injured man's face.

Someone begins to confront Thom but cowers away when he sees that Thom is wet with sweat and all his veins are thick underneath his skin, like pipes about to burst. Thom quickly forgets the scene and runs towards the exit. He passes many people, he barges through the barrier behind someone else, he dodges the cars in the road, yet he feels immune.

If Thom had been thinking, he would've known there is no other place he can go. With the DVD clenched in his aching hand, he looks up at the building. It has become his comrade, the friend he keeps around who reflects his mood. It is the place that still connects him to her.

As he unlocks the front door, he thinks about where he is. He thinks about how there is only a slight chance she will actually be here. Yet Thom feels his heart honing in on something or someone and with each step, he feels more certain. As he turns the key in the lock, he can see her turning towards him, smiling?

Yet he is greeted by no one when the door of the bedsit creaks open. He sags against the door frame for a moment, before accepting it and wandering inside. He slumps onto the bed, the DVD still fastened to his hand, almost cutting through his skin.

The bed is still unmade since he was last here. He looks at the disc in his hand and shoves it into the covers, burying it.

Thom gets up and walks to the window. He tweaks the blind, the dust coating his fingers. He leaves his fingerprints on the slats, so if a policeman investigates later, he will know that Thom has been here. He will be implicated. They can accuse him of stealing something or hurting someone because he has left something behind.

"Thom?" a voice says from behind him. He wonders why it is a question. She must know it is him. Who else would be in her bedsit? Who else looks like him? Except Daniel... That thought makes Thom's chest flush cold as if someone has pulled the toilet handle.

"Sarah", he says, turning. Sometimes when he says her name now, he blushes. After all, it isn't really her name but he is holding onto it, as he is holding onto her.

After seeing her in the video, he thought when he saw her, he'd attack her. He thought he'd scratch her pale cheeks, tear at her bouncy curls. Yet, as he looks into her eyes and she smiles at him, the coldness rushes out of him and his blood flushes instantly warm instead.

"I hoped you'd be here", she says, closing the distance between them. At first, Thom jumps back, crashing against the blinds. Her face momentarily twitches, yet she shakes out her curls, dismissing it. "I've missed you". She smiles, holding up her hand in openness. Thom stares at her fingers, shaking in the air and finally locks his hand with hers.

"Have you really missed me?" Thom asks quietly. She reaches up with her other hand and plucks at some of Thom's hair. He shakes her touch off, but smiles faintly. He feels like he is seeing her through a heavy fog. He can't help grasping onto her hand for fear he will lose her, for fear he'll slip further into the fog and never climb his way back out.

All the time he is looking at her, half of his mind is preoccupied with the video. He is playing the scenes over in his head. They are flashing across half her face like a horror film, and he is helpless to change the ending. He wants to rewind everything, never let the clock reach 15:32. Yet it isn't to save Daniel as much as to save himself.

"Where have you been?" he asks, pulling her into him. Her heart drums against his body. He wonders what she has to feel so anxious about. Has she seen the DVD buried in the covers somehow? Is she going to leave him? Thom squeezes her tighter at these thoughts, trying to decide which option is worse.

"I've been thinking a lot. I've been resting", she answers simply. Yet Thom knows there is much more she is leaving out. Does she know she killed Daniel? Or has her damaged mind hidden it from sight underneath the madness and delusion?

"You feel better". Thom nuzzles his words into her neck. She smells like soap and toast. Thom thinks about eating breakfast with her, about reading the paper with her – ordinary things they have missed out on since they met. How can he really have a relationship with this woman? This murderer?

Yet the word murderer offends Thom. How can he possibly attach that evil concept to his beautiful Sarah? Even if she pushed him, there must be a reason. Daniel must have hurt her, or he has imagined it all.

"I'm much better than I was". Sarah nods gently. Thom presses his thumb against her cheek, her pulse and his pulse mixing together until he can't separate them. Thom doesn't think he can ruin her now, after all, she has made progress and she looks happier. When she smiles at him now, it makes him want to slap her and squeeze her in the same moment.

"I'm so happy for you", Thom croaks. Yet his eyes are welling up with water and threatening to spill over like an avalanche gathering momentum. Sarah grabs him by the wrists.

"You're *not* okay though are you?" Thom wants to let his legs melt. He wants to sink. He wants her to love him so much that he will forget everything on that disc and everything he knows.

"Sarah, I need to..." Thom begins, yet he can't finish. He won't only be finishing a sentence; he will be finishing both of them. He digs himself a burrow in her arms. Her chest is sticky against his cheek. As he inhales her sweat, he looks down and sees the top of her breasts.

Thom thinks then about the day of the phone call. The moment he stopped, as though in preparation for the news that would jar his routine forever, jab a stick into the spokes of the wheels that make his world turn. He'd been worried he wouldn't be able to move from the desk, wouldn't be able to meet Emma and lie next to her in bed. And now, all he can think about is touching Sarah instead.

Thom lifts his head up, catching the softness in her expression as she'd been looking down at him. She instantly corrects herself, as though her feelings are a secret she doesn't want him to discover. Thom stands face to face with her, their toes touching, their hands grasping onto one another's. He is thinking about how it is so simple to kiss her and, at the same time, how his fingers are tingling in anticipation of strangling her.

275

So Thom kisses her instead. The throbbing anger and confusion suck desperately at her, trying to recover something caring instead. It strikes him that getting these things from a murderer is a paradox but he can't stop. Her lips seem even softer than only a few days before. The longer he kisses her, the more he wants to kiss her and get dragged into her mouth, into her body.

She brings him closer and slides her hand underneath his top. It feels cold, so he tracks its every movement over his stomach and chest. She digs her nails into his side and feels the grooves of his ribs that have become more prominent over the last few weeks. Thom wonders whether he should touch her and decides that she made the first move, so why not? He has one hand on her hip, on top of her clothes and he now moves the other underneath her top and up her back.

Her backbone curves beneath his touch. Her body wriggles in his arms; pressing so hard into him he almost falls backwards. In the next moment, she is pulling off his shirt. It almost pains them to part for those few seconds. Their lips instantly spring back together as Thom's top lands on the floor.

The longer Thom kisses her; each second feels like he is withering inside. As his hands grip onto her and his muscles tense and relax, he feels like he is shrinking inside. He begins to feel like he is floating or that he is standing on top of a high building, staring at the dizzying lights below.

Sarah pulls back, sensing Thom's distraction. His eyes directed at the floor, as though they are being circled by sharks. She takes him by the hand and leads him over to the bed. Thom suddenly remembers the DVD buried there and rushes forward, flinging the duvet towards the wall.

Sarah raises an eyebrow at Thom, worried by his sudden surge of energy and by just how keen he is to get her into bed. Thom realises these same things as Sarah thinks them and instantly says, "The sheets haven't been changed", blushing. Sarah nods dismissively and sits beside him.

Thom has forgotten that the last person she kissed before him is Daniel and, before that, she was raped. And Sarah has forgotten that he attacked her brother, that he is Daniel's relative and that he is slowly losing grip on reality. There are only the two of them, in this darkened room, filled for once, with life.

As the thought that she has murdered his brother flickers through his mind, it sparks him into leaning forward and giving her a long hard kiss. She grabs hold of his face and pulls him even closer, moaning quietly and pushing her lower body into his side. He imagines he can feel her clit, hard against his hip.

He forces himself to pull away, staring into her eyes for a moment and slowly moving his hand up to unbutton her shirt. She watches his hand moving down her top, smiling faintly to reassure him, until her stomach and breasts are exposed. He gently releases her bra, then instantly presses her body against his.

Sarah pushes Thom down onto the bed, moving on top of him. She closes her eyes, imagining he is already inside her. She bends down, kissing him and reaching down to undo his belt and trousers. Thom almost gags at the speed of this, and can't help remembering the man who hurt her. Why does she trust Thom? He is a violent and reckless person who knows her secret.

Thom thinks about confronting her then but his resolve is broken. He is torn between the curiosity he has inexplicably felt for her since he first saw her in the front garden and the desire to avenge Daniel. Yet as Sarah eases his trousers off and her own, and continues to move against him, the moment overtakes. All Thom wants then is to get inside her.

Sarah is afraid but thinks taking control will help her. She reasons she also trusts Thom, that she loves him, and therefore he is the right person to open up to once again. Feeling certain of this, she eases herself onto him and presses her body down until he is fully inside her. She winces half in pleasure and half in pain, adjusting to the feeling again. Thom feels her getting wetter, his eyes closed as he moves her up and down by guiding her hips.

Thom lifts his hands up to her breasts, rubbing them over her erect nipples, making her squirm for a moment but then relax, pushing her body down on him harder. He is watching her, the display of her pleasure, still asking her in an unspoken way if this is all okay.

She presses down on his chest, his heartbeat thudding under her hands, sweat gathering on their skin. Time seems to have slowed down but only a minute or two has passed.

When Thom sees Sarah close her eyes, leaning backwards and her chest reddening, Thom allows himself to come. He thrusts hard several times and finally feels release. Sarah moans softly.

As Sarah falls on top of him, her breaths rapid against his cheek, Thom finds he can't do the same. He tries a few deep intakes of air but his chest feels constricted. Sarah unknowingly nuzzles into his neck but he pushes her off. Looking hurt, she begins to speak but stops as Thom jumps to his feet.

He presses against his chest, trying to force an opening for air. Yet, he still can't breathe. Sarah gets up and tries to comfort him but he shakes his head, his vision beginning to recede. A huge circle of darkness begins to burn at the corner of his eyes and slowly spreads. He thinks that this must be how it happens – this must be how he dies.

The darkness is nearly complete and Thom is being surrounded by a tunnel, closing its mouth around him. In the last flash of light, he sees Sarah. Staring out of the darkness, Thom knows she is waiting for him, as she waited for the train to emerge from that tunnel, in order to kill his brother. Falling now, Thom realises he can't escape the truth, the video, the tunnel. For one last moment, his body tries to keep him from all these things.

Chapter 50

Blood and Truth

Thom screams and claws himself out of the dark. He can't help thinking this is a familiar feeling since the moment he answered the phone and had been told about Daniel's death. The ink on the note only dragged him further into the darkness, the unknown, the unrelenting pull into a set of jaws that keep chewing him apart inch by inch.

He realises Sarah's arms are around him. He smells the dampness of the room before his eyes slowly adjust to the light. As he rolls onto his side, he notices a few dead insects on the floor under the window and a layer of dust coating the floor. His body is aching as though he has been running for miles. Part of him thinks that this is apt, as he has been running from his old life and the truth for far too long.

"I know", Thom grunts as he heaves himself to a sitting position. Sarah is still only a fuzzy shape to Thom. Despite this, Thom feels a definite alteration at his words. It is as though a sudden beam of light has appeared or the room has slowly begun to slant.

"What do you mean, Thom?" she asks quietly. She is pulling on clothes as she talks, as though planning to flee. Thom refocuses on her face. He realises then that he is still naked and grabs at his t-shirt that has been deserted on the floor. Then he struggles to pull on his jeans, nearly toppling as he tries to zip them up.

"I think you know exactly what I mean", Thom sneers and adds for emphasis, "I mean that what you've been running from is exactly the thing I've been chasing".

Sarah narrows her eyes at his words, trying to decide whether he is hinting at what she thinks he is. He wonders what questions are going through her mind like a whirlwind: what does he know? *How* does he know? What should she do now?

"Thom..." she starts but he cuts in.

"No". He stamps his foot. "I've had enough lies from you".

"I don't want to lie to you anymore..." she whines, holding her hands out to him. He takes them without thinking. When he looks at them, he can't see Daniel's blood covering them but at the same time, he can't ignore the fact that they are the reason he is dead.

"I saw the video of the day he died", Thom tells her. When he had imagined this moment as he'd run away from the station, there was shouting and crying and perhaps even blood. Yet looking into her face now, seeing her struggling to meet his eyes and her shoulders weighed down with guilt, he feels calmer. He loves her, despite everything.

...

I shudder inside as he says the words. Why did I never think of a video? I should've got there first, to stop him ever finding out.

281

Surely he will lash out now? I have killed someone, and this someone was his cousin.

Lots of pointless words come into my head at once. I filter each one, deciding they will be even more useless to Thom. Although, one feeling overwhelms everything: relief. No more hiding, no more running – I can stand before him and he can see every dark crevice and glaring scar.

Mum, I'm coming clean about everything. You would be proud of me for that at least.

"You haven't said anything", Thom notes, looking for something to fill the heavy silence. I inhale deeply, my head beginning to swell out like there has been a tumour hiding behind my eyes for some time, waiting to pounce.

"What can I say Thom?" I swallow heavily. "That I killed him? That I knew who you were when you chased me out of your garden? That I have no idea why I pushed him and I still don't?" As I speak, Thom bites his lip so hard it nearly disappears underneath his teeth.

"You're admitting it, just like that?" Thom asks, shifting on his feet. He hasn't expected it to be this easy but I am tired, ready to let the stone, I have been holding in place, roll out of me and disappear into the distance.

"I've tried to hide this from you for too long".

It seems like we are discussing a tea party or what we watched on TV last night, not a murder. Where is the shouting? Where is the heart wrenching emotion? Perhaps we are both too exhausted. I can

282

see the bags under Thom's eyes; they are parachutes that have deflated before they have left the ground.

"You know what I don't understand?" Thom exclaims suddenly, raising the sounds levels, throwing my hands down. "How you could lie to me all this time, how you could sit there and listen to me going on about what he did and how I don't understand it all... Didn't you feel bad? Didn't you at least feel sorry for me?" His hands are in fists; his teeth clenched as he stares at me, like a dog I have kicked for no reason. I instantly feel the ceiling sagging above my head, threatening to collapse.

"It's the worst I've ever felt in my life", I answer honestly.

"Worse than you felt after you pushed my brother onto those tracks?"

...

"Your brother?" She asks dismissively, thinking he has made a simple error and will correct himself. Yet Thom gives her a twisted smile, almost mocking her for being so stupid all this time, as he has been for most of his life.

"*Of course*. Didn't I tell you that Daniel and I were actually brothers?"

"What are you talking about?" Sarah grabs him by the arms and squeezes gently, trying to bring him back to sense. Thom doesn't push her away now. He thinks that her gesture is born out of affection for him and part of him enjoys it, despite everything.

"Aunty Val had a secret all these years. Apparently Daniel found out and he wanted me to know too".

283

"Are you saying Val isn't your aunt? She's your... *mum*?" Sarah pronounces each word carefully, except the word 'mum'. That word falters on her tongue, partly held back as if she doesn't want to let it go.

"Yes. Apparently she's my real mum. She and my dad put their genes together and ended up with twins. So they flipped a coin and decided which one she should keep and which she should give to my parents".

"I'm sure it wasn't as easy a decision as that", Sarah says quietly. Thom laughs and reverses the hold, so he is now holding onto her, and pulls her close to his face.

"You really think so, do you?" he spits.

"Thom, I'm sorry". She stares into his face, determined not to be frightened by him. Thom shoves her away roughly but she manages to catch herself and doesn't fall.

"You're sorry, she's sorry, we're *all* sorry". Thom counts on his fingers. "All it means is that my whole life has been a big fucking lie. And Daniel's too". He closes his fist around his own fingers, cutting himself down.

"You must feel completely betrayed", Sarah hazards. Thom raises his head, one side of his lip hooking into a smile. His cheeks are reddening and even from here, Sarah can see his eyes flashing with water.

"You know..." he begins, twisting his hands as he talks, "I

284

wanted to believe you so much". His words have a twang of tears. "I guess that's why it was so easy for you to fool me".

...

"I didn't try to fool you Thom", I insist. I am desperate to close the space between us, have him against me again, skin on skin. Yet I can't move, knowing I will be rejected.

"Oh so what do you call it, Sarah?" Thom can't stop a few tears escaping from his eyes and running down his face. "I mean, that's not even your real name. *I'm* a fucking joke". Thom digs his nails into his arms. His body is shaped like an arch weighed down by tonnes of stone. As he coughs out his words, his tears fly towards me in the air and land on the floorboards.

"Please Thom. I never meant to make a fool of you". I falter, knowing that my intentions and my actions are completely separate. He is right.

"But you did Sarah. I believed in you, despite everyone telling me I shouldn't. Richard didn't trust you, Emma didn't believe you, and even *I* wasn't convinced". He chokes on a suppressed sob. "But I am so broken that it was easy for you".

"I'm broken too", I tell him. He jolts as though his body is offended by this comment but after a moment, he nods gently.

"Did you know what you'd done at the station that day?" Thom asks cautiously, seemingly jabbing a lion in the eye with a stick.

"My body and my mind weren't connected properly. I remembered I'd done it but my mind wasn't connected to reality. I can't even tell you what I was thinking", I pause heavily, "even now, my mind isn't right…"

It feels like I am talking to a therapist again, but this time, I am making some progress at least. However, looking at Thom, each word I say seems to punch him down. His body is swaying slightly, his eyes squinting at the world he can't escape.

"So when you met me, you already knew. And you didn't feel shame or remorse?" He is pacing the room now, trying to look like an excellent sleuth but his wobbly steps defy him.

"I didn't really feel remorse then. You helped me with that".

"Me?" He stops.

"Yes. Spending time with you taught me how to feel again. You really saved me Thom", I tell him earnestly, grabbing at his hand. He glances down at my touch, as though he has forgotten he has hands.

"But you're still a murderer". He shakes me off roughly.

...

Thom watches her body droop. For a few seconds, he thinks she might faint, but she slumps onto the bed instead. A strange stab of guilt pricks Thom in the side. How can he still care about her? Shouldn't he be getting his revenge for Daniel? Or did he feel she is just as much a victim as Daniel? Even after all these weeks, he is just as torn as he was when it first began. It seems like since the note, he has been torn in two – the grieving relative and the detective. Although his detective work leaves a lot to be desired; the

286

culprit has been right in front of him for weeks and he has been blind to suspect her.

"I sometimes thought you were alike", she says, playing with her hands in her lap and peering up to see his response. Thom allows her to speak this time.

"Every time I saw you, your hair or your voice, would remind me", she pauses, "and every time I saw your grief, I felt like I was killing you too. But I realised that although what I have done is completely wrong and unforgivable, I wasn't aware of what pushing him really meant".

"You're defending yourself?" Thom scoffs, kicking the floorboards. A haze of dust floats up between them.

"Not defending, Thom, *explaining*".

"Should I really care about your explanation, your reason or whatever you want to call it?" Thom says, his limbs flailing as though independent of himself.

"You're right", Sarah admits, shrugging, "but there is something I want to tell you". She lets the silence fill the room for a moment until Thom can stand it no more.

"What then?"

"He said something to me, Thom".

"Well you knew him before, didn't you? At the hospital? It's hardly surprising he spoke to you!" Thom turns away, laughing to the side of him, as though he has an invisible friend standing there.

"No, I don't remember all that", she corrects him. "I meant when he fell".

Thom's head jerks back towards her. She instantly feels as though a stark light is shining into her eyes and she lifts her hand to shield it.

"Don't people always say something when they get pushed in front of a train?"

"Not like this", she insists, "I thought at first I imagined it, as you might expect a crazy person could. I thought I'd seen it wrong... but I'm so sure that I'm right..."

"Are you ever going to tell me?" Thom cries, bouncing on his feet like a man standing on hot coals.

"Yes", she reassures him. "As he fell, he said *right on time*". She stares into the distance. She expects Thom to react to this, yet he seems almost unflustered.

"Right..." He agrees, as though they have been comparing notes.

"You don't seem that surprised'.

"I'm not really". He nods, a small smile growing on his lips.

Sarah isn't sure what to make of this so she continues talking: "I thought about it for days and days afterwards. And I decided I had to know what he meant".

"So you came to our house?"

"I followed you first. I tried to find out more about him by watching you".

"You were following us?" Thom says; looking more disgusted than when she admitted she is a murderer.

...

Looking at myself through Thom's eyes is now an altered and disturbing experience. From his unrelenting faith in me, he is now losing his adoration word by word.

"I told you I was very sick".

"You love telling me that, don't you?" he says roughly.

"People find it hard to see. Even I did before this happened to me..."

"Talking isn't helping. It doesn't change all this, does it?" Thom looks so tired that all I want is to lie him down and let him sleep for days, forgetting everything.

"We should've talked more before", I tell him, unsure of what else to say.

"You're right", he says quietly, pained by the fact he agrees with a murderer and a crazy person. "The thing I'm most sad about – how all this started – is the lack of talking". He leans against the wall. For a moment, he looks like a tramp hitching a ride to another town. His hair is unwashed, his brow dirty with sweat and dust, his eyes darkened by lack of sleep.

"If she'd just told us in the first place, if she'd been honest enough, Daniel wouldn't have been so angry. I could've saved him, *and you* wouldn't have pushed him. He must've made you do it, I don't know how… But all *this* could've been avoided". Thom gestures to the room around them as though it holds their lives. He walks towards me, his gaze so focussed that I believe it is compensating for his broken mind. He takes my hand.

"But the person I'm most upset about is you", he tells me, his lips trembling uncontrollably. Yet he doesn't cry. He is too shattered and drained to actually cry again. "I loved you. I really loved you". He squeezes my hand until it feels numb but I say nothing. "If after everything, I could've trusted you, maybe I wouldn't feel like there isn't anything left".

"Please Thom…" I say sadly but can't think of how to end the sentence. Please Thom, change your mind? Please Thom, let me love you? Please Thom, let's forget everything and start again? None of them seem right so I say nothing.

"I wish you knew what to say to help me now". Thom's words transform into a moan. "But you've *all* let me down". He snatches his hand back, although he is the one who initiated it. "And I let Daniel down because I am so stupid that I never saw the truth… I let everyone lie to me because I can't handle things".

"Thom, don't say these things about yourself".

"Well it's true", he spits. "I've never been able to deal with anything. I've sat in a cosy office talking to people on the phone, never really dealing with anything. And do you know why Sarah?"

"Why?" I ask reluctantly.

"Because I don't really know who I am". Thom shrugs, not even sure his words are true. "I thought I was a son but then my parents died. I thought I was a cousin but it turns out I'm a brother. I thought I was a nephew but I'm a son. I thought I was an insurance officer but I can't even remember where I work. I thought I was a detective but I've been fooled all along. I thought I was a boyfriend but I'm a cheat. And I thought I was a man in love but... *I don't know anymore*". Thom stares at his palms as though they are morphing before him.

"I know you don't want to hear this but I can understand how you feel".

"Oh, you can?" Thom sneers, clearly unimpressed by my empathy. "I can't believe you're trying to liken yourself to me. After everything..."

"We're not so different, Thom. Daniel fooled me too", I say quietly. Thom's face instantly softens as he digests this.

"You're right", he croaks. "He changed your life forever. You can never go back". Thom pauses briefly, finishing, "just like me".

When he moves, I think he may be coming to embrace me but he brushes past me. I don't move, too drained to really think of doing so. What's the point? I know I can't leave him here. But I should be out of this house, since I tried to escape it for months and have been so close...

Thom's presence arrives behind me. I turn towards him. His eyes are bloodshot, his body straight like a nail sticking out of the floor trying to catch my toe and drag me down, his arms bulging with veins, the knife sparkling in the light from the half-opened blind.

I open my mouth but he grabs me roughly with his free hand before I can protest, plead or even utter a syllable. His mouth is wet with spit, a few specks on his beard. I am frozen for a moment, staring at the knife in his hand.

Mum, I know I said I'd stop talking to you but I'm really afraid…

"Sarah", he whispers, looking down at the knife himself. He moves it between them and pulls me even closer. I can feel it through my top, like a vein throbbing beneath the skin; subtle but something that cannot be ignored. I meet his gaze, wondering what has happened behind his eyes. What has happened to the man I can trust? What has happened to his hope?

"Thom, you don't have to do this", I tell him firmly.

He shakes his head. "I have to do something", he insists, pulling me even closer. My stomach leaps at the thought of it being punctured, but the pressure of the blade only increases, although doesn't draw blood yet. Our foreheads are touching, and from afar, I imagine we look like lovers.

Thom begins to shake, his unrealised tears making his whole body shudder. I want to grab hold of him, keep him still but the knife lingers between us and I'm afraid I will push it into one of us, or both of us. Instead, I reach up and touch his face. I move my fingers across his bristly beard, the softness of his lips amongst it, his clammy skin.

His body slowly stills again. He nuzzles his head against mine, moaning gently. Yet all I feel is his grip on the knife, which doesn't falter. My wrist is still clamped in his other hand, drawing me closer to his body and perhaps closer to death.

As I move over the back of his neck, he jolts suddenly. His body shoots up straight, his expression darkening. I feel the knife press harder into my stomach, the pressure beginning to mark the skin underneath. His eyes are wet but his mouth is hardened by his clenched teeth.

"While I've been standing here..." He speaks in a throaty voice, as though he has been screaming for hours. "All I can think about is two things", he pauses, "kissing you and... *killing* you". The space between us is now non-existent; there is only the knife to separate us. His face is close. I can feel his breath on my lips and as he moves his head a millimetre forward, his beard scratches at my skin.

"You can't let him do this to us", I insist. I don't want to plead with him. I don't want to be the murderer who can't face up to death. If anything, he should've killed me as soon as he found out.

Thom finally lets his tears throb out of him like lava pulsing out of a volcano. His face flashes with sadness and anger each millisecond. It seems like I am watching him through a kaleidoscope. Then he moves a millimetre forward and presses his lips against mine. They are shivering and cracked.

I see the red before I feel it. But it's the sudden push backwards and a thrust that really occur first. It punctures the skin violently, delving inside where no one can see what's been ruptured. It is seconds later that the blood actually begins to swell out of the hole. Yet, after the initial swell, the blood spreads like a fire tearing through the material. The shock follows. Neither of us moves. Our eyes are locked, our mouths gasping for air.

Still locked together, we fall to the floor.

The door bursts open as we land. The blood covers my arms. I'm holding onto the knife so hard that my hands are sliced open. "Alice, *no…*" A voice says. I realise Michael is pulling me up, leaning me against him. He is searching for the wound, flailing his jacket around, ready to plug the hole. I have forgotten he had been waiting for me at all.

"No", I push away, as he realises what has happened. I scramble towards Thom, lying on his side, staring towards the blank TV screen. I lift his head onto my lap. Michael belatedly presses his jacket against Thom's stomach, causing Thom to groan and recoil. Yet after a few moments, he doesn't seem to notice anymore.

"Why did you do it?" I shake him. He looks dazed so I slap him gently on the cheek until he focuses on my face. He smiles gently, as though he has forgotten everything. Perhaps this is exactly what he wanted – numbness, oblivion. Yet I don't want to let him go. I start to sob as Michael calls an ambulance.

For once, I don't find blood beautiful. It makes my head dizzy. It makes my chest tighten and spasm. It makes my stomach twist as if the knife is actually stuck inside me, ripping my organs apart.

"I had to", Thom says quietly. "You're getting better..." He whispers, leaning his head into my chest. Does he mean that only one of us can survive? That he thinks he will never 'get better'?

He closes his eyes but I refuse to let him leave me. I shake him awake. He drowsily reopens his eyes, and I think he will start telling me how he is cold or numb. Yet he doesn't need to. His body is shivering in my hold and he seems unaware.

"Don't die", I tell him. Thom barely responds. He is going limp.

And all I see is you, Mum. I am holding you in the hallway. The line of blood is drawn down your chin as though you have misapplied lipstick. I can't feel a heartbeat as I lay my head against your chest. You are still. The world is still. Yet somewhere in my mind, I refused to accept it.

I rest my head against Thom's chest and hear his heart beating, slowly, slower, slower, slow. I think I hear the ambulance wail somewhere in the street. Yet I can't be sure I haven't imagined it. All I know is this time; they will need the sirens. He isn't dead. Not like you or Daniel. We can get out of the tunnel. We aren't paused forever.

Still beating, beating, beating, beating, it still beats.

Chapter 51

Red Fingerprints

Michael pulls me closer. I let myself flop onto his shoulder, not knowing what else to do with my body. My arms are covered with Thom's blood, now dry. Somehow I believe this is the blood that should've marked me after I pushed Daniel. After all, they were made of the same bloodline.

Even though all the information is before me, I can barely draw faint lines to connect them. I know I pushed Daniel. I know he planned it. I know he left clues for Thom. I know Thom and he were actually brothers. And I know that Thom uncovered my secret.

Losing a relative is enough to break anyone, I completely understand. But finding out your whole life is a fabrication... that is enough to destroy someone. And Thom knows this now. Everything he trusted has twisted out of familiarity and transformed into something else. No wonder Thom has responded to everything as he has.

Destroying a person takes time. And Daniel had had that time. Creating questions and doubts through his clues, bringing unfamiliar people into Thom's life to unbalance him and distract him, holding back the vital clues to keep Thom chasing him, making Thom's whole life flip upside down until his head was so full of blood it needed to explode. He'd been clever and perceptive and, most of all, evil.

Even now, I can't recall the hospital properly. I have faint flashes of him sitting on a bed, perhaps holding my hand? Yet I can't trust my thoughts. I have the letters now and they give me enough ideas to create something. It makes me shudder thinking about what he must've said to me, how he influenced me, how he somehow knew me better than I did. However, I guess a fragile mind is easy to manipulate.

As I followed Thom down to the ambulance, I saw the DVD lying on the floor. Picking it up, it seemed to scream in my hand. I didn't need to put it on to know what I would see. I shoved it into my coat pocket and it is still hiding there now. I wonder what I should do with it.

The moment I pushed Daniel seems like a dream. I have rehearsed the simple action in my head but it never seems to be real. The only thing that makes me believe I will live with the guilt is the fact that he led me there.

It is then that I realise Michael has fallen asleep beside me. I slowly lift myself off him, only making him stir for a moment before I slip away. I have to wash off this blood. Looking for the nearest toilets, I see they are down the hallway. I shuffle towards them, clamber inside and rush straight to the sink. I pull the taps on to full and let the spray lash at my clothes. My torso is instantly soaked and I imagine it is me that was stabbed, not Thom. Yet there is no pain for me.

297

Splashing the water up my arms, I scratch at the stained skin until the blood grudgingly re-moistens and slides off. The sink water turns pink and eventually drinks it all. I only stop when the water turns clear again.

I switch off the taps but as I do, catch myself in the mirror. My hair, my left cheek, and the bottom of my neck are specked with blood. I grab some paper towels, dropping a pile of them in the process, and hurriedly rub at the stains until all is left are red tension marks. I douse my hair and hope it has caught most of it; but I will have to wash it several times when I get home.

Although, this will never truly wash off.

As I leave the toilets, water dripping onto the dusty floor from my hair and the bandages on my hands, I see them. Richard and Val are standing in the corridor, holding hands. Richard has his head down and even from here; I can see him holding onto Val so tightly that his arms are bulging with muscles. He squeezes her and lets go of her. I begin to duck but thankfully he walks in the opposite direction, digging into his pocket as he walks, filling his hand with coins.

I watch Val for a moment. She is looking around as though she is lost. I can already see the withered tissue peeking out of her sleeve. I am taken back to the first time I saw her, leaving the house I'd been watching for days, her eyes sore and a tissue flapping behind her. I consider turning away and even take a step backwards but in the end, I walk straight towards her.

She barely notices me approach. She only looks up when a drop of water lands on her arm. She lifts her face up with great effort, her wrinkles appearing deeper with each movement she is forced to make. She stares at me for several seconds before she nods in recognition. "Sarah…" she says in a raspy whisper. Her cheeks are raw with tears, her lips cracked. She reminds me of the last time I saw Thom. The only difference is a purple bruise making a small bulge on her lower lip. Where did that come from?

Considering her now, I see the similarities with Thom. She has the same shaped face; a slightly rounded nose, long eyelashes (although hers are glued together in clumps by the mascara and her sobbing), the same downturn of the mouth that makes a smile even harder.

"How is Thom?" I ask. She instantly begins to sob as though I have flipped a switch. I hesitate but finally draw her into a hug, wondering if by being this close she will be able to feel that I am a murderer. She doesn't seem to flinch though. She simply buries her head in my curls.

"How is he?" I repeat, more urgently. She says something into my hair. I have to push her backwards slightly, yet her words are still muffled like she is speaking through a pillow. "Val, please". I shake her gently.

"He's not good", she finally manages.

"What did they say?"

"They say he's struggling. He's lost a lot of blood", she tells me shakily, digging her fingers into my arms. "What will I do?" she asks me desperately. I deliberate on how to answer the question: *"you'll cope, we all do", "he'll be okay, I'm sure of it", "don't think about that now, let's wait"*. I can't help thinking I am the last person who should be comforting her. If Thom had punished the right person, he wouldn't be 'struggling' to stay alive.

"Let's see what happens first". I choose a variation on one of them to comfort her. She nods but her face is still twisted in anguish.

"The only thing is; it's all I can think about", she admits.

People are filtering by but she doesn't seem to notice that they are staring at her, wondering if we know each other and wondering if there is somewhere they can move her, so they don't have to see her pain.

"It must be horrible for you", I tell her. I feel terrible imagining how I would respond at the possibility of losing two children within a few months; especially as one has only just found out he is her child.

"I don't think I can cope with this again…"

"I know". I squeeze her.

I imagine she is you, Mum, alive again. I let her warmth smother me. Her salty tears sting my cheeks. If only you hadn't left me, maybe I wouldn't need to drain this poor woman of her last drips of energy.

"You were with him", she says, easing away from my hold. "Did he say anything about me?"

I remember every word that Thom said in the bedsit. I could've recited every word and every intonation to her. Yet now I have begun to feel normal again, I recall that the truth doesn't always help. If I tell her how angry he'd been, how confused and desolate he felt, would it really make her happier?

"He told me what happened. But he didn't say too much".

"Then why did he do that to himself?"

"I'm not sure. He didn't make much sense". I shrug, hoping she is as confused as she looks. She shivers as though I have thrust an icicle into her chest and wraps her hands around herself.

"Did he do it because of me?" she asks quietly, unable to meet my gaze. I think about this carefully before even thinking of opening my mouth. It's definite that she has some weight in his anger and pain, but is it because of her? I decide the answer is safely no. Without Daniel and myself, he wouldn't have done it. Under normal circumstances, I believe he may have even reconciled with her one day, despite the years of lies.

"It wasn't you", I say, bending towards her lowered gaze to emphasise this.

She nods weakly and says, "I'm his real mother, you know".

"He told me". I nod. She seems satisfied, looking away to compose herself.

"Do you want to see him?"

"Yes", I answer instantly. Since I'd been forced to let the paramedics take him away, I have only thought about the moment I can see him again. I want to see how they have repaired him, fixed the gaping hole in his skin. She takes my arm, the broken leading the broken; towards the person we both love.

As we approach the cubicle, with the curtains drawn around the bed, I try to catch my breath. I can't believe I will actually see him again.

Unlike you Mum, I won't be losing him forever. I won't have to stand at a funeral and feel my mind float up above my body, never quite able to reconnect.

Val peeks through the curtain discreetly, as I hop on my feet. She lets out a small yelp. I push her aside and tear the curtains apart. Before us, the sheets are dishevelled and twisted, alarmingly empty, like a robbed grave. The machines beside the bed are dead. I bend down and see the plugs have been pulled out. The wires connected to the machine are tossed on the bed like haphazard veins leading to nothing. There are a few bloody finger marks on the sheets, on the bedside table, on the curtain to the left.

I follow the blood marks, chasing them into the next cubicle where a surprised family turn to face me. I run around the bed and keep following the marks, diminishing with each gauzy curtain, becoming more elusive with each bed. There are three I pass before I reach the corridor at the end. I check all the doorways for signs of him and after several; I find the faintest mark on the door to the stairway. I fling the door open and fly down the stairs.

I imagine I am a policewoman in pursuit, only a whisper behind. Yet, when I reach the bottom, the door is firmly closed. No one has been here recently. I open it anyway, feeling the cold night rushing towards me. I think about Thom's clothes and how the knife has torn them, how he could be shivering in an alleyway, or worse, dying.

I step out into the night, looking to both sides. Ambulances are pulling in, a few people loitering in the car park, a few nurses smoking near the corner, but no Thom. I focus my eyes on each spot in my sight but see nothing unusual. I somehow believe that if he is out here, I will find him, despite the darkness and the stinging wind.

Checking the floor for blood, I pace up and down. I look in doorways. I walk in between the cars and search for bloodied fingerprints or smashed windows. I walk to the street and search for movement or a group of people huddled over a body. Yet I find nothing.

I can't find Thom.

Wrapping my arms around myself, I let myself sink against a car. I look at my arms and remember the stains of his blood and now can't believe I ever washed it off. This was my last link to him. I may never see him again and I have washed him away out of guilt.

"Thom", I call into the wind. "Thom!" I scream. The only response I get is from a fox that is slinking across the road which casually glances over and, after a long stare, continues padding onwards. I slide further down the car, leaning my cheek against its cold body.

I know he can't hear me, wherever he is. Yet I hope he knows I came looking for him, that I called for him, that I am frozen by the heartbreak. This is all I can do for him now. Unlike me, I hope he knows that someone is thinking about him and believes in his ability to heal.

Oh Mum, what should I do with myself now?

Several minutes later, when I drag my body from the floor, I wonder if wherever he is, he will think about me too. And when he does, will he think of me as a lover or a murderer? No matter what I do in the future, there will still be a person who knows what I am.

Yet if I saw him again, just once, perhaps I could tell him I love him and it would change his mind.

Sparkling Books

Tony Bayliss, *Past Continuous*

Anna Cuffaro, *Gatwick Bear and the Secret Plans*

Daniele Cuffaro, *American Myths in Post-9/11 Music*

Alan Hamilton, *Two Unknown*

David Kauders, *The Greatest Crash*

Amanda Sington-Williams, *The Eloquence of Desire*

L. A. Abbott, *Seven Wives and Seven Prisons*

Harriet Adams, *Dawn*

Grace Aguilar, *The Vale of Cedars*

Gustave Le Bon, *Psychology of Crowds*

Carlo Goldoni, *Il vero amico / The True Friend*

M.G. Lewis, *The Bravo of Venice*

Alexander Pushkin, *Marie: A Story of Russian Love*

Ilya Tolstoy, *Reminiscences of Tolstoy*

For more information visit:

www.sparklingbooks.com

Sparkling Books